PRAISE FOR STANLEY EVANS

"Evans' combination of [Coast] Salish lore and solid plotting is a winner." —*The Globe and Mail*

"A fast-paced, entertaining story with enough plot twists to keep the reader guessing." —*Times Colonist*

"A mystery novel worth reading and lingering over."
—*Hamilton Spectator*

"A gritty murder-mystery with some violence and suspense thrown in for good measure." —*Oak Bay News*

"Tightly written mystery . . . a pleasure to read." —*Comox Valley Record*

"Evans does not disappoint." —*WordWorks*

"Well worth reading. Evans knows how to set a scene, creates vivid minor characters, and is capable of spitting out the requisite snappy dialogue." —*Monday Magazine*

"An exciting introduction to a Coast Salish cop with a lot more entertaining stories to tell." —*Mystery Readers Journal*

"Sharp, calculating and extremely convincing style of writing."
—*Victoria News*

"Evans is a forceful story teller." —*Parksville Qualicum News*

"[An] evocative series." —*Montreal Gazette*

SEAWEED ON THE ROCKS

SEAWEED ON THE ROCKS

Stanley Evans

TouchWood
Editions

VICTORIA • VANCOUVER • CALGARY

TouchWood Editions
#108 – 17665 66A Avenue
Surrey, BC V3S 2A7
www.touchwoodeditions.com

TouchWood Editions
PO Box 468
Custer, WA
98240-0468

Library and Archives Canada Cataloguing in Publication
Evans, Stan, 1931–
        Seaweed on the rocks/ Stanley Evans.

ISBN 978-1-894898-73-7

I. Title.

PS8559.V36S41 2008   C813'.54   C2008-903109-1

Library of Congress Control Number: 2008905352

Edited by Betty Keller
Front-cover photo by Evelin Elmest / iStockphoto

Printed in Canada

TouchWood Editions acknowledges the financial support for its publishing program from
the Government of Canada through the Book Publishing Industry Development Program
(BPIDP), Canada Council for the Arts, and the province of British Columbia through the
British Columbia Arts Council and the Book Publishing Tax Credit.

The author is indebted to the British Columbia Arts Council for its financial support.

This book has been produced on 100% post-consumer recycled paper, processed chlorine free and
printed with vegetable-based dyes.

to Marlyn Horsdal, Vivian Sinclair and Pat Touchie.

THE WARRIOR RESERVE DOES NOT EXIST. The Mowaht Bay Band does not exist. All of the characters, incidents and dialogue in this novel are products of the author's imagination. Any resemblance to actual living persons or to real events is coincidental. Depictions of Native mythology and religion are based on ethnological research and do not necessarily reflect the present-day obser- vances and practices of Canada's West Coast Native people.

The author is grateful for the expert help and advice of Dr. John Marsden, Dr. John Tibbles, James Clowater, George Easdon and Michael Layland in the preparation of this manuscript.

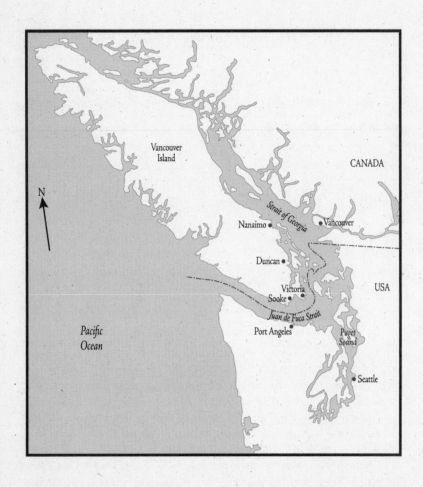

Vancouver
Island

CANADA

N

Strait of Georgia

Nanaimo • • Vancouver

Duncan •

Victoria •
Sooke •

USA

Juan de Fuca Strait

Pacific
Ocean

Port Angeles •

Puget
Sound

• Seattle

THE SALISH SEA

According to Old Mary Cooke, Canada's northwest coast and its many islands were once collectively a big raft anchored near the South Pole. When people living on the raft got tired of penguins and ice, they hoisted their anchors and let the raft drift loose. Some people dived off it and swam ashore in places like Hawaii and New Zealand. That's why, Old Mary Cooke says, Hawaiians and New Zealanders look like West Coast Natives.

After many years the raft crashed into North America, where chunks broke off, thereby creating Vancouver Island and a large rocky inland sea that my people call the Salish Sea. You won't find that name on ordinary maps, even though its waters include the Strait of Georgia, Puget Sound, and Juan de Fuca Strait. Old Mary Cooke's account of things may not be strictly true but, true or not, it is incontestable that Coast Salish people spend much of their time studying the watery horizon.

One morning, not so very long ago, a Coast Salish man was looking out at the Salish Sea when he spotted a dugout canoe manned by a single paddler. It was blowing a gale, the sea was wild and full of driftwood, and the canoe appeared to be taking on water. The alarm was raised. Soon lifeboat men began launching a Zodiac inflatable. One of them tugged the Zodiac's starter rope while another used a pole to hold its bow into the wind.

But before the outboard kicked into life, a rogue wave buckled the Zodiac's rubber hull and flipped the boat upside down.

The lifeboat men were still scrambling back to shore when a lookout pointed out to sea. "Over there!" he cried. "The canoe just swamped! The paddler's been washed overboard!"

An hour passed before the waterlogged canoe washed onto the beach. Sloshing about in its flooded bilges they found a baby porpoise, along with a small wooden coffin daubed with ghostly red-and-black heraldic crests. Chief Alphonse tipped the porpoise into the water and opened the coffin, which contained a small human skeleton. At the same moment, a brilliant light flashed out on the horizon and travelled towards the canoe in zigzags like lightning, and the air smelled of forest mould, salt water and sulphur.

Eventually the lifeboat men got their Zodiac launched, and they combed the Salish Sea and its beaches for ages, but no trace of that paddler was ever found.

CHAPTER ONE

It was a Welfare Wednesday in late April and nearly quitting time when an anonymous tipster phoned to say that a woman on my Wanted List was living on Donnelly's Marsh. The tip sounded phony, somebody's idea of a joke, and I was half-inclined to ignore it. Still, I cranked up my steel-bumpered, wire-wheeled '69 MG coupe and joined the afternoon commute along Highway 1 out of Victoria. Half an hour later I reached View Royal, where the monotony of rush-hour traffic was relieved by glimpses of Esquimalt Harbour. A flock of massive yellow cranes and derricks were poking their noses at the sky above the naval dockyards, while warships aimed their guns at the strip malls and used-car dealerships. I couldn't help remembering that before all the trees and farms had been subdivided in that area, there had been fresh air, and fruit stands and orchards and country roads to look at instead of payday loan sharks and the Great Canadian Casino.

The sky above the Salish Sea had darkened to a menacing purple by the time I reached an area of broken-down shacks and live-aboard buses and neglected yards—places where nobody came from, where busted gambling addicts and other sad cases drifted in and out, waiting for their luck to change. It was a relief to turn off the highway onto Donnelly's Marsh—a thousand acres of duck-hunting country—and when the blacktop petered out, I ploughed on along dike roads within hailing distance of the sea. After another half-mile I saw a crooked signpost warning all comers that these were Native lands and honky trespassers would be shot on sight.

A lone coyote was feeding on watercress in a ditch, and for no particular reason I pulled up and got out of the car. As I followed the coyote's tracks across sand dunes peppered with yellow sand-verbena and dwarf pines, a red-winged blackbird's throaty cry broke the silence. I came out on a bluff overlooking the Salish Sea. The coyote, crouched amid driftwood the same colour as its bristly fur, was hard to spot until it broke cover and loped into the trees. In the evening calm I watched bufflehead ducks performing aerials and skating on the water as mallards and Canada geese dabbled in the shallows. A doe and two fawns were nose-down amid the sawgrass greening along the water's edge. Backlit by a single beam of sunlight, they made a pretty picture.

My people have lived here for at least ten thousand years, but human activities in this part of the world were cramped by the last great ice age, which lasted thousands of years, and most of the record of Coast Salish occupation up to that time was destroyed by glacial activity. Some of my hardy ancestors endured, however, because a few coastal refuges stayed relatively ice-free, though even that record was hidden beneath the sea when the icecaps melted.

Nowadays Vancouver Island—285 miles long and 85 miles at its widest point—has pulp-and-paper mills, sawmills, logging camps, four-lane highways, and a few cities and towns of which Greater Victoria, with its population of about 300,000, is by far the largest. But the Island still has its primeval forests and isolated regions where wolves howl for an audience comprised principally of bear, loon, elk and cougar. Many snowy peaks and alpine meadows still remain where people seldom or never set foot. And there are dozens of small, tenacious Native Indian bands that continue to inhabit remote coastal villages, many of them unreachable by road.

Long ago, Donnelly's Marsh was one of these remote coastal villages. Then, in 1838, Haida warriors sweeping down from the Queen Charlotte Islands in giant, ocean-going dugout canoes landed here one night, encircled the village and massacred most of its sleeping inhabitants. Every Coast Salish man in the village was killed. The Haidas kidnapped a few women and children and carried them back north, where they ended their days as slaves. Nowadays, few Coast Salish set foot on Donnelly's Marsh at any time—and practically never after dark.

I went back to my car and started driving again. Five minutes later, the gaunt shape of a derelict, two-storey house rose up. Shrouded in English ivy, it stood in lonely isolation on the marsh, the only building in sight. Gazing at it, my head full of memories, I saw a pale shade move across a windowpane—a passing gull, its fleeting image reflected by the glass. Two Cape Cod chairs mouldered on the house's wraparound porch. Nailed to the front door was a hand-painted plywood sign: DANGER. DO NOT ENTER. The door had a thumb latch instead of a knob, but it wouldn't open, and I hammered on the door in vain. Adjacent to the door, the bottom half of a sash window had been partially raised. I put my hands under the frame, heaved, and made an opening wide enough to squeeze through. I had one leg across the sill and was crouching to get inside the house, when the front door opened. I exchanged startled glances with a bone-thin Native man, aged about 35. He had long yellow hair with black roots, a pear-shaped face, a receding chin, fat lips and slitty black eyes. He was wearing a grimy fleece hoodie, baggy cord pants and baseball shoes with loose laces. This was Hector Latour—a crack addict with a rap sheet as long as a sermon. A small object fell from the backpack he was carrying when he slung it across his shoulders as he scurried away.

As I scrambled back onto the porch, my jacket caught on the latch inside the window and before I could unhook it, Hector had vanished along a boggy footpath. The object that had fallen from his backpack turned out to be a white ballpoint pen marked DR. LAWRENCE TREW, HYPNOTHERAPY. I put the pen in my pocket and stepped into the old house's vestibule, which reeked of urine, its ancient, ragged carpet spotted where birds had flown in and out. As I peered around, a feral cat nibbling something in the darkness fled upstairs.

I heard—or thought that I heard—somebody open a door at the back of the house, and I began moving cautiously along a hallway lit only by a vertical sliver of daylight at the far end. Then a sudden draft slammed the back door shut and plunged the hallway into darkness again, and I became aware of tiny scratching sounds behind a side door. When I opened it, another cat darted past me from a gloomy kitchen. Light from a window set high in the kitchen wall revealed heavy dark counters, wooden shelving, a white enamel sink and a lot of dust. A loaf of bread was turning black atop an old-fashioned icebox.

Suddenly the light in the kitchen dimmed as something appeared outside the window. A massive grizzly bear was standing on its hind legs and staring straight at me. The bear's head, covered with dark reddish fur, seemed a yard wide and filled the whole window frame. Before I could reconcile this improbable apparition with my normal cognitive functions, it had vanished.

As my eyes adjusted to the gloom, I saw Marnie Paul sprawled in a kitchen chair. She was wearing a black leather jacket and black cotton pants, and the rest of her was just thinly fleshed bones, lip rings and earrings. She had meth mouth—rotten teeth and lips covered with blisters and sores from sharing hot crack pipes with other meth addicts—and her fingernails were blue from cyanosis. Two years earlier, Marnie Paul had been a healthy Coast Salish high school student. Now she looked older than Hector Latour. Her eyes were closed and she was apparently dead, but I felt for a pulse. It was barely discernible. I lifted her off the chair and laid her on the gritty floor.

Things looked bad. Marnie's brain had been denied oxygenated blood for God knows how long. I checked her foul-smelling airway for obstructions, made sure she hadn't swallowed her tongue, nipped her nostrils shut and started a combination of mouth-to-mouth respirations and chest compressions. After working on her for a while, I took a few seconds to grab my cellphone, call 911 and tell the operator that I had a very sick woman on my hands. By then my lips were greasy and my throat felt like I'd been gargling grit.

It took forever before I saw an ambulance's blue lights flashing in the kitchen window. To judge by their tortured expressions, the medics didn't like the kitchen's sweaty reek any more than I did. One of them was Tony Roos, a Nimpkish guy from up Gilford Island way whom I'd known for years. He got to his knees beside me, jammed a plastic-tube safety gizmo into Marnie's mouth and kept the CPR going. His partner stuck a syringe into her arm and gave her a shot of something—probably intracardiac epinephrine. After they had her stabilized, I helped them lift her limp body onto a gurney and wheel her outside to the ambulance. When the gurney was loaded and strapped, Tony Roos gave me a bottle of antiseptic mouthwash, told me that I was a bloody fool and then said, "Rinse your mouth out with this but don't swallow any of it. Then get to a hospital and have yourself checked for Hep C and HIV."

The ambulance's diminishing siren was still within earshot when I began to search the house's grim, ugly rooms. I had to kick a few doors in, although why they were locked in the first place made no sense—the furniture consisted of valueless, worm-eaten three-legged chairs, threadbare carpets, warped tables, bare iron bedsteads and massive mahogany and rosewood wardrobes ruined by the damp. My head full of dire forebodings, I phoned police headquarters and brought the duty sergeant up-to-date.

Occasionally rinsing with mouthwash, I left the house. A sliver of moon showed between ragged black clouds, and bats had replaced the swallows that had been feeding on flying insects all day. Half a mile away, waves boomed against the shore with metronomic persistence.

I took a good look at the kitchen window and estimated that its bottom sill was at least 10 feet above ground level. If the thing that had shown its head at that window earlier had been a bear, then he was a really big, dangerous fucker. But Donnelly's Marsh is spook country, and given the jumpy state of my nerves on that dark, evil night, I began to think that maybe what I'd confronted had been a signifier in the shape of a bear sent from the Unknown World by a trickster. I turned away from the house in time to see a coyote—perhaps the same one I'd seen on my way here—sniffing along the black lines of a hedge. He seemed real enough, anyway, and he paused to give me a cheeky, inquisitive stare before trotting away.

I was suffusing my lungs with moist sea air when an unmarked black Interceptor arrived. A full minute passed before its driver's-side door opened, and Detective Inspector Manners got out. A tall, dark-haired, angular man with a sharp jaw, narrow eyes and a nicotine-stained moustache, "Nice" Manners was wearing a smart charcoal grey suit, a silver-coloured necktie and the insincere grin of a man harbouring disagreeable thoughts.

"You again," he said provocatively.

"Uh-huh," I said.

Manners flicked away the stub of the cigarette he had been smoking, fumbled another from a pack in his breast pocket and said unpleasantly, "They told me it was an empty house with a murdered girl in it."

"The murdered girl is inside the ambulance that you passed driving in here—except she isn't dead yet."

"So she wasn't murdered?"

"Oh, she was murdered all right. And keep your eyes peeled for bears ... I spotted a big one earlier."

By then more crime-squad vehicles were arriving, along with rain, and chilly gusts were ruffling the ivy growing on the house. After declining my offer of assistance, Manners went up onto the porch out of the rain and barked instructions to the flatfoots milling around in their white bunny suits.

It was dark enough for headlights when I woke the MG up, got safely off the marsh and headed back to Victoria without spotting Hector Latour. At Hillside Avenue I stopped the car and wound the side window down. Rain was moving in sheets across the rooftops, and the traffic lights suspended across the street swung in the wind. A hustler named Claudette minced from the shadows on stiletto heels. He didn't recognize me at first and offered to perform an illegal procedure for a hundred bucks. I told him to fuck off and asked him if he'd seen Hector Latour. "Not lately," Claudette lisped, smiling at me with botox-bloated lips as fat as frankfurters.

I told him to watch his ass, turned south onto Government Street and ended up parked on a yellow line across from Fran Willis' Chinatown art gallery. Taking a POLICE card from the MG's glove compartment, I clipped it to the sun visor, got out, locked up and walked along to Fisgard Street. Most of the buildings around there are brick tenement houses, the rest being old warehouses, rooming houses, Chinese restaurants and shops. It was raining hard by then— what Canada's west-coasters call Prince Rupert weather—and Fisgard Street's black pavement shone like a brightly flowing river. But rain or no rain, Chinatown was crowded. Pyramids of vegetables and fruit sat beneath flapping canvas awnings, and here and there, open doors and windows emitted waves of laughter and music.

However, I was headed for the Good Samaritan Mission, and there is nothing Chinese about it. A cube of concrete the size of a city block, it is topped by a giant neon crucifix. I waited for a break in the traffic, ran across the street and went inside. The mission's free clinic smelled of bodily secretions and disinfectant, and it was jammed with the walking wounded—people debilitated by years of poverty and homelessness who just needed a place to escape out of the wet.

An emergency room nurse—who obviously rated my hypothetical condition very low on the triage scale—took my name, gave me a number and told me to wait. I sat next to a scabby crack addict, sweating and ill and covered in bandages, who appeared to have fallen through a window. The whole room had that junkie constipation smell. When I grew sick of it, I nipped out of the emergency clinic, went down a flight of stairs and ended up in the clinic's detox department, where a middle-aged woman with heavy purple stains under her eyes was working behind a U-shaped nursing station. She had a stethoscope around her neck and was wearing one of those white, smooth-fronted collarless shirts buttoned down one side.

She gave me the once-over and saw a tall, 40-year-old Coast Salish Native with long black hair. From the look of my red Sierra Designs Gore-Tex jacket over an open-necked plaid shirt, my thirty-dollar wranglers and my caulk boots, she assumed I had lost my way to the soup kitchen and was telling me how to find it when I interrupted to explain that I was a cop. I asked to see Marnie Paul.

"She's not allowed visitors," the nurse told me.

"I'm Marnie's uncle," I lied. "Her only living relative."

"It doesn't really matter. She's just had surgery and is on life support."

The nurse was adamant, and the door to the detox wards was locked. I was pondering my next move when the Good Samaritan Mission's founder and CEO waddled in. This is Joe McNaught—three hundred pounds of assertive Christianity wearing a black robe large enough to house a troop of Boy Scouts. Your average crack addict could easily squeeze through the white ecclesiastical collar that encircled his neck.

Joe McNaught had figured significantly in my past. Once upon a time the preacher and I had been in the boxing racket together, but all he had to show for it was scar tissue, ears like broccoli, and the faint spasmodic tremors associated with early-onset Parkinson's. But that was before he found Jesus. Now he had his own TV show, a waterfront house in the Uplands area of Victoria and a ski lodge at Whistler. McNaught grinned at the nurse and said, "Open the door, Leslie, and show us the way to Sergeant Seaweed's niece."

Marnie was lying in a dimly lit hospital ward with tubes coming out of her body. She looked dead. Even her hair seemed lifeless, and deep wrinkles were etched into the blotchy skin of her face. Tattoos covered her bare arms like vines. After glancing at her charts, the nurse left the ward.

I followed her into the corridor and asked, "How bad is she?"

The nurse shook her head, folded her arms, gazed at the acoustic ceiling tiles, shuffled her feet and said regretfully, "I'm sorry."

I waited.

"There's a lot of bad heroin on the street. Your niece isn't the only dire case we've treated lately," she explained in a low voice. "Doctor Auckland worked on her when they first brought her in, and afterwards she rallied a bit. You could see her eyes moving behind her closed eyelids. She even mumbled a few words."

"About what?"

"It was mostly meaningless babble. Don't hold me to this because I wouldn't swear to it, but for a bit she seemed to be talking about Truth."

"Wait a minute—are you telling me there's brain activity?"

"Marginal brain activity. It doesn't look promising." Evading my eyes, the nurse went on, "Have you read Kübler-Ross' books about death and dying?"

I shook my head, no.

"Maybe you should. To me they were a revelation. Dying patients who haven't been inside a church in fifty years suddenly get religious. Maybe Marnie has a guilty conscience about something and is trying to get it off her chest."

I returned to Marnie's ward and found McNaught down on his knees. I think he was praying because his lips were moving, although he wasn't making any sounds. When he got through praying, it was interesting to watch this three-hundred-pound man get to his feet. Without that hospital bed to cling to, he probably couldn't have done it. After he got his breath back, he made the sign of the cross over Marnie and went away.

I checked the cabinet beside Marnie's bed and found her black leather jacket, a pair of black Doc Martens boots and a half-dozen of Dr. Lawrence Trew's white ballpoint pens. I was sitting there thinking about the kind of danger that naive young Native women fresh off reserves can drift into—prostitution, for example—and the vicious pimps who do their heads in, when Dr. Auckland came by. He glanced at the blood-pressure monitor that was pulsing spasmodically. Then he lifted Marnie's wrist and checked her pulse the old-fashioned way, with his fingers. Maybe it's a conditioned reflex.

Dr. Auckland said, "They say that you're related to the patient."

"Actually she's an orphan. Her dad was a fisherman. Her mom

used to knit Cowichan sweaters. But Marnie and I were born on the same rez, so we're undoubtedly distant cousins. I'm a cop, by the way. Silas Seaweed."

"I've heard of you," the doctor returned absently, looking at me with the alert, slightly wary expression that grows on physicians like patina grows on old silver.

Joe McNaught, waiting for me in the corridor, offered to share the bottle of orange juice he'd been drinking from. I declined, but followed him into his office. It's about the size of a badminton court, with a hardwood floor, Persian rugs and oak shelves filled with dark leather-bound books. McNaught has also spent a lot of money on bureaus, tables and other expensive trappings, including two oil paintings. One is of Mother Teresa wearing white castoffs. The other is of McNaught himself dressed like the Archbishop of Canterbury in red ermine-trimmed robes and a gold cap. The place was as dimly lit as Marnie's ward and had the peaceful atmosphere of a funeral chapel. I looked around the room for a crucifix but didn't see one.

Instead of sitting in his specially reinforced steel chair, McNaught rested his backside on the edge of his huge rosewood desk, a lemon danish in one hand, a cup of coffee in the other. He stared balefully out the window at Chinatown's passing parade as he sipped a little coffee. I was remembering the man that he used to be, when he said, "I'm sorry about your niece."

"She's not my niece—I was fibbing earlier—though I've known Marnie her whole life. When she was little, she wanted to be a ballet dancer."

"She lived on the Warrior Reserve?"

"Until two years ago. Then she left suddenly without saying goodbye."

McNaught's mouth opened, but whatever he had intended to say did not come out. After fidgeting for a minute, he pushed himself away from the desk and wobbled across to the window. "It's my fault," he mumbled. "I killed her."

"She's not quite dead. Not yet."

He produced a tissue and blew his nose with a noise like a surfacing whale. "Poor little kid. She's been hanging around the mission all winter, off and on. Her and a great fucking big mongrel dog. We don't allow dogs. We can't have dogs bringing fleas into the place."

"That would be intolerable," I replied with just a touch of scorn in my voice.

"My board makes the rules. All I do is enforce 'em," McNaught blubbered. "You let one mutt in, it's the end. We'd be knee-deep in dogshit in no time. I built this mission for people, not animals."

"Yeah, it's a no-brainer," I jeered. "Suffer little children, fuck mutts."

"I used to see her sheltering in doorways. I'd say, Marnie, for Christ's sake, drop your dog off at the pound and come into detox. Find Jesus and dry out. She never listened."

"It's a shame."

"And now she's dying. She's going to a better place."

"She's going to the morgue. This place is better," I retorted, pointing my finger at the world outside the window. "In a couple of weeks, what's left of Marnie will be bottled in formaldehyde."

"How about the Unknown World that you Aboriginals are always yakking about?"

I thought about Hayls, the Transformer, and said, "The Unknown World is probably more dangerous than this one."

Beyond McNaught's window, across the street in a Chinese herbalist's shop, a man wearing a black skullcap and red silk robes with dragon embroideries was arranging bottles on his shelves. I left Mcnaught to do whatever he does when people are not watching him, and returned to the emergency clinic. After I waited in line for a while, my number came up. Another tired nurse sitting in a glass sentry box asked me to describe my symptoms. I told her I felt fine, that I just needed checking for Hep C and HIV.

"Tests are expensive," she grumbled. "What makes you think you need them?"

I told her.

Her face expressing disgust, she said, "You've had persistent mouth-to-mouth contact with an open-sore meth addict?"

"She was dying. I didn't know what else to do."

"In that case, you're a reckless idiot," she snapped.

Tony Roos had told me the same thing.

The nurse checked my medical card, made me sign a few papers, gave me an information sheet, advised me to read it and ordered me to wait some more. I sat down in a moulded plastic chair beside an elderly asthmatic and read the brochure.

ABOUT HIV TESTS

When HIV enters the body, your immune system springs to action, producing antibodies to fight the infection. Unfortunately, the antibodies cannot destroy HIV, but their presence in bodily fluids is used to confirm HIV infection.

STANDARD TESTING

HIV testing most often begins with an ELISA (or EIA, enzyme-linked immunosorbent assay) test performed on the blood. If this test shows a reaction, it is repeated on the same blood sample. If the duplicate test is reactive, the results are confirmed using a second more specific (and more expensive) test, most commonly the Western blot. A person is considered infected following a repeatedly reactive result from the ELISA confirmed by the Western blot test. Results can take up to two weeks.

RAPID TESTING

A rapid HIV test is a test that usually produces results in 20 to 40 minutes. There are currently four rapid HIV tests licensed for use:

1) *OraQuick Rapid HIV-1 and Advance HIV 1/2 Antibody Tests, manufactured by OraSure Technologies, Inc.*

2) *Reveal G2 HIV-Antibody Tests, manufactured by Med-Mira, Inc.*

3) *Multispot, manufactured by Bio-Rad Laboratories*

4) *Uni-Gold Recombigen, manufactured by Trinity Biotech The availability of these tests differs from one place to another. These rapid HIV blood tests are considered to be just as accurate as the ELISA. As is true for all screening tests (including the ELISA and EIA), a positive test result must be confirmed with an additional specific test before a diagnosis of infection can be given . . .*

By the time I finished rereading the information sheet for the third time, the emergency clinic was full of twitchy, whacked-out addicts who'd blown their welfare cheques on drugs, and I was beginning to feel like a man who'd fallen from a fire escape and landed among trash bags. I phoned Acting Chief Detective Inspector Bernie Tapp to alert him about Hector Latour. I didn't tell him about the HIV test. Time enough for that later. I was feeding coins into a coffee dispenser when I became aware that my name was being paged.

The triage nurse was trying to calm a weepy, snotty-nosed kid—probably a rent boy—and the nurse who had given me the brochure had apparently forgotten what I looked like. I re-identified myself. She led me into a white booth with a white bench to sit on and a white curtain instead of a door, told me to take my jacket off and roll up a shirt sleeve. While taking a blood sample, she warned me to refrain from sexual activity, sharing needles, and otherwise exchanging body fluids with anyone until the results of my tests came in.

"How long will that take?"

"It depends. Up to four weeks."

"According to your brochure, you can get results with the rapid HIV test in less than an hour ..."

"Perhaps," she interrupted impatiently, "but we use the standard testing model. I'm sorry if this is inconveniencing your life, but if you made sensible choices, you wouldn't be in this predicament. You'll have to wait. In the interim don't exchange bodily fluids with anyone."

"How about if I use condoms?"

"Condoms help, sure. Only condoms have been known to leak. Are you selfish enough to risk your partner's life?"

"Why not?" I replied flippantly. "I'm a typical male."

"This is no joking matter!" she snapped. "Don't share needles or pipes. Don't share eating or drinking utensils. Don't kiss anybody, either! Have I made myself clear?"

Jesus Christ, I thought. Four weeks! Twenty-eight days at least before I can have sex, share Felicity's wineglass ...

CHAPTER TWO

My steps slow and heavy, I left the mission, turned up my collar against the rain, plodded up Fisgard Street and along to Fan Tan Alley, wending through the crowds past curio shops, artisans' workshops, head shops and a room like a barbershop where a man sticks slivers of burning bamboo in your ears if you want to quit smoking. At the end of the alley I turned right and descended Pandora Street.

An elderly man with eagle feathers poked into his long, dark braids was sheltering from the rain in a doorway. He was wearing a green rubber raincoat and knee-high moccasins and holding a large, flat parcel beneath one arm. People called him the Chief, but he wasn't a chief. He was a suicidal, alcoholic artist with a BFA from the University of Washington, Seattle, and his name was Harvey Cheeke. If you threw more than five dollars into his cap, he would reach into his cardboard portfolio and give you a little painting or a drawing. I have acquired half a dozen Cheekes over the years for a total investment of less than fifty dollars. I keep them hidden because I don't want monochromatic stick figures and four-legged inkblots hanging in my house, but luckily I saved them instead of just throwing them away. Nowadays signed, genuine Harvey Cheekes are as valuable as signed, genuine Norval Morrisseaus. But on this night, before I reached him, he had detached himself from the doorway and walked off into the rain on sluggish, rheumaticky legs.

As a neighbourhood cop, I'm supposed to keep an eye on Victoria's runaways, slackers, junkies, pushers and the likes of Harvey Cheeke. And I usually assist the detective squad in serious crimes—occasionally murders—that involve Native Indians. My one-man office is located on the ground floor of a no-longer-young, three-storey brick building. My door is the first on the right along a corridor that ends at the door to my private washroom, though a lot of people seem to end up with keys to it. I get the lock changed every now and then. I let myself into my office, draped my jacket over the hat tree and left it to drip on the linoleum.

I picked up a couple of advertising flyers lying beneath my mail slot and dropped them onto my battered, wooden, seven-drawer desk. PC—my very own feral cat—was taking her ease on the blotter. Indignant at being disturbed from her slumbers, she leapt to the floor and bolted into the bottom drawer of my filing cabinet where, out of spite, she's been shredding important documents.

Queen Victoria, in her picture frame on the wall, gave me a stern look as I reached into my desk and brought out the office bottle. I poured two inches of Teacher's into a Tim Hortons mug and, sitting down, gazed up at the plaster cornice mouldings on the high ceiling while I tried to think. One way or another I was going to do something about Marnie Paul. In my opinion she'd been murdered. I sent a silent toast to Marnie's spirit—and to whichever Coast Salish spirit is in charge of sexually transmitted diseases—and poured myself another drink.

PC had exited her nest and was standing on a scrap of carpet with her back arched, talons exposed, purring ecstatically, but when she saw me looking at her, her eyes glazed with hatred. She and I have this hot/cold relationship. At that moment our relationship was heavily biased towards the blue end of the spectrum because I had kidnapped her last batch of kittens and then delivered her to the spay shop. My conscience is clear, though. The kittens went to good homes and PC's mothering days are over.

After brooding about grizzly bears for a while, I phoned Chief Alphonse at the Warrior band's business office. Nobody answered, and I left a message on the chief's machine. Mr. Teacher's was doing a great job on my sore throat, so I had another. After that, I put the bottle away, checked PC's kitty litter, emptied half a can of cat food into her saucer, locked up the office and went out.

Harvey Cheeke was back on station near Swans pub. Winds gusting up from the harbour were whipping his long hair around his scrawny, bristled face, and his moccasins were soaked. He was staring at the dark interior of an empty wine bottle when I spoke to him. I asked if he needed a flop for the night.

"I've got a place I can burrow into if I want. Pull the lid over myself and I'm cosy as a . . . clam," he told me.

I gave him a few bucks. Harvey reached into his portfolio, brought out a big manila envelope and shoved it into my hands.

I LIVE IN A two-room waterfront cabin on the Warrior Reserve. Out back I have my own little secluded garden and a one-hole privy hidden among a stand of cedars. When I got home that night, the cabin was as cold and dark as my mood. I switched a light on, placed Harvey's unopened manila envelope on a window-sill and exchanged my boots for fleece-lined moccasins. After that, I put Big Mama Thornton on the turntable and let her 33-rpm blues wash over me while I lit my woodstove, opened the damper on the stove's sheet-metal flue and let her rip.

I lit a couple of candles, flipped the electric light off and stood at the window. Limber trees were shaking in the wind. Out on that portion of the stormy Salish Sea that is known as Juan de Fuca Strait, ships were inward and outward bound between

Victoria and the Orient, but closer in I could see a black-hulled fishboat pushing its foaming white bow wave towards our jetty.

One of Thrifty's deep-frozen lasagnas had been thawing on top of my refrigerator since breakfast. When I poked it with a finger, it felt a bit squishy, so as soon as the kettle boiled, I made a pot of Red Rose, then melted a little butter in a skillet and dumped the lasagna in. By that time Big Mama Thornton had fallen through the hole in her record, and to deflect my thoughts from HIV, I put Bessie Smith on. She was singing about pigs' feet and beer, and the lasagna was bubbling nicely on the stove when somebody hailed the house.

"Yah hey!" I shouted back.

Chief Alphonse came in. "Seen your lights on," he said in his soft voice. Haggard and barefoot, he was wearing a bearskin cloak and a red-cedar headband with hemlock twigs poked into it. The chief is an old man now, but to me he has always been old. He seems immune to time and death.

He turned his wrinkled, hawk-nosed face towards the stove. "You're not going to eat that?" he said, sniffing the lasagna as I jiggled the skillet.

"Certainly, Chief. Have you had supper?"

"I haven't eaten since last Tuesday."

"Help yourself to a cup of tea."

Ignoring my words, the chief brought a candle to the stove, peered closely at the lasagna, and said, "It's green in places, Silas. There are enough bacteria in that pan to kill the whole tribe."

"Not if it's heated enough."

"Maybe you've got stiqa'yu."

"Stiqa'yu? I don't know that word."

"It's an old Snohomish word for wolf spirit," the chief explained. "Wolves eat carrion, so people with wolf spirit make good deer hunters. Snohomish Steve had stiqa'yu. He was the man people hired to dig up corpses and put them into new graves. Stiqa'yu helped him to handle the half-decayed bodies. He would put decayed flesh in his mouth to show his power."

"How long ago was this?"

Instead of answering my question, the chief said, "Why do you use candles?"

"Ambience."

"Do you like listening to that noise or would you rather hear music instead?"

I can take a hint, so I put Bessie Smith back to bed. The cabin was heating up nicely.

"I phoned the band office earlier, Chief. Did you get my message?"

"Yes. Maureen told me that you'd found Marnie Paul up Donnelly's Marsh way. Thank heavens. The poor little kid has the heebie-jeebies, I guess?"

"Marnie's not a drunk, Chief. She's a methamphetamine and heroin addict."

"We'll work on it, you and me, get her healthy again."

"That might be tough. Marnie's pretty far gone. They're treating her for an overdose at the Good Samaritan Mission."

"How would you rate her chances?"

"Not as good as mine," I suggested.

The chief folded his arms and stood gazing out the window at the slivered moon in the windswept sky as I described Marnie's mouth sores and told him about the grizzly bear that I may or may not have sighted at the old Donnelly house.

He remained silent for a long moment and then, instead of addressing my topic, said mildly, "Johnny Scranton came in just now and I watched him unload his catch at the jetty. He was trolling off Sooke in eighty feet of water, picked up some nice twenty-pound springs and an eighty-pound halibut."

"Not bad. What was he using?"

"Herrings," the chief said. "Frozen herrings and crocodile lures."

The lasagna was burnt black around the edges, but I dumped it onto a plate, carried it to the table and ate it. It was delicious.

The chief sat down on my sofa and said, "So Marnie was hiding out at the marsh. That took some nerve."

"Her and Hector Latour. The Donnelly house is a perfect hideout."

"If you're not afraid of ghosts . . ."

"Or ghost stories. People see something a little unusual and it triggers big crazy ideas."

"And some people think with their heads too much. There are other ways of seeing. I hear about weird sightings all the time."

"What kind of sightings?"

"Dancing *hamatsa* men with human skulls tied around their waists. Bears with noses like pigs. Ghosts."

"For drug addicts there are worse things than ghosts. Besides, Marnie and Hector are stoned most of the time. With them, hallucinations are normal."

Shaking his head absently, the chief said, "I've been meaning to ask you, Silas. This methamphetamine stuff I keep hearing about. What is it?"

"It's a cheap chemical stimulant, very addictive, and it sells on the street for about a quarter of the price of crack cocaine. You can get instructions how to make crystal meth on the Internet. The ingredients are all readily available, but it's not as easy to make as people think. Kids get burned trying to make it . . . or blow themselves up."

The chief was silent for a while. Then he said, "I was thinking maybe the Donnelly's Marsh curse had run its course because nothing lasts forever, but it's still a very evil place. Pity. There's good clamming along that shore."

I poured myself another cup of tea.

"Okay," the chief said, "I'm out of here. Got any Imodium?"

I shook my head.

"Too bad. I just hope you don't have to spend all night on the crapper," he said, standing up. "I got business to attend to now."

Turning to leave, the old man staggered slightly and as he walked out into the cold night clad in his bearskins, he looked exhausted and feeble. This put me in a predicament. I knew the chief was on Vision Quest business, and as such, it was a strictly private affair between him and his personal spirits. Oh, the hell with protocol, I thought.

The moon, sliding between rain-sodden clouds, was throwing grotesque shadows when, against all the rules, I followed the chief into the night. There was barely enough light to see him moving slowly along the seldom used waterfront trail. After half an hour he reached a small, bag-shaped cove encircled by forest, and he paused there for a moment gazing out to sea. A screech owl hooted, and suddenly in that queer, murky half-light, the chief dematerialized—one second he was there, the next he'd gone.

Rain began to fall coldly again. I hunkered in the dryish area beneath a big old cedar tree and settled down to wait. After a while Chief Alphonse emerged from the bush carrying a bundle of nettles and leafy twigs. He walked right past without seeing me and went down to the water's edge, laid his bundle down and began to collect handfuls of gritty seaweed. I stayed where I was while the old man took his bearskins off and scrubbed his naked body with seaweed, nettles and twigs. Then, scratched and bleeding, he walked chest-deep into the sea. I don't know how long he had been in that frigid water when out at sea something flashed and came towards the land in zigzags like lightning. I closed my eyes but I could still see that lightning. It was accompanied by an icy wind that whistled in the trees, making noises that sounded like unhappy children.

I never go into the bush without matches or a lighter, so I went looking for and soon found an old fir stump that was full of pitch. I cut slivers of kindling with my pocket knife and got a fire started inside the stump. The rain had stopped again, and the slivered moon had reappeared from behind dark clouds, and in that queer half-light I could see that something limp and white was flopping about in the surf like a giant fish. It was Chief Alphonse, bleeding at his mouth, ears, temples and from the pits at the base of his neck. I wrapped him up in his bearskins and carried him to the fire.

CHAPTER THREE

The vacant lot behind Swans pub where I usually park my car is being developed, and I had to cruise Victoria's rainy streets for five minutes before finding a spot near the Store Street kayak shop. A hairy piss-bum trudged past, pushing a shopping cart loaded with the burden of his life. His trousers were several inches too short for his skinny legs, and his arms and head poked through holes in the green plastic garbage bag that he wore instead of a raincoat. He paused at a phone booth, checked it for quarters and resumed his endless trek.

Lou's Cafe—crowded with raincoats—smelled of damp clothing, fried food and coffee. Lou, sweating over his grill, was busier than a cat in a doghouse because the latest in a long line of his waitresses had quit to work in Alberta's oil patch. Men in hard hats and steel-toed boots were sitting in the booths quarterbacking last Saturday's Ducks versus Canucks game. Graveyard-shift workers, homeward bound from Esquimalt's dockyards, swigged coffee. I filled a cup for myself at Lou's percolator and stood in a corner to wait for an empty seat. When the eight-o'clock whistle sounded, the hard-hat brigade trooped off to work, and I bagged a table by the windows.

After a while, Lou came over to take my order. He is a short, angry former Yugoslavian guerrilla fighter with eyebrows like worn-out toothbrushes. I think he is bald, but I've never seen him without a hat on. That day he was wearing a Boy Scout's beret covered with merit badges that were a perfect match for the tomato stains splashed down his white apron. "Is crazy," he said. "What I going to do about getting girls?"

"Use deodorant," I kidded him. "Smile more."

"Sonsabitch. Already I paying waitresses ten bucks an hour plus tips. What more they want?"

"Thirty dollars an hour plus benefits in boom towns full of sex-starved oil millionaires."

"Oil patch wages is disgrace. Construction wages is disgrace. Government got to do something."

"How about three eggs over medium, crispy bacon, hash browns and whole wheat toast?"

Lou hurried away.

Gales of laughter were erupting across the room, where Cynthia Leach and a clutch of highly buffed women were exchanging obscene jokes about George Bush and Tony Blair. After paying her bill, Cynthia came over to say hello. A rookie porn-squad constable on VPD's entrapment detail, she had been strolling all night, and she looked sexier than Cialis in black fishnet stockings, red shoes with six-inch spikes and a faux fox jacket barely long enough to cover her Kevlar vest. She gazed at me with dreamy blue eyes that—if she stayed with the porn squad much longer—would acquire a cynical cast. After the usual palaver, I asked if she had any idea where I might find Hector Latour.

"Hector the Protector? I don't know diddly-squat except somebody told me he'd gone to ground. Why?"

"Sit down and I'll tell you about it."

"Sorry, can't. Gotta run." But she paused long enough to study my face closely and then ask, "You all right, Silas?"

"Sure. Why shouldn't I be?"

"No reason. You look a bit peaky is all. Now I really gotta run. If I don't get some shut-eye, I'll collapse."

After breakfast I went next door to my office and let myself in. PC was out, and the room smelled like dirty laundry. I left the door ajar, changed PC's kitty litter and opened the window blinds. Puddles reflected Victoria's grey morning sky, but the trees in the vacant lot beside the Janion Building showed fresh green leaves, shiny with rain. A Slegg Brothers truck was backing into the construction site behind Swans pub, where hard hats were doing things with concrete vibrators and steel-reinforcing rods. In the damp morning air, I heard a locomotive shunting back and forth near the E & N roundhouse a half mile away.

Headquarters had sent me a framed photograph of Queen Elizabeth II. She wore a jewelled crown, a remote smile, blue silken robes and her purple Honi-soit-qui-mal-y-pense sash. I borrowed hammer and nails from the janitor's closet and hung today's majesty on my wall next to her great-great-grandmother. After that, I stood at the window gnawing thoughts while I watched a truck-mounted crane dump construction debris into heavy-duty trucks. I phoned Acting Chief Detective Inspector Bernie Tapp to ask for the latest on Hector Latour.

"Everybody's looking, but Hector's cleared off somewhere. If we're lucky, he's on a slow boat to China. And what's this I hear about you having AIDS?"

"Somebody blabbed?"

"No, I'm a mind reader," Bernie replied, treating my banality with the derision it deserved. "The point is, is it true?"

"Possibly, except it's not AIDS. It's HIV and Hep C. I'll know for sure when I get the test results in four weeks."

"Okay. Meantime, keep your dick in your pants."

The dialtone kicked in to tell me he'd gone. I was still processing my indignation when the phone rang again. This time,

Fred Halloran, a newspaper reporter, wanted to know if I had anything to say about the squatters illegally camped in Beacon Hill Park.

"Why should I care?"

"Two hundred acres of prime Victoria real estate is being used as a tent city, and your people used to own it."

"My people? I suppose you're referring to the Coast Salish people."

"You catch on quickly sometimes. So how about it, Silas? Any remarks?"

"In the olden days the Coast Salish used to cultivate camas lilies on that land. They're full of calories, but they taste awful, make you fart and give you the trots. You want to get rid of squatters, feed 'em camas bulbs, then stand back and watch 'em run," I said and hung up.

As I usually record such calls, I reached for paper and pen. The pen was dry. Then I remembered the white ballpoint that had fallen from Hector Latour's backpack—the pen marked Dr. Lawrence Trew, Hypnotherapy. It was still in my jacket pocket, and I used it to write my note. The next thing I found myself doing was phoning Trew's office. All I got was his voice mail. I looked up his home number and tried that with the same result.

I closed the blinds, locked up and went out into a light drizzle. PC was perched on the construction hoarding across the street, keeping an eye on things.

THE MATBRO BUILDING ON Fort Street is another of the old brick holdovers that date back to Victoria's gold-rush era. I know the building well because Henry Ferman—a private eye who specializes in video surveillance—has an office on the second floor. I entered the lobby through a door located between a one-chair barbershop and a used-book emporium. The wall directory told me that Lawrence Trew had an office on the second floor. The elevator was out of order, so I hiked up the stairs.

The legend on the glass panel in the door read "Dr. Lawrence Trew, Hypnotherapy". Intriguingly, the paintwork between Trew's door and its jamb was damaged—splinters of bare wood showed where somebody had inserted a jimmy or a heavy screwdriver. But the door was locked, and nobody answered when I pounded on it. I was gazing speculatively at its shiny new brass lock when a cleaning woman emerged from a broom closet down the corridor.

I watched her plug an extension cord into a wall socket and began shoving a vacuum cleaner towards me along the hall carpet. "You'll be lucky," she said, looking me over with good-humoured curiosity. "Nobody's seen Dr. Trew all week."

Her accent told me she was English. She wasn't as handsome as Queen Elizabeth, though she was nearly her majesty's age, and I imagined that if she were to remove her headscarf, she'd reveal the same tight silver curls as well. A plastic ID tag dangling from her neck said that she was Mrs. Irene Adams.

"Is he on holiday?" I asked.

"No, he's ill," Mrs. Adams said. "Because he was robbed, wasn't he?"

"Was he?"

"Two layabouts broke his door down. Bold as brats at nine o'clock in the morning," she said, cigarette ash cascading down her apron whenever her lips moved. "They were filling their pockets when the doc walked in on 'em."

I had a feeling that Mrs. Adams and I were going to get along.

"Tell me more," I said, showing her my badge.

"Oooh! You're a policeman, and the doc told me never to tell nobody," she said in consternation. "Now I've put my foot among the pigeons."

"It's all right, don't worry about it."

"It's too late to worry—the horse is out of the barn, isn't it?"

"So Dr. Trew was robbed?" I said to encourage her.

"Robbed and beaned," she said, warming to her tale. "Brained him they did, with one of his own brass candlesticks."

"Dr. Trew's not in hospital . . ."

"Oh no, he wasn't hurt serious. Just a bit shook up and a head-ache."

"Did Dr. Trew tell you what the burglars looked like?"

"He didn't have to, did he? I saw 'em myself, didn't I? Indians like you they was, only a bit scruffier. One was a thin little runt with yellow hair—I suppose he dyes it. The other was a young girl—dressed all in black she was. They ran right past me, the pair of 'em. They gave me such a fright I haven't had a good night's sleep since."

Mrs. Adams removed the half-smoked cigarette from her mouth, nipped off the butt with calloused fingers and dropped the stub into her apron pocket. I waited while she vacuumed the still-glowing butt off the carpet. Mixing burning cigarette butts with highly combustible carpet dust causes many fires, but instead of cautioning Mrs. Adams, I asked her if it were possible to view Trew's office. Without hesitation, she produced a master key and unlocked the door. She tried to follow me in, but didn't make any fuss when I shut her out.

The hypnotherapist had a two-room-plus-washroom suite—a swanky reception room stocked with up-to-date editions of *Vanity Fair* and *Vogue*, where clients could swoon over pictures of Paris Hilton's jewellry while the client ahead was being mesmer-ized, and a consulting room that lay behind a soundproof door. The entire suite had oak wainscotting, antique wallpapers, crossbeamed ceilings and comfortable leather chairs. Trew's glass-topped desk, steel-and-leather recliner and red-leather chaise lounge must have cost nearly as much as the Canucks had paid to acquire their latest goalie. What appeared at first glance to be a carved oak sideboard turned out to be a filing cabinet. An oak bureau concealed a safe. Built-in shelves displayed dark leather-bound books that were interchangeable with those in Joe McNaught's office. A framed certificate dated 1989 indicated that Lawrence Trew had graduated with his MD from McGill, another one declared him a licentiate of Portmann's Hypnotherapy College.

After poking around ineffectually among Trew's files, I checked out his desk drawers, which contained the usual—paperclips, staplers, a bottle of liquid paper, an eraser, elastic bands and stuff like that. I didn't find any alcohol, drugs or complimentary ballpoints. The only thing on the desktop was an ivory telephone, and when I picked it up, it beeped intermittently before the dial tone kicked in. The secrets lodged in Dr. Trew's telephone would soon be known to Victoria's detective squad. I swivelled around in Trew's chair, preparing to stand, when something caught my eye. On the parquet floor between the Persian rug and the wall was a small faint rusty stain that looked like dried blood.

I was still sitting behind Trew's desk, looking at the stain, when a lovely Native woman entered. She was about thirty and moved with an athlete's fluid grace. She was tall with huge golden eyes and skin the colour of cappuccino. Her hair was parted in the middle and fell to her shoulders in loose waves. Beneath her unbuttoned oatmeal-coloured tweed coat, a creamy turtleneck sweater and a short tartan skirt with a lot of red in it showed off her shapely figure.

"Who are you and how did you get in here?" she asked. Her eyes were cool and—given half a chance—I'd have been willing to put some warmth in them.

"I'm a policeman, who are you?"

"One of Dr. Trew's clients."

"Do you have an appointment?"

"That's hardly any of your business," she informed me tersely. "Do you know where he is?"

"Not at present. When is the last time you saw Dr. Trew?"

She tilted her head. "Ten days ago, perhaps more." Then she demanded with a little more force, "How do I know you're a policeman?"

I showed her my badge. "Now I think it's your turn to tell me who you are."

"Well, I don't," she said with the same calm enunciation.

I grinned at her—or thought I did until I saw my leer reflected in the window. Miss Wonderful walked out without smiling or saying goodbye.

I gave her a minute. Then, leaving Trew's office unlocked, I went downstairs and stepped into the street just in time to see her get into a late-model blue Lexus SUV. Before she drove off I noted its licence number and then traipsed back up to Trew's office. Using his desk phone, it took me all of five minutes to determine that the blue Lexus was registered to Charlotte Fox. It took me one minute more to find Ms. Fox's file in Trew's cabinet. The file's bare-bones information was to the effect that she'd presented for grief counselling following the death of her father. I also learned that consulting Dr. Trew was an expensive pastime. Ms. Fox had been seeing him once a week for two years, more or less, at a cost of two hundred and fifty dollars per visit. Her account was overdue, and a reminder had been sent. As I returned the file to the cabinet, I was thinking that the name Charlotte Fox sounded vaguely familiar. I thought I'd give her a call one of these days.

There was a soft thud as something struck Trew's outer door. When I checked, I found a morning newspaper lying in the corridor. Obviously he hadn't expected to be away this long, or he would have cancelled his paper. I glanced at the headlines. Another roadside bomb had killed six Canadian soldiers in Afghanistan. In Victoria the average price of an ordinary house now exceeded half a million dollars, and militant squatters had declared Beacon Hill Park to be a free state.

I went back into Trew's office and sat behind his desk. After some heavy thinking, I used his phone to call Cynthia Leach. Answering after the sixth ring, she sounded sleepy. I apologized for waking her up.

"Never mind me, Silas. What's this I've been hearing about you having AIDS?"

"I'm fit as a fiddle. It's nothing, just a few routine medical checks. Have you any idea how the rumour got started?"

"No, but didn't somebody say that rumours are condensed facts?"

"The reason I'm calling is, do you remember me asking you about Marnie Paul and Hector Latour?"

"Yes . . ."

"You told me that you didn't know diddly-squat about Hector. Then you added something about Hector going to ground. Correct?"

"Yes?"

"Well, I'm curious about the actual words you used. I don't think you're the sort of person who'd usually say 'going to ground.'"

There was a long silence followed by, "Funny you should say that. I ought to have mentioned it earlier, but there *was* a bit of street buzz about Hector and Marnie last night. Some John was driving around in a BMW asking for them."

"Did you get the BMW's number?"

"No, I didn't see the car myself. I was told about it is all. But I think there are people out there who do know where Hector's hiding, because one of the people I spoke to said she didn't know, quote, diddly-squat about him, unquote. Then she said she guessed he'd gone to ground, making a kind of a joke of it, you know."

"I'll need that BMW's registration number."

"It's probably in my bad-date book. I'll look my BMW numbers up and email them to you."

I thanked her, put the phone down and leaned back in Trew's very comfortable leather chair. After some unproductive brooding, I left the office thinking that I'd like to have a chair like that one day.

Out on Fort Street, a pavement princess was sitting on the sidewalk with her back to a lamppost and her legs stretched out. From a distance of five yards, her shaven head resembled a skull. Up close her face was too pale, her lips too red, her gaze too dreamy. It was still only April, but she was dressed for summer in shorts, flip-flops, and a cotton tank top decorated with yellow butterflies. Tweaked out on crank, she was using a cigarette lighter to singe the downy golden hairs off her pale skinny arms. A baseball cap lay between her feet, but there was more copper in her ear rivets than in the cap. I told her to move on. She flipped me the bird and called me a nasty name—as was her right. Besides, under Canada's nitwit legal system I had no power to influence her behaviour whatsoever, and she knew it. If she wanted to incinerate her arms and turn the colour of verdigris every time it rained, that was strictly her business. I wished her good luck and left her to it.

CHAPTER FOUR

Victoria's Beacon Hill Park is two hundred acres of ornamental ponds, cricket pitches and tree-shaded bowers. Cooper's hawks, bald eagles, nervous squirrels and numerous species of waterfowl inhabit the park full time, but during the past few weeks the wildlife had been sharing its space with illegal human squatters.

After driving over to the park, I tramped a woodsy trail past the Cameron Bandshell and around the children's petting zoo to reach a sloping meadow overlooking the sea. The lush grass was colourfully varied with balsamroot, satin flowers, blue camas, chocolate lilies and blue violets. Hummingbirds buzzed among purple and pink rhododendrons.

About a hundred of Canada's homeless had set up camp on a stretch of level ground. Some had built semi-permanent shacks using salvaged wooden pallets, bits of canvas, sheet metal and old planks. Others had pitched tents. Smoke drifted up from tin stovepipes and open fires. A large white banner strung between trees read: BEACON HILL ESTATES—CHOICE LOTS STILL AVAILABLE.

Death camas—so-named because the whole plant is poisonous—was flourishing amid the construction debris and the garbage. The scent of lilacs and apple blossoms was leavened by the stink of rotting vegetation, human waste, woodsmoke and skunk cabbage. Broken glass lay here and there. Two trees—their root-balls loosened by the squatters' ill-advised digging—had blown down in a recent gale, and their craters were now filled with rainwater. Dogs barked. People moped around, smoking joints. But apart from three teenaged boys riding around on trail bikes, nobody seemed to be having any fun.

A thin woman with grey hair and slightly prominent blue eyes was on her knees beside an open fire, trying to heat milk in a fry-ing pan. She held a sleeping baby in one arm. The wide nostrils of her upturned nose showed darkly. "What do you want?" she asked suspiciously as I approached.

"I'm looking for Hector Latour," I told her. "Maybe he's around here someplace."

She cocked her head and gave me an empty stare. "I wouldn't know, I'm sure," she said in a ladylike way. "What's his name again?"

"Hector Latour. A Native man who dyes his hair yellow."

"Oh, Natives," she said inscrutably.

She seemed sad and pathetic. I wondered if she was the baby's mother, but she seemed too old. I tried to guess her age. Forty? Fifty? She seemed out of place here, but just thinking about the route she'd travelled to reach this hopeless dead end was enough to give me a headache. I smiled at her and was moving on when she called me back.

"On second thought, I might have seen him," she said, stand-ing up and rocking the sleeping infant. "A Native man with dyed yellow hair, I mean, although I don't think he's here now. What did you say your name is?"

"Roger Bannister."

"And I suppose you and Hector used to run around together," she said with a smile that took twenty years off her face.

As I turned away, Fred Halloran walked up to me. He'd been skulking around the camp, his notebook open, digging up dirt for the next edition. Fred was always on the spot when things happened, and when things didn't happen, he was on the spot inventing stories about things that might happen. He asked me where all the camas bulbs were.

I pointed to the blue flowers that were blooming profusely as far as the eye could see. "The bulbs are underneath those things. In the old days the Native people dried them out then buried them in sand. When they were completely dehydrated, the bulbs were warmed in hot water and served in big white clamshells."

"In the old days?"

"Hell yes. We've moved on, Fred. Tonight the band cafeteria is offering us our choice of consommé au citron or lobster bisque, hearts of palm salad and noisette of lamb à l'Indienne with a bit of sabayon au Grand Marnier to follow."

Fred was scribbling in his notebook when I went back to my car. I sat in it for a while, gazing down Douglas Street towards the sea. Most people don't know that Beacon Hill is an ancient Lekwungen burial site and as such is hallowed ground to Coast Salish people. Stone memorial-cairn remnants can still be found on the park's southeastern slopes. I'd been thinking about burials and ghosts and hauntings a lot lately, and now an unbidden ghost from my distant past had showed up to remind me that long ago I'd smoked plenty of dope and tobacco. Sometimes—not often—I regret giving them up. After all, cigarettes have their uses. Cigarettes and matches give fidgety hands something to do. For tongue-tied swains, offering women cigarettes and the whole ritual of lighting them are valuable social gambits. In the good old days before cancer and chronic obstructive pulmonary disease, everybody smoked. This was a boon to Christmas shoppers—if you had smokers on your list, you could always give them another ashtray. And there was something irresistibly sexy about the way film goddesses like Rita Hayworth used to lean back in their chairs, cross their legs and blow smoke into the eyes of adoring male actors.

I occupied the time it would have taken me to smoke two Export As brooding about where Hector Latour might be. Then I watched an old woman pushing a walker come out of an apartment building across the street, and I marvelled at a gull's flight mirrored by its passing shadow on the sidewalk. And that, too, reminded me of something.

WHEN I GOT BACK to my office, I found two reports had been slipped through my mailbox. The first, dropped off by Cynthia Leach, was the bad-date driver's-licence list she'd promised. The second, from headquarters, was an updated missing kids list. Two eight-year-old Harris Green boys had failed to return home overnight. I posted their pictures on my bulletin board.

The sun was shining by the time I'd caught up on routine business and walked back across town to the Matbro Building, this time headed for Henry Ferman's second-floor office.

Henry's one-room suite plus washroom is like Lawrence Trew's suite in the same way that a garbage scow is like the royal yacht. The only magazines in his waiting room are dog-eared circa 1970 issues of *Popular Mechanics*. His inner sanctum smells like oily rubber, and it resembles an electronics-repair shop more than a private-eye's office. He has a couple of filing cabinets, a computer with more ports than the British Navy, and a fax machine. Most of his remaining space is devoted to floor-to-ceiling metal shelves laden with microphones, cameras, video monitors, long-distance listening devices and boxes filled with other electronics junk. A six-inch TV monitor mounted on a swivel bracket bolted to his desk displays a grainy image of his waiting room.

I found him sitting behind his cluttered desk reading a paper-back copy of *The Sun Also Rises* and wearing a toupée that would have gone unnoticed on a coconut. In 1964 Henry had been in Canada's far north, checking traplines, when he and his dog team crashed through the ice of a frozen lake. Henry lost his rig, but crawled ashore and made it back to camp with nothing worse than frozen ears and frozen feet. Hence the toupée and the fact that indoors (and sometimes outdoors) he now wears padded car-pet slippers. His top speed wouldn't challenge a tortoise. But what Henry lacks in velocity, he makes up for in acuity.

When he saw me, his frown was as meaningful as an evic-tion notice. "Sorry," he said mournfully. "I've already donated. The policeman's benevolent association may have better luck next door."

I sat down, looked at Henry and said, "Lawrence Trew's office was burgled recently. I think you'd know something about it."

"Why should I?"

"Because you're a private investigator, not a whirling dervish."

Henry chewed his lip and shrugged. "What's to know? The only thing Larry Trew and me have in common is we work in the same building. I like Larry—which makes two of us."

"Is he a portly, bald, harried-looking man who beats his chil-dren and wears dowdy brown suits?"

Henry shook his head. "Larry's a single dude who looks like Leo DiCaprio. Wears blue-chalk pinstripes and five-hundred-dollar Mephistos."

"Vain?"

"I'd be vain if I had Larry's looks, clientele, sex drive and money. What he's doing with an office in this building is beyond me."

"It's beyond me, too. According to Mrs. Adams, the cleaning lady, Trew hasn't been in his office all week."

SEAWEED ON THE ROCKS   41

"Right. He told me he'd be out of town for a few days—business."

"He didn't say where?"

Henry shook his head. "I'd like to help, but there's nothing else I can tell you. We're not exactly pals. All I do is pass him in the corridor sometimes. We just nod and say hello."

"You haven't done any PI work for him, put bugs in his office, shined his five-hundred-dollar shoes?"

Men who spend years sharing remote Arctic wildernesses with grizzlies and wolves don't scare easily. Instead of answering my questions, Henry took his toupée off and placed it carefully upon a moulded Styrofoam head, which he then set gently on the floor by his feet. The shrivelled nubs of Henry's ears resembled the hallucinogenic mushrooms my people eat when they get tired of ordinary reality.

I said, "You've never discussed the burglary with Mrs. Adams?"

"It's all we talk about now. It's the most exciting thing that's happened in her life since Donald Trump's hair fixative let go on TV."

"Trew's office could have been burgled by Hector Latour and Marnie Paul. Hector had a string of hookers till drugs fried his brains. Marnie was the only girl he had left."

"What's it to you, Silas?"

"Marnie and I lived on the same reserve. When she was little, I used to drive her to ballet class."

Henry flushed and his glance shifted to a wall clock.

I said, "Lawrence Trew has dropped out of sight. It makes me wonder if he's dead."

Henry licked his lips, the wrinkles on his brow deepened, but he didn't say anything.

"This is the way I've got it figured," I continued, leaning

forward. "If Hector and Marnie did break into Trew's office, I expect they were looking for drugs. They may have thought he was a real doctor of medicine instead of a hypnotherapist. Once inside Trew's office, they didn't find anything they could snort, smoke or inject, so they mitigated their damages by stealing everything they could carry. A gold-plated desk set, maybe a picture or two. Complimentary ballpoint pens with Trew's name on them. Candlesticks."

In the silence that followed, I could hear the distant whine of the vacuum cleaner. Henry transferred his gaze to the window. Three miles away the white observatory dome atop Saanich Little Mountain was reflecting the sun's strengthening rays. He lit a cigarette, blew smoke out the side of his mouth, and said, "Well, Silas, how is life otherwise?"

"Less of the other, none of the wise."

"So it's true then what I've been hearing?" he said. "You've only got a few months to live?"

"There's some crazy talk about me right now. Tell you what, though. You'll know the stories are true when you see me driving around town in a rented Porsche and smoking cigars."

Henry brought out his office bottle, splashed some of its contents into a couple of transparent plastic cups and slid one cup across his desktop for me to pick up. It was Italian Red, and I figured Henry's taste buds must have disappeared along with his dog team, because he poured his drink down with evident relish. Licking his lips like a dog that's just scarfed up a hundred millilitres of Russian caviar, he said, "Why do you think Larry needed candlesticks in his office?"

"Hypnotherapy aids?"

"I thought they used gold watches and chains. You know, swinging them like pendulums."

"Quite possibly. You said he was a swinger."

"Don't get me wrong—I really like him. Maybe I'm a little jealous."

Henry's glass was empty. He filled it up again, sighed and said, "Yes, Larry did consult me. There's that burglary you already know about, and as you guessed, the burglars didn't get any drugs because Lawrence isn't a real doctor anymore, but they did steal a bunch of small stuff. Pictures, some other knick-knacks of little value. Larry didn't care because he was insured. What bothered him was the thieves took a bowling trophy."

"A little statuette of a guy balanced on one leg holding a bowling ball?"

Henry squinted at me. "I'm trying to imagine a guy balancing a bowling ball on his leg."

"A guy balanced on one leg holding a bowling ball in one hand."

"Hell no, this trophy was a silver cup. It was an engraved sterling silver cup that had been awarded to Larry's mom. It had sentimental value, so he asked me to try and get it back."

"Keep talking."

"Hector and Marnie, if that's who the thieves are, unloaded the stuff at Titus Silverman's place."

"You're certain about that?"

"Like I said, the cup was engraved. I found it in Titus' shop."

I thought that over. Titus Silverman was a mid-level, mid-career villain who enjoyed shooting BB pellets into people's eyes. "Then what? Did you talk to Silverman about it?"

Henry scowled. "Speak to Tight-ass? Hell no, he's a maniac. Think I'm nuts? I haven't told anybody till now. I was going to tell Larry, but I haven't had the chance yet."

Henry got up, shuffled to a cabinet on his obviously aching feet, opened a drawer and brought out a jeweller's presentation box. He handed the blue box to me. I opened it. It contained an engraved silver cup wrapped in tissue paper.

"Every time I talk to a cop it costs me money," Henry complained. "I'm out three-fifty and change on this deal so far."

"You paid three hundred and fifty dollars for this cup?"

"Why not? It's sterling silver."

"Has Lawrence always been single?"

"He was married till his wife fell off a balcony. Now he's a widower."

"His wife fell off a balcony?" I said, taken aback.

"A high balcony."

"Thanks for being so explicit. Maybe you can clear something else up for me. Trew has an MD from McGill, so why doesn't he practice regular medicine?"

"Because he's barred. He practised in Quebec for a few years till something happened and he was struck off the register, which is when he pulled up stakes and moved to Toronto." There was a pause before he continued slowly and, perhaps, reluctantly.

"Ontario yanked his licence because he went nuts at a conference, beat the bejesus out of another delegate. He ended up in Vancouver, where he sold securities until he got his licence back and was registered with the BC Medical Association. The BCMA yanked his licence, too, after a patient accused him of slapping him around during a "consultation." Larry didn't even contest the accusation, just relinquished his licence, came to Victoria and turned to counselling. Anybody can set up as a counsellor."

"So he's kind of volatile."

Henry shook his head. "Larry seems like a sweet guy, but I guess he has a violent side."

"Like Titus Silverman?"

"Hell no. Tight-ass is a psychopath—front, back and sideways."

"Do you know Charlotte Fox?" I asked casually.

Henry stiffened. "Sort of. I've seen her with Larry Trew. She's kind of nice, which is more than I can say for her brother, George."

"George Fox?" I said, still acting the innocent. "What's the scoop on him?"

Henry shrugged—he'd told me enough for one day.

I drained my plastic cup, carried it and the blue box as far as the door. Turning back, I said, "Henry, I need to keep this cup. Evidence. Do you want a receipt?"

"No. I want three-fifty."

"Don't worry, you'll get the money. Make out an invoice and send it to me."

"At least give me the plastic cup back."

"No can do. I'm keeping it as well."

"That it, Silas? You sure there's nothing else you can do to screw up my day?"

"Just one more thing," I said, pointing to his copy of *The Sun Also Rises*. "Is it true that men who read Ernest Hemingway all have small penises?"

"Yeah, but I must be lucky. The women I make love to all have small vaginas."

I made him wait ten seconds before I smiled.

CHAPTER FIVE

Back on the street, I dropped Henry's plastic cup into a garbage gobbler, spoke sternly to the bongo-playing deadbeats polluting the airwaves outside the Bay Centre and went back to my office. PC was out. I ran a computer check on Lawrence Trew. I was able to confirm most of what Henry Ferman had already told me about him. He was a 44-year-old widower whose wife had died in Toronto in 1999 after falling from a fifteenth-floor balcony.

While I was at it and for lack of something better to do, I ran a check on Charlotte Fox's brother, George. His resume was impressive. In 1992 he had bilked a salmon canner out of a million dollars in a money-market swindle. Two years later he was arrested in Jamaica in connection with a salted gold-mine scam. Legal fees and fines ate up his capital, and he ended up serving two years less a day in a tropical prison ruled by ganja-smoking thugs. His weight dropped to 95 pounds and he lost all of his toenails.

Using forged documents, George Fox then went to California, where he convalesced, joined a spiritualist cult, learned how to manipulate Ouija boards, overturn tables with black wires hidden beneath his sleeves and produce ghostly cracking sounds using a compressive device strapped between his knees. In a matter of months he had developed a devoted following in Los Angeles.

Things went swimmingly, and George did very nicely for himself until one night during a séance, US marshals showed up instead of visitors from the astral plane. They confiscated his forgeries and, out of pure malice, turned him loose on the Tijuana side of the Mexican border with nothing in his pockets except air. How he got back to Canada is anybody's guess.

After pondering this information, I hoisted the phone and called the Good Samaritan clinic. A woman called Tracy told me that Marnie's condition was listed as critical but stable. I asked Tracy if she could transfer my call to Joe McNaught's office, which she did. McNaught wasn't there. I didn't leave a message.

LAWRENCE TREW'S HOUSE ON Terrace Lane was a big, two-storey, black-beamed Tudor with a cedar-shake roof, cream-coloured stucco and red-brick trim. In Victoria only the snootiest residential lanes are allowed to remain unpaved, and the unpaved lane leading up to Trew's residence was barely wide enough for two wheelbarrows to pass side by side, and it had hedgerows instead of fences. The only thing missing was an Olde English varlet with a pitchfork across his shoulder, tipping his cap as I went by.

An octagonal sign stuck in Trew's front lawn told me that Total Alarm Systems protected his house, and I could see conspicuous strips of shiny metallic tape bordering the windows. Nobody answered the front door when I rang the bell, so I strolled around to the back of the house. A pillared oak portico sheltered Trew's rear entrance. What I saw from that elevation was a long stretch of pristine grass flowing down to fieldstone walls beyond which, far away in the misty distance, America's San Juan Islands floated like giant green frogs in the Salish Sea's twinkling blue waters. Forty miles east, Mount Baker's regal white pyramid rose up in Washington State.

When I rang the bell, I could see dozens of fat houseflies

buzzing inside the diamond-paned panels set in the back door. Another minute passed, during which a pair of blue jays that had been squawking up in a mountain ash flew down to the pampered lawn and hopped around joyously. After standing on tiptoes and flapping his wings, the male jay began his soft courting song.

When nobody answered the back door either, just for the hell of it I tried the doorknob. It turned easily. As I opened the door and went inside, those fat houseflies flew out. Although Trew's house had an intruder alarm, that wasn't a problem because the alarm had apparently been deactivated. The back door gave onto a small mud room with built-in cabinets and wall pegs for outdoor clothing. There was an pew-like oak bench for people to sit on while they changed footwear. A door to the right led to a kitchen. Another door opened onto a wide hallway leading to a large living room with stuccoed yellow walls, heavy upholstered chairs, side tables with heavy turned legs, and—incongruously, I thought—walls covered with outrageous modernist paintings. Leather straps studded with horse brasses draped both sides of a fireplace big enough to roast an ox. The house was uncomfortably warm, and it had a peculiarly foul closed-up smell.

I went back to Trew's ultra-modern kitchen, which contained everything you'd expect to find in an ultra-modern, fake-Tudor house, including an Italian coffee machine that probably required a licensed operator. But what interested me more were the tiny splashes of what looked like dried blood discolouring some of the kitchen's floor tiles. More red splashes were visible on the adjacent baseboard. There were no obvious signs of a disturbance, but I began to wonder—if those red splashes consisted of human blood, had Lawrence Trew been involved in another fight here?

By the time I came up with this idea I was sweating, though at the same time I felt chilled. I went outside and circled the entire house, checking every window and door for signs of a forced entry. When I didn't find any, I went back inside and searched every room.

The house did not appear to have been burgled. Nobody had tipped out any of the drawers or defecated on Trew's expensive carpets. Just the same, I looked inside every drawer, cupboard, cabinet and bag and examined their contents. I checked clothes closets and bathroom cabinets. What kept me searching and poking and prying was that awful smell, because now I suspected that it was the reek of putrefying flesh. Those houseflies, of course, had smelled something days earlier, had laid their eggs in it, and baby maggots had feasted on it. Only there was no large dead thing lying in the house—at least not anymore.

The stink drove me out to the front lawn again, where I used my cellphone to call HQ. I was telling Bernie Tapp where I was and what I'd found when a couple of Trew's neighbours showed up. The man was short, bandy-legged, tweedy and sixtyish with a shaved head and a military moustache. Perhaps a golfer, he was holding a five-iron in a manner that suggested that, if provoked, he was ready to bend it over my head. His wife, twenty years younger, was skinny where her husband was stout, fluttery where he was pompous.

"Hey! Who are you and what are you doing here?" the man said, glaring at me suspiciously.

I showed my police badge.

"Delighted to meet you, I'm sure," the woman announced.

"We're the Treeloves," the man said, lowering his five-iron. "We live next door. Something wrong, officer?"

"Why? Did you expect something to be wrong?" I had addressed myself to Mr. Treelove.

His wife answered, "No, not necessarily. It's just that we haven't seen Dr. Trew for a week."

"Ten days," Mr. Treelove corrected.

"No, it was exactly a week ago," his wife corrected him. "Don't you remember, darling? We were looking after Dorothea's children. Julian lost his ball and we all came over here to look for it. Dr. Trew was standing right where you're standing now, Officer, having an argument with that chap."

"Yes, that's right, but it wasn't a week. It was ten days ago," Mr. Treelove responded impatiently. "A week ago we spent all day organizing things for the church jumble sale."

"Flea market, dear," the woman said. "One doesn't say jumble sale anymore."

"So," I said, "a few days ago you saw Dr. Trew arguing with a stranger. Can you describe him?"

For once the Treeloves agreed on something. The stranger in question had definitely been tall. Other than that, they were at odds. Mrs. Treelove insisted he had been wearing a pale-coloured suit, possibly linen, and a Hawaiian shirt. Her husband said the man wore a tweed jacket, green corduroy trousers and a blue-checkered shirt. To clinch the truth of his version he added, "I'm a trained observer. Spent twenty-five years in the military, not to mention being involved with Neighbourhood Watch. Needless to say, living in a wealthy part of town like this, we get a lot of opportunistic thieves. They keep stealing our garden ornaments, you know. It's pure bloody jealousy, of course. Why don't these people go out and get a job and work like the rest of us?"

"Is that a rhetorical question, darling?" his wife asked.

"So," I said yet again, "Dr. Trew lived alone?"

"Yes. He's a jolly bachelor."

"If he's a bachelor, I suppose he has a cleaning woman."

"Yes, of course," Mr. Treelove answered. "And that's another thing. We employ the same woman, Mrs. Widderson. She was telling us that she hasn't been able to do Larry's this week because she can't get in."

"Because of the burglar alarm?"

"Exactly. Mrs. W. does him on Saturday mornings, but if he's not home, she's stumped."

"Is your home equipped with a burglar alarm system?"

"Oh yes. This area, they're an absolute necessity. The chap that bought that house across the lane last year thought he'd economize. The poor fool went away for a month's holiday without telling us, and when he came back, his house had been stripped clean, absolutely clean. Furniture, antiques, built-in washer. Hah! We laughed our heads off."

Smiling broadly and swinging his five-iron, Mr. Treelove wandered off between the evergreens and flower beds. His wife followed discreetly a few paces behind. By then, police emergency sirens were closing in on Terrace Lane. A blue-and-white arrived a few moments later, followed immediately by Nice Manners in his unmarked black Interceptor. This time he was dressed in smart casual—pressed jeans and a suede jacket over an open-necked blue shirt. He lit a cigarette and said, "You again."

"This is getting to be a habit," I said.

"And there's no body this time either, Tapp says."

"And no bears. Just a couple of suspicious bloodstains and a very nasty smell."

"That's exactly what Tapp said—suspicious bloodstains and a rotten stink. I thought he meant you."

"Right. Well, you would, wouldn't you? Still, those stains in the kitchen should be checked because you never know . . ."

"What I do know, Seaweed, is that you're wasting a helluva lot of my valuable time."

CHAPTER SIX

Bernie parked his car outside the Ogden Point Cafe, and we went in together for a late lunch. As we slid our trays along the counter, the women behind the glass display cases filled my order for Melton Mowbray pie, Caesar salad and a pot of Earl Grey. Bernie chose spinach quiche and a beer. We carried our trays to a table overlooking Victoria's cruise ship terminal.

Bernie, dressed in a scruffy green bomber jacket, whipcord trousers held up by black suspenders and high-top leather boots, looked like somebody who'd just spent the last ten years pumping iron in the joint. Except Bernie is a very smart man who happens to be the Victoria police department's acting chief detective inspector.

"Tony Roos told me you gave mouth-to-mouth to a crankster," Bernie said. "You're a hero in my book, pal, but you're a fucking idiot as well. Now there's gossip that you're dying of full-blown AIDS from diddling hookers."

"There's been gossip I should make horse noises and gallop away ever since I joined the VPD."

Bernie forked some quiche into his mouth. "So give me the scoop about Marnie Paul and Hector Latour."

"Marnie was born on the Warrior Reserve. She was a bright, good-looking kid and we thought she'd been streetproofed, but two years back a pimp shattered that assumption. He moved her to Calgary. Then we heard she was in East Vancouver. A few weeks ago she was spotted back in Victoria. By then she was dog meat and had hooked up with Hector. By the time I caught up with her on Donnelly's Marsh, it was too late."

"So you're personally involved, and now you want to break Hector's balls, right?"

"What? I sound angry to you?"

"No. Funnily enough, you sound calm to me. Just the same, I know you're angry."

"If I am angry, I'm not angry at Hector . . . well, maybe a little bit, but he's an addict, too. In a way he's as much a victim as Marnie. The guy I really want to get my hands on is probably the handsome young stud who met Marnie coming out of a Saturday matinee and took her to Starbucks. Maybe he sprinkled a little angel dust in her triple-shot café latte. The next thing Marnie knows she's doing crack and working the streets. So if it's all the same with you, Bernie, I'm going to put some more time into this case."

"That's okay. You're entitled, since Natives are involved. But try not to get up Nice Manners' nose too much."

I shrugged.

After finishing his quiche, Bernie pointed to the fishermen out on Constance Bank and said, "Think they're having any luck?"

"There's a good run of spring salmon in the Strait right now. People are catching 'em on herrings and crocodiles just off the bottom. Halibut fishing is supposed to be hot out at Sooke, too."

Bernie stood up and said, "I'm going to get myself another beer. You want one?"

I shook my head. Out on the water, sports fishermen and a couple of commercial boats were trolling their lines. A catamaran ferry, outward bound from Victoria to Seattle, exchanged horn signals with an oil tanker. A Coast Guard helicopter, hovering above Ross Bay, made a sudden 180-degree turn and headed at speed towards Mount Douglas.

When Bernie came back, he sipped a little beer, burped noisily—to the amusement of four Japanese tourists occupying an adjacent table—and said, "Just run the Trew office story past me one more time."

I told him what Henry had told me about Trew's medical career, vicious temper and the fact that Trew's wife had died after falling off a balcony.

"A suspicious fall?"

I hesitated. "Given the advantage of retrospective knowledge, I'd have to say yes. It happened years ago, when Trew lived in Toronto."

"You think he gave her a push?"

"I don't know about her, but I'm beginning to think that the guy was born to end prematurely in a zip-up body bag." Then I added, "Hector and Marnie broke into Trew's office, probably after drugs. Trew was practising hynotherapy instead of medicine so they came up dry, but they were burgling the place when he walked in on them."

For about the third time, Bernie asked me how I knew all this. I told him.

Bernie said, "The Hector Latour that I know is a weedy ninety-eight-pound addict who'd be overmatched against Paris Hilton. And Trew sounds like a guy who can handle himself."

"So what?"

"So this—if Hector and Trew got into a fight, I wouldn't expect Trew to lose hands down."

"But Hector brained Trew with a candlestick."

"Sure, but when Trew came into his office, he surprised Hector, so Trew had the initial advantage," Bernie said, grim lines etching his face. "Trew is a bad 'un. It's as plain as the nose on your face."

"It's as plain as a steak on a dartboard," I countered.

"Plain as an old boot in a dish of fettuccini alfredo," Bernie was saying when his cellphone rang. He looked at it, groaned and said, "I gotta run. Keep your nose clean and your head down."

"Am I in quarantine? Do people think I'm contagious?"

"Certainly. People are scared shitless. Mention AIDS and their brains go down the toilet."

Victoria's "Viagra Triangle" is based at Rock Bay, the area lying between Douglas Street and the Gorge Waterway. Fifty years ago it was largely residential, but now the few remaining houses share Rock Bay with pawnshops, one-hour motels, used-car dealerships, warehouses, hole-in-the-wall consignment shops and British Columbia's liquor-distribution headquarters, which occupies a whole block. But when I parked my car on the street in front of it, it was after five o'clock and all the liquor employees had gone home. I strolled to the corner of Government and Bay streets and stood with my back to an ivy-covered concrete building that, as soon as it gets dark around there, provides a windbreak for street hookers and the swaggering pimps who own them body and soul.

Hidden beyond the masonry walls and tall steel silos across Government Street was Rock Bay itself—one of Victoria's minor navigable backwaters. When the traffic light changed to green, I crossed over, walked past the Ocean Cement concrete plant, turned a couple of corners and ended up looking at the treasures displayed in Titus Silverman's hockshop window. The only thing I coveted was a shipbuilder's 1/75 scale model of the SS *Princess Marguerite*, priced very reasonably at $15,000. I went in and idled my way between display cases containing the abandoned souvenirs of anonymous lives until I came face to face with Frankie Nichols. Fifty years old, a matronly ex-Las Vegas showgirl, she was sitting behind a wire-mesh wicket with her elbows on the counter and her chin in her hands. She gave me a long cool look, sighed and half-lowered her eyelids.

"Hiya, Frankie," I said. "I'm making inquiries about an engraved silver cup purchased from here last week."

"Sorry I can't help you, Silas, because nobody here's sold nothing in silver cups in months."

"That's not what I heard, Frankie."

"I can't help that," she replied mulishly.

"In that case, I need to see your pawn book."

"No chance. Not without a court order," she said, her soft lower lip sticking out. "You know Titus hates cops. If he knew that I was even talking to you now, it'd be more than my job is worth."

"Is Titus here?"

"No, he don't come in here much, thank Christ."

"What's the matter?" I said, puzzled by Frankie's less-than-welcoming attitude. "Don't you like me any more?"

"I don't even like my kids any more," she responded listlessly. "Why don't you scram over to the recycling depot and bother them guys instead?"

Titus Silverman's recycling depot was a rectangular, flat-roofed, corrugated-iron building that had been spawned as a machine shop. At the tables on the sidewalk in front of it, a continuous flow of binners traded bottles and cans for cash. Abandoned shopping carts lay everywhere. The whole scene was like a Baghdad street market after a suicide-bomb attack. As I arrived, a helmeted biker drove a Harley chopper out of an alley beside the depot and roared off downtown.

Walking down the same alley, I glanced through a doorway set in the depot's otherwise blank wall. A man wearing plastic goggles, a face mask and earmuffs was heaving bottles and cans into crushing machines. The clatter of gritty materials racing down steel chutes was almost loud enough to drown the noise of the German shepherd guard dogs going nuts inside their wire cages. I tapped the man's shoulder. When he emerged from his trance, I asked him where Titus Silverman's office was. The mumble emerging from his face mask was probably words. I went out again, walked to the back of the building and entered a door marked NO VISITERS—TRASPASSARS KILLED. Inside, surrounded by mountains of cardboard boxes, six men were sitting around a felt-covered, octagonal poker table playing five-card stud. One of them directed me to a small, square, windowless room with unpainted gyproc walls, a concrete floor with a square of brown furry carpet on it and the kind of furniture appropriate to a recycling facility. It stank of poor digestion and dirty clothes.

Sitting in the middle of a filthy black velvet couch, poring over a dog-eared *Hustler* magazine was a Mexican with a long grey ponytail and a tight face. According to the poker player, the guy's name was Tubby Gonzales. He had the consummate liar's frank unblinking gaze, and it focused on me as I entered and took his measure. Gonzales was about forty years old, on the short side and a little overweight. His shoulders were probably no wider than an ordinary door. The hubcap he was using as an ashtray overflowed with butts.

"Mr. Gonzales? Good afternoon," I said. "I am Sergeant Seaweed of the Victoria Police Department."

"You the guy was in the hockshop earlier, pushing Frankie around and asking after Tight-ass?" he asked in a chilly voice. He had a cleft palate and spoke a queer variety of English.

"That's correct, and I hope you don't try to fuck with me as well, because I might lose my patience, and putting uncooperative civilians in handcuffs raises my blood pressure."

"Tough guy, eh? So what you want?"

"I'm trying to trace objects stolen in a recent burglary. You or Mr. Silverman may be able to help with my inquiries."

He lit another cigarette. "We don't handle no stolen property."

"Of course not, it's out of the question," I retorted sarcastically. "Still, sometimes things go missing, and sometimes those things turn up in pawnshops."

"What should I do, lay an egg?"

After counting silently to five, I said, "One of the stolen items was an engraved silver cup. That cup was found in and purchased from Mr. Silverman's pawnshop a few days ago."

"That's bullshit."

"Excuse me?"

"Silver cup, my ass," he said in a voice as excited as an iceberg. "I just told you—we don't handle no stolen property."

"The gentlemen playing cards outside tell me that you manage things during Titus Silverman's absence. Now how do you think Mr. Silverman will feel when he gets back from wherever he is and finds that his business licence has been lifted?"

Gonzales' laugh sounded like a backfiring diesel. "It won't happen. I mean, somebody brings us something, and a shop assistant makes a mistake. Hey, mistakes happen. People don't lose business licences just like that."

"They do if the infraction is integral to a murder investigation."

"Murder?" Gonzales returned with less assurance. "Who's been murdered?"

"Who do you think I am, a newsboy? You want information, buy a paper," I said, putting some menace into my voice for the first time. "All that concerns you is that I'm looking for stolen property."

Gonzales got up from the couch, carefully folded his magazine, put it down on the French provincial dressing table that served as his desk and sat behind it on a wooden kitchen chair. He leaned back in the chair, blew a smoke ring and asked innocently, "Is Tight-ass dead?"

I let that ride and allowed the tension to build for a minute before I said, "When's the last time you saw Titus Silverman?"

"We ain't seen Tight-ass since the early part of last week, which is funny," Gonzales answered, a hint of confusion now wrinkling the flesh between his eyes. "He never said nothing about going nowhere, so we been wondering."

"You are sitting in the middle of a nasty piece of business, Mr. Gonzales, so you'd better tell me what you know about those stolen items and the person who brought them in."

"I don' know a goddam thing!" he snapped back. "For Chrissake, you think we can account for every candlestick that comes into the shop?"

I let the tension grow before I asked, "When's the last time Titus Silverman took an unexplained absence lasting more than a week?"

Gonzales sighed. After butting his smoke in the hubcap, he said, "It's not like Tight-ass to take time off—not ever. I tell you the truth, I been wondering where he's at."

"Does Titus ride a Harley?"

"Nah. He rides a BSA."

"Have you contacted his family?"

"Tight-ass ain't got no family since the bitch moved out."

"Which bitch?"

"His old lady! Jesus!" Gonzales snarled, speaking as if only a hermit after years of solitude in a remote cave could be unaware of such an important fact.

Gonzales declined to identify the old lady in question, but he did provide me with Titus Silverman's home address. I said good-bye. He ignored this, but I thought that his exasperation seemed a bit overdone. And I'll say this for him—he was exactly what Titus Silverman needed in the way of a lieutenant, and if I ever meet him in a back alley, I want to be the one carrying the baseball bat.

I went out of his office and stopped to watch the poker game. The players took no notice of me until I asked them what the ante was.

"Fuck off," somebody said.

By that time I'd figured out where the sucker was sitting.

I drove over to Fisherman's Marina, parked my MG near the houseboats and walked down a wooden ramp to Barb's floating cafe. While waiting for my order of cod and fries, I phoned Tubby Gonzales. I said, "I'll bet you five I know the make of car and approximate year of that hubcap on your desk."

"You're on."

"It's an A40 Austin, vintage 1953 to 1956."

There was a short pause.

"You owe me five," I said.

With a click Gonzales broke the connection.

CHAPTER SEVEN

Given Titus Silverman's lurid reputation, I'd expected his house to be a mini-Fort Apache or a concrete bunker with gun ports. It turned out to be an ordinary 1960s split-level in a crescent off Admirals Road. Located behind a lawn flanked with beds of well-tended tulips and heathers, the house stood adjacent to an empty lot covered with Scotch broom and mature cedars where kids had built a tree fort.

As Acting Chief Detective Inspector Bernie Tapp and I went up the gravel path to the front door, I looked inside the garage and saw a BSA motorbike. Bernie had seen something else—bolted to a metal post set into the ground was a cast-iron plaque bearing the symbol of a pistol and the phrase "We don't dial 911." The combined weight of the post and plaque was probably about the same as a sack of cement, but showing no visible exertion whatsoever, Bernie tore the whole assembly out of the ground and tossed it over the fence into the vacant lot. He then dusted off his hands and pushed the doorbell.

After a longish wait a slender young Asian woman answered the door. She was wearing diaphanous silk lounging pajamas, lip gloss like freshly applied tomato ketchup and enough perfume to deodorize a pulp mill. "No goo. Titus no hoe," she said, batting her long mascaraed eyelashes seductively.

Bernie put his foot against the door to prevent her from closing it and pushed his way into the house. I followed, and she didn't try to stop us. She just folded her arms, leaned against a wall and said, "Ha-hah."

"Don't I know you?" I inquired.

She shook her head. She wasn't beautiful, but she looked like she'd be plenty of fun on a stag night after she popped out of the cake.

"We'd like to talk to Titus," Bernie said.

"Titus no hoe."

"Where can we reach him?"

"No hoe. Titus no hoe."

"What's your name?"

"Ming," she said demurely. "Titus no hoe."

"I think we've got that," Bernie said. "Titus is not home. What we'd like to know is what you are doing here?"

"Titus throw me ow. I come back when I fine ow Titus no hoe."

Bernie and I went past her and into a living room heavily scented with the woman's perfume. The room had too much furniture, all of it new and expensive. Some of the upholstered chairs were still draped in transparent plastic shipping wrap. There was a small modern kitchen with stainless steel appliances and polished granite countertops. A bedroom in the back of the house was full of a king-sized bed. A second bedroom had been fitted out as an office. The bungalow's single bathroom had pink accoutrements that included a Jacuzzi and a bidet. While Bernie tried to converse with Ming, I poked around. There were no suspicious letters, phone numbers or any of Lawrence Trew's ballpoint pens in Titus Silverman's office—or if there were, I didn't see them.

"I've half a mind to take her back to headquarters," Bernie said. "Use an interpreter and question her under oath."

"I doubt if she's a Christian."

"You're Chinese, right?" Bernie asked her. "From the Mainland or Hong Kong?"

"Vietnam," Ming said.

"Chinese, Vietnamese, what's the difference? I'd swear her on the chicken oath," Bernie told me. "Ever seen it done?"

Instead of answering Bernie's question, I bulged my bottom lip with my tongue.

"The chicken oath is swearing to tell the truth after cutting off the head of a live hen with a sharp knife," Bernie explained.

"In court?"

"Certainly. In an open court with the judge and jury right there watching."

"Why not?" I said. "Nixon swore he wasn't a liar. Clinton swore he never had sex with a White House intern, and they were both Christians. Maybe we should forget bibles, see if swearing on chickens works better."

"I go' chicken," Ming said, pointing.

We looked out the window into a backyard consisting mostly of chicken coops and fenced runs where handsome red banties were scratching up dust.

Bernie's stern expression faded. "My dad used to raise chickens. And homing pigeons."

"I never knew that."

"We raced 'em on weekends for years and years."

"You raced chickens?"

"I wish I had chickens in my yard now," said Bernie, smiling absently, "instead of paving slabs, a gazebo and pre-cast concrete fucking gnomes."

"What's stopping you? It wouldn't cost much to build a chicken coop and a run. We could do the whole job in a weekend."

"Can't. There's a bylaw against keeping live poultry in my

neighbourhood," he said. Turning to Ming he said, "I'll be in touch."

On the way out I asked Ming, "Didn't I see you perform at a fire-hall smoker last Christmas?"

Giggling, she hung her head.

We went out.

Bernie said, "What do you think?"

I stopped outside the garage. Instead of answering Bernie's question, I said, "Did I tell you that Titus Silverman rides a Beezer?"

"No, you didn't. So what?"

"That's one, right there."

"Correct. A BSA Lightning Rocket with a custom tank. Six hundred and fifty cubic centimetres of sheer terror. Ever been astride one of those babies in top gear?"

"Hell, no."

We went back to Bernie's car.

"Maybe it's time we said hi to Frankie again," I suggested.

Bernie drove us over to Titus Silverman's hockshop. The *Princess Marguerite* was no longer on display.

I said, "Hiya, Frankie. What happened to that ship model?"

This time Frankie smiled. "Why, did you want it?"

"Sure, in the same way I want to win the 6/49."

"You'll need lottery money if you start collecting quality ship models. We don't get many, but those we do get sell for a ton."

Bernie, who didn't like Frankie as much as I did, said, "Have you heard from Titus Silverman lately?"

Frankie stared at Bernie without expression.

I said, "Level with us, Frankie. You were on duty the day Hector Latour and Marnie Paul came in here with a silver cup and some other stuff, right?"

Time passed. Eventually Frankie nodded.

"Tell us about it, Frankie," Bernie suggested heavily.

She folded her arms, thought for another minute and said, "They came in with a cardboard box full of stuff, just a bunch of crap. I was making them an offer when Titus arrived. He took Hector and Marnie into his back office and made his own deal."

"We need to see the record of that transaction."

"No way," Frankie said firmly. "Not a chance."

That's when Bernie decided to get tough. "Wait here," he said to me. "Make sure Frankie stays put till I get back with a search warrant."

He had reached the door before Frankie said, "Okay, you win. Just hold it."

Bernie sauntered back to the counter.

Frankie thought things over for another minute before reaching into a drawer and bringing out an account book. She said, "Remind me what date you're interested in."

After consulting his notebook, Bernie did so.

"There's no record of that transaction," Frankie said, pushing the account book across the counter. "Look for yourself."

She was right. Neither Hector Latour's nor Marnie Paul's name appeared in the pawnshop's account book on the date in question.

Either Frankie's girdle was too tight or she was nervous, because she was becoming fidgety. Bernie looked at me and winked.

I said to Frankie, "You were making a deal with Hector Latour and Marnie Paul. Titus Silverman comes in, they talk for a moment then Titus takes them into his back office?"

"Right. One day is pretty much like another in here. I couldn't remember the actual day it was, but I remember what happened because Titus doesn't spend much time here now. Generally he's over at the recycling depot."

"Why?" Bernie said.

"Ask Titus."

Bernie, lying relentlessly, said, "Listen, Frankie, I hope you understand that you are complicit in a violation of the Pawnbroker and Moneylender's Act."

"Technically I am in violation of the Minimum Wage Act, but I need money for food and rent so what the hell . . ."

"Well, technically is all that counts," Bernie said. "I think you'd better let us into Titus' office."

Frankie picked up a phone behind the counter and spoke to the Mexican over at the depot. She put the phone down and said, "Titus is still AWOL. To be honest, I don't know what to do."

"Frankie, you have two options," Bernie said. "You can stall us or you can let us in now. Either way we are going to have a look at Titus' office."

Frankie sighed, shook her head, came out from behind her wicket, hung a CLOSED sign on the front door and led us through the back of the shop. She was wearing high-heeled shoes, and though she had become a bit thick-bodied, her legs were still gorgeous, and when she remembered to, she could still move like a thirty-year-old. I wondered what had happened to all the money she'd earned kicking poker chips off mantelpieces in Las Vegas.

Titus Silverman's office was small, dusty, windowless and cob-webby, and the roaches scurried for cover when Frankie switched the light on. She leaned in the doorway with her arms crossed while Bernie and I looked the place over. The walls were lined with cheap, pressboard bookcases entirely filled with paperback mysteries. By the light of a naked 60-watt light bulb dangling from a ceiling cord, I observed that the books were all filed in strict alphabetical order. Most dated back to the 'thirties. There appeared to be complete sets of Dashiell Hammett, James M. Cain, Carroll John Daly, Raymond Chandler, Mickey Spillane, and many others from crime writing's golden age. Other than the bookshelves, the only other furniture was a leather recliner in one corner and beside it, an old-fashioned four-bulb pedestal lamp without a shade, a metal seven-drawer desk with an Underwood typewriter on it and a swivel chair behind it. The room's green shag carpet looked as if muddy buffalos had trampled it. Bernie sat behind the desk to look in the drawers, while I opened a Peter Cheyney first edition at random and read about crime detection in Blitz-era London.

Bernie brought an address book out a drawer and, after studying it for five minutes, laid it on top of the desk. I put Peter Cheyney back on the shelf and picked up the address book. A brief glance revealed a *Who's Who* of Vancouver Island's crooks, fixers and politicians, past and present. The desk's bottom right-hand drawer was locked, but Frankie drew the line when Bernie asked her if she had a key.

"Come back with your search warrant first," Frankie told him.

Bernie appeared to put the address book back in the drawer. He thanked Frankie for her cooperation. As we walked back to the car, I said, "Did you get it?"

Bernie nodded—the address book was in his pocket.

I said, "I suppose it's possible that somebody broke into Trew's office before Hector and Marnie got there. If so, it's likely that the same person left the Matbro Building's street door open as well."

"I wouldn't believe anything that little punk Latour told me," Bernie scoffed.

WHITE FAWN LILIES and ancient rhododendrons were in full bloom around the ivy-covered Donnelly house where on my previous visit I'd found Hector Latour and Marnie Paul. But this time it wasn't the house I was interested in, and I drove my MG along the well-marked track that went past it, following it across waterlogged meadows and between the isolated ponds that lent a half-marine atmosphere to the scene. Even so, the sodden ground was drying out as the water levels beyond the dikes got lower. After a few hundred yards the track began a slight ascent and I came upon a newly painted sign: PRIVATE PROPERTY. NO VISITORS. A minute later I brought the MG to a standstill— a clear creek burbling with knee-deep water ran right across the track.

I left the car beside the creek, took my boots off, rolled up my pants and waded across. I put my boots back on and started walking. The track wound around some high dunes, and terminated a few hundred yards farther on where the moss-covered ruins of a Coast Salish longhouse created a dead end. This is what I had come to see. Two cedar mortuary poles with mute, carved animal faces gaping out towered above the ancient site. The woodpecker crest figure perched atop one of the poles, a shaman's memorial totem, seemed to be watching me. Halfway down, the pole had been notched to accommodate a wooden box. When the old shaman died, they folded his legs up close to his chest, with his arms between his legs, and put a blanket around him and sat him in the box with his rattles and medicine bag and strings of sea otter teeth and other regalia and put the lid on. He was still there in his box.

Crows swooped and dipped among another half-dozen collapsed poles, their carvings now barely distinguishable, that lay mouldering upon the earth. A hundred years ago several poles and a thirty-foot dugout canoe were removed from this site and housed in Vancouver's Anthropology Museum. I stood for a moment with hands in my pockets, looking at the longhouse. Fortunately, the Donnelly family had used it as a hay barn and had kept its roof tight, otherwise it would have collapsed long ago. Its roof sloped gently from front to back, with its front end facing the sea, and the roof planks overlapped like tiles. On the front, the ghostly image of a painted killer whale was still vaguely perceptible, and the entrance was in the form of a giant carved frog with a swinging door set between the frog's green legs.

Many years had passed since my first and only previous visit to this lonely house, haunted as it was by the ghosts of the past, and now, though the evening wasn't cold, I found myself shivering. It was sheer nervousness compounded with wonderment and awe. People say they get the same feeling visiting ancient European cathedrals. My uneasiness increased when a ray of yellow light suddenly flashed upon a fallen pole. It appeared to emanate from behind the longhouse, but it wasn't lightning—the ray was stationary. I went behind the longhouse for a closer look and saw that it was caused by the slanting rays of the sun reflecting off an SUV's chrome front bumper. The SUV was Charlotte Fox's Lexus.

I was standing by the Lexus when a nebulous object materialized from the darkness of the forest beyond. It seemed to be an immense bear, standing upright on two very long legs. Black bears are common on Vancouver Island—they are often sighted inside the city limits. But this was no ordinary black bear. For one thing, it was twice as big. For another, it was the wrong colour—its fur was reddish brown, almost golden in the sunlight. I watched the apparition move silently across the ground before merging invisibly with the shadows thrown by the longhouse.

I backed away and returned to the front of the longhouse. The hinges of the door between the frog's legs had been recently oiled and didn't make a sound when I pushed the door open and went inside. A faint odour of burnt sweetgrass, balsam and wood ash breathed from the interior, and light fell through narrow chinks in the planked walls, painting gold stripes across an area large enough to accommodate two small airplanes. More light came from the smoke hole that had been cut in the roof directly above a circle of fire-blackened stones. The place was almost exactly as I remembered it from the time Andrea Crandon had come here with me. We were just thirteen years old. She had been beautiful then, before she became sick with an illness that aged her prematurely, made her strange and finally killed her.

Except for Andrea's ghost reaching out across the years, I thought myself the building's only occupant until suddenly the same immensely tall bear, rematerialised and faced me in the silence. My mouth went dry. Andrea receded into the past. I knew this was no earthly bear, although its woodsy smell was palpable enough. The creature—whatever it was—now wore a cedar-bark cloak and a strange hat. It had neither legs nor arms and appeared to float in mid-air. I didn't move or speak, and after a few minutes the shape drifted silently towards me. It was within twenty feet of me when it made an abrupt 90-degree turn and faded completely into the planked wall.

When I'd pulled myself together, I checked the section of wall through which the ghost had dematerialized. That wall was solid. Once or twice I heard heavy footsteps as the creature moved about unseen. Then a tiny flame appeared in the middle or close to the middle of the longhouse. The flame brightened, became larger, and I perceived that some *thing* was lighting a long wax torch. Holding the burning torch aloft, the dark shape moved towards me, did another abrupt turn and vanished through the wall in the same place as before. A minute later the front door opened for an instant and closed again. After waiting for a minute or two I went outside, walked around to the back of the longhouse again and stood there looking at the SUV. The sun had set and the light was fading, but I glanced down and saw something white gleaming on the grass at my feet. Idly I picked it up. It was one of Lawrence Trew's business cards.

Suddenly some crows began cawing in the trees nearby, and sensing a presence behind my back, I dodged automatically and twisted around to face it. Standing there on its hind legs was the massive bear again. It was still wearing the strange hat, but now it had a square pig-like snout that was immensely wide and at least a yard long. When a huge paw swung towards my head in a downward arc, I jumped aside, and instead of crushing my skull, the blow continued on its downward swing and set the monster off-balance. I leapt across a fallen mortuary pole and ran into the forest. The ground was well drained here and thick with timber that blocked the light as effectively as a roof. I kept going until I ran straight into a barrier of loose jumbled rock. Now the animal was only a few feet behind and I started to climb. Ledges covered with evergreen huckleberries provided handholds, so that I was up some twenty feet before the bear came to a stop below me. I kept going. Reaching the top of the rocky barrier, I found myself overlooking a boulder-strewn beach. I was thinking that getting down would be trickier than getting up—on its seaboard side the rock face was pocked with barnacles and limpets and strewn with flat, slippery, green seaweed—when I realized that the bear hadn't attempted to climb up after me. It had disappeared among the trees. For the time being, I was safe. I made myself comfortable on a bed of sea plantain and closed my eyes.

CHAPTER EIGHT

A skeleton was sitting on a carved wooden throne surrounded by his many wives, and in front of them eagle masks floated in a sea of red sparks. Abruptly I opened my eyes. While I'd been dozing on the rocks, night had fallen.

As I scrambled down to level ground in the dark, the eagle masks and throned skeletons returned to dreamland. Moonlight silvered the ground except where the longhouse and its totem guardians threw their long shadows. I waited in the trees while I checked the clearing for bears, but the longhouse had an abandoned, empty look, and the Lexus had gone. I worked my way back to the MG and was surprised to find it undamaged. I got in the car, started the engine and leaned back in the seat. Besieged by memories of the past, I couldn't think straight. I put the car in gear and headed back to town.

A dozen sheep sleeping in the nearby field fled for cover when I pulled the MG up beside one of the barns at Felicity Exeter's farm and switched the engine off. I sat for a while adjusting to the silence before getting out. While it was almost totally dark beside the barn, every light in Felicity's house was on. I was walking in that direction when she emerged through the French doors arm in arm with a man I'd never seen before. They paused to kiss passionately, and then strolled down the sloping meadow together and disappeared into a stand of pines.

I let myself into the house. The living room felt cold and empty, but I couldn't help noticing an empty wine bottle on the coffee table, along with two unwashed glasses. Feeling like a love-sick kid or a middle-aged voyeur, I checked Felicity's bedroom. Her bed was warm, and I smelt the slight musk of perspiration instead of her usual perfume.

I drove away from the farm without turning on my headlights.

When I woke on Friday morning, I felt the sun's pleasant heat spilling through the window and onto my bed. But as soon as I opened my eyes, my head began to ache, and I blinked the way you do when you're drunk and trying to clear your head in the hope, soon dashed, of diminishing the haze. Trying not to think about Felicity was going to be difficult.

I booked the day off and decided to spruce up my cabin. As I don't own a vacuum cleaner, what I had to work with was a five-gallon pail, soap, water, assorted rags and brushes. I began by cleaning the windows till they sparkled. I dragged all the rugs outside, gave them a good shaking and afterwards draped them to air across my backyard hedge. I removed all the crocks and pots from my kitchen cupboards, washed everything and wiped the shelves with bleach. Chief Alphonse came in while I was on my knees scrubbing the floor.

"You look bushed," the chief observed.

"I was out on Donnelly's Marsh last night poking around. Perhaps I shouldn't have been. A grizzly wearing a strange hat damn near blindsided me."

The chief scratched his chin. "A grizzly wearing a strange hat?"

"It was really strange . . . weird, you know? It was bigger than any ordinary bear but shapeless, almost as if it was made of smoke. Copper-coloured smoke."

"That's the second time you've been out Donnelly's Marsh way lately. Dark, was it?"

"It was getting on towards dark. I was feeling nervous, to tell you the truth. Maybe I was overwrought. But this creature with the strange hat—I saw it the last time I was there, too."

"We don't see grizzlies on Vancouver Island much, not since what's his name came here, that Spaniard who showed up here in his galleon?"

"Manuel Quimper?"

"That's the one," Chief Alphonse said laconically. "Grizzlies are good swimmers, as good as polar bears. Matter of fact, polar bears and grizzlies interbreed sometimes. I guess maybe they're the same species evolved to different colours. Once in a while a lone grizzly will island-hop this way from the mainland. He won't stay long. Come mating season he wants the company of his own kind."

I thought about that. Southern Vancouver Island is separated from the BC mainland by the Strait of Georgia, which is twenty miles wide in many places. But north of Desolation Sound, the Strait is packed with islands, and a fit and determined outdoorsman could walk and swim his way down the whole coast to Vancouver if he really set his mind to it.

The chief moved so I could scrub the floor where he was standing. "Donnelly's Marsh is a very spooky place," he said after a few minutes. "Maybe you seen things that aren't there. Every think of that?"

I nodded.

He looked at me sideways. "Is the longhouse still standing up all right?"

"Yes, and the roof is still tight. It's dry inside."

"So you went inside? Then what?"

"This weird shape—like a bear—appeared. It didn't make any

sound, and after a bit it vanished through the wall . . . the solid
plank wall. A bit later I saw the thing again just briefly until it disappeared. There was something else funny as well—a Lexus SUV
was parked behind the longhouse. It belongs to a Native woman
named Charlotte Fox. After seeing that spook, I went back out
to where the Lexus was parked. I was standing there looking at
it when some crows started cawing at me, and I managed to duck
before something tried to hit me."

"Could it have been Charlotte Fox?"

"No, I think it was a real bear, a ten- or twelve-foot giant bear
wearing a strange hat."

The chief grunted. "Grizzly bears were Coast Salish people
before Transformer changed the world. That's why an ordinary grizzly will never kill a Coast Salish. In fact, considering
the amount of aggravation we put them to, it's surprising that
ordinary grizzly bears seldom kill anybody." It was a minute or
two before he continued, "So that thing you saw—it might have
been a ghost. Real ghosts are foolish because they have very
small brains and what brains they do have don't work too well.
But I never heard of a ghost that could blindside a human being.
I'll talk to Old Mary Cooke." He spread his hands, his face calm,
his eyes soberly appraising. "Maybe we'll do some medicine, just
in case."

I went back to scrubbing floors.

"I've been meaning to ask you, Silas. Why do people like
Marnie Paul and Hector Latour do heroin and crack cocaine?"

"They use heroin to make themselves feel normal. They smoke
crack to get high."

The chief was giving me a hand to move my chesterfield away
from a window so that I could wash the floor underneath when
he said, "Hold it a minute."

The manila envelope Harvey Cheeke had given me had fallen

from the windowsill. I threw it on the table and went back to scrubbing the floor.

Chief Alphonse kept looking at the envelope. Grinning slyly, he said, "I hope there's nothing important in that letter."

"It's just another of Harvey Cheeke's pictures."

He looked at me questioningly. "Same-old, same-old buffalo painting?"

"I guess. I haven't looked at it yet."

My collection of carved wooden masks needed to be taken down from the walls one at a time and dusted. I have about thirty, the most valuable being an articulated Nootka mask with moveable eyes and jaws that I found washed up on a remote shore near Ucluelet. Arthur Gottlieb once offered me ten thousand dollars for it. While I dusted and cleaned them, the chief spent his time commenting on my masks and their genealogical history.

When the job was nearly finished, I put the kettle on, and a half hour later we were in my backyard eating smoked salmon sandwiches, drinking Red Rose tea and watching the rufous hummingbirds feasting on insects and pinesap. After a while the crows that were doing house renovations in the trees were making such a mess that I had to raise a patio umbrella.

The chief's ritual fast had ended and now he was making up for lost time. As soon as we finished the first batch of sandwiches, he said, "I'll take smoked salmon sandwiches over whale blubber any day."

I can take a hint. As I was returning to the cabin, he said, "When are you going to look at Harvey's picture?"

I made another plateful of sandwiches and took them back outside along with the manila envelope. "Here," I said. "Open it and have a look. Tell me what you think."

Chief Alphonse reached for the envelope, changed his mind and said, "No, Silas, it's yours. You'd better see it first."

Harvey Cheeke had spent a lot of time drawing this one. Instead of the usual stick figures, it was a realistic, carefully composed study of a child lying naked in the sun on a west coast beach. The sun's rays, however, were reflecting from the child's eyes. As a composition, it was a wholly unexpected surprise.

A gust whistled in from the sea, rustling the patio umbrella's canvas.

The chief's face tightened up. "About a hundred years ago there was this young Coast Salish boy who lived on Puget Sound. People said he was advanced for his age. When he was two, they had a potlatch ceremony where he received an ancestral name that had never been spoken in half a lifetime. After the naming dance, the boy's family distributed a fortune in eulachon oil, deer meat and other gifts. That boy disappeared shortly afterwards, and when he returned many years later, he had a strange glow about his body and beams of light radiating from his eyes. And he wore a strange hat that could produce lightning and thunder. He demanded many wives and received them atop a great mountain in a house made of newly woven rush mats. The boy's ancestral name was Filligan and people believed that Filligan was a god.

"Two of the cuckolded husbands attacked this so-called god and killed him. The way they did it, Silas, one of the husbands held a sealskin over Filligan's head while the other clubbed him to death with a poker heated in a fire. After Filligan died, amid thunder and lightning his spirit changed into a bird and flew into the sky."

"What did this strange hat look like?"

"I don't know," the chief replied slowly, lifting his clasped hands a little. "Just strange. You'd have to see it."

"I have seen it," I said.

CHAPTER NINE

That night I couldn't sleep. A northeasterly whistled along the shore, making the trees ruffle and creak. After some heavy tossing and turning and thinking, I got dressed, equipped myself with a roll of duct tape, a flashlight and a cellphone embedded with a GPS chip, and then woke up the MG. Traffic was light. Downtown the bars and cabarets had closed, but on Government Street the hookers still tottered back and forth beneath the streetlights, and late-night revellers were doing their noisy best to keep the party going as another long night stretched towards morning.

Tall laurel hedges sheltered Charlotte Fox's house from prying eyes. I drove on down the street to the next corner and parked before walking back to the house. It turned out to be one of those dark, shingled, three-storey Gothic mansions with turrets, wide porches and bay windows. Such residences are generally too large for modern families and have been converted into B & Bs or apartments, but this one had survived as a single-family home. Charlotte's Lexus SUV was standing outside a two-car garage. A BMW was parked on the street directly across from the house. I noted the BMW's licence plate number.

It was about four o'clock and still very dark, so I was well concealed as I stood just inside the yard against the laurels. But when I moved little by little towards the Lexus, a motion-activated lamp set on a high pole came on and showed me the grass on the front lawn, shiny with dew. I crouched beside the Lexus and kept still for a while. When the lamp went off, I tried the SUV's front passenger door and found that it wasn't locked. Using my flashlight, I located a suitably inconspicuous metal bracket beneath the dashboard and taped the cellphone to it.

By the time I was finished, the sky was faintly dusted with glimmers of dawn, and I returned to the MG, fired it up and pulled away from the curb. A Volkswagen beetle parked fifty yards behind started at the same time and followed me with its lights off. It was still on my tail when I reached the Moss Street/ Fort Street intersection. I stopped my car, grabbed my flashlight and strolled back to the Volkswagen. Its driver—a kid who looked about fourteen years old—had three silver rings in his lower lip and another dangling from his nose. Those faint clues—and the large black swastika tattooed on the crown of his white shaven head—told me a lot about him. He gave me a cheeky grin and said, "What's wrong, Dad?"

"You're driving without lights."

He switched his lights on, backed up, drove around and past my car and turned in the wrong direction down Fort, which happens to be a one-way street. I thought about giving him a ticket but dropped the idea. Life would punish him later when he collided with an eighteen-wheeler . . . or male-pattern baldness kicked in.

THE SUN'S RAYS STREAMING onto my face woke me up. The overnight wind had blown itself out, and the sea was a limpid deep green. I opened my door and windows, put Mr. Coffee to work and shaved before I made my morning bacon, eggs and toast. At nine o'clock I switched on my Apple laptop. After figuring out how, I began tracking the GPS chip on Charlotte Fox's Lexus. It had been driven away from Moss Street while I slept and now it was stationary on Meares.

With the laptop on the passenger seat beside me, I drove over to View Royal, filled the MG's gas tank at the Esso station there, measured the oil and checked the Michelins with my own pressure gauge. By then the Lexus was in Victoria's Yates Street parkade. My bill for gas amounted to $35, and I went into the Esso convenience store to pay for it. Two middle-aged, over-weight tourists in Hawaiian getups were cruising the food aisles, gobbling Mars bars. The kid behind the cashier's desk had a star tattooed on the crown of his shaved head, and he put down the graphic novel he was reading to make change for me.

"That book you've got there," I said. "Does the boy get the girl, or does the monster get the girl?"

"Usually the monster gets the boy," he said.

"That tattooed star gives your bean a distinctive look."

"Until it washes off," he said, handing me my change.

"It's a transfer?"

The kid nodded. "And watch out for traffic cops, Granddad," he said with a pitying shake of his head. "Right now they're staked out behind the Six-Mile Market."

"Those monsters!" I said.

The male tourist thought I was referring to him and called me a smartass. I informed him that his mouth was smeared with sto-len chocolate. Star boy and the tourists were in a shouting match when I went back to my car. The sun was hot and there was no wind. I drove across the Esso lot, pointed the MG's nose west-ward and waited on the apron until I could merge into traffic. Two Hummers, going past at eighty, created a backdraft strong enough to wobble my little coupe.

It was about noon when I got to Donnelly's Marsh, left my car at the creek and waded across it. Crows, hopping about on the roof of the longhouse, flapped away as I walked up. Even in full sunshine, the deep shadows, the nearby forest and the carved animal faces staring down from those ancient totems lent a sinister air to the place. I poked around in the nearby bush, searching in vain for bear scat or places where black bears or grizzlies might have bedded down. Then I had a good look at the longhouse, and I realized that parts of the roof and wall cladding had been recently renewed. I hunted for hinged planks or secret doors without seeing any.

I walked between the frog's legs into the longhouse and stood just inside the doorway. This time the interior had the faint aroma of fresh paint, and it was dark in there except for a square of yellow sunlight below the smoke hole. This, I remembered, was the place where Andrea Crandon and I fell in love, where some of my ancestors had lived before northern warriors killed them.

I went outside. This time, instead of walking back along the road to my car, I found a winding forest trail that brought me to a steep-sided creek tangled with blackberry vines, ferns, and stinkweed plants with leaves the size of elephant ears. A bald eagle, perched on a treetop with its beak half open, was scanning the terrain. The creek terminated at a muddy beach covered with broken clamshells. A rising tide was flooding depressions where deer had walked and where the ubiquitous raccoons had been digging. Buried clams squirted water. The eagle had scared away most of the waterfowl.

I didn't see any grizzly tracks.

CHAPTER TEN

I needed a drink and strolled over to Bartholemew's to get one. Fred Halloran was sitting alone in a corner booth. It was overly warm that night, but as usual Fred was wearing a scruffy raincoat.

I went over and said, "Expecting global colding, Fred?"

"Sit down," he said. "Keep me company."

"Who, me?"

"No, the bartender's dog."

I sat down.

"Enjoy your dinner?" he said cryptically, smiling at me the way cats smile at mice.

"I haven't had dinner yet."

Fred's dark eyebrows moved upwards. "Somebody told me you were dining with Felicity tonight."

"And who might that somebody be?"

"Never mind. It's not important. Somebody just mentioned in passing that Felicity and her boyfriend had booked a table at the Deep Cove Chalet."

Trying to conceal my agitation, I signalled the waiter. Fred wanted a glass of red wine. I wanted something stronger and ordered a double Haig with no ice and water on the side.

"This one of your regular hangouts, Fred?"

"It is. Because there's many a night when I'm sitting around the house, knitting balaclava helmets for our gallant fighting men in Afghanistan or playing solitaire in my fur pajamas, just me and the cat, and all the time I'm thinking how much more exciting it might be to have a little drinkie in a place like this."

I said offhandedly, "So what's all this about Felicity's boyfriend."

"*You* are Felicity's boyfriend? At least that's what I've long thought. Am I wrong?"

"Well, I can't be, can I? I mean, if Felicity's in the Deep Cove Chalet with some guy and I'm in here with you."

"God, Silas, you're such an idiot," he said, smirking unhelpfully.

As frequently happens when I'm around Fred, I had the feeling that I'd ventured out of my depth. A few drinks later I dragged him out of Bartholemew's and we walked down to the causeway. It was a lovely evening. Jugglers, painters, puppeteers, musicians and mimes entertained the crowds thronging Victoria's Inner Harbour. On a wooden quay below Wharf Street large white tents had been erected and a music festival was in full swing. A hundred yachts were moored at the floating docks fronting the Empress Hotel. Floatplanes, ferries and sailboats came and went.

Fred and I bought hot dogs from a street vendor, found a bench in Bastion Square and had dinner. Fred burped, put a cigarette into his mouth and lit it with a match struck on the zipper of his raincoat.

I said conversationally, "Did you know, Fred, that we're occupying almost the exact spot where, a hundred and fifty years ago, malcontents such as yourself used to be hanged in public?"

"Hanged?"

"A multi-strand knotted hemp rope and a six-foot drop, followed by a quick burial in unconsecrated ground. After public hangings were officially abolished, people still managed to watch. Crowds would gather on rooftops. Young boys would climb trees. Raise a cheer when the trap door banged open."

"I knew that talking to you would cheer me up."

"Did you also know," I went on undeterred, "that this area has been important commercially since the 1840s—which is when the Hudson's Bay Company appropriated it from my ancestors?"

Fred sighed. Maybe he was thinking what I was thinking: that once the HBC had controlled the whole of Vancouver Island and most of the American West. The Company's presence in Victoria is now marginal. Its wooden palisade vanished long ago, as did the original HBC trading post where Scottish-born adventurers gave my Native forebears glass beads for telling them where to find gold and beds of coal.

A kid came by shoving an ice cream cart. I asked Fred if he wanted a cone.

"Sure," he said. "I'll have vanilla. Two scoops."

I stopped the kid, ordered what Fred had asked for and, after rejecting various options including a double maple ripple, ended up getting the same as Fred.

"That'll be ten bucks, mister," the ice cream kid said.

"Things have come to a pretty pass," I said. "An ice cream now costs the same as a line of coke."

"It's your choice," the kid said. "We aim to please."

By then, it was growing dark. Fred finished his cone and drifted off home. After walking the streets of Victoria's Old Town with its souvenir and specialty food shops and cafes, I wandered back to Bastion Square, lined with old houses that have been transformed into art galleries and restaurants. The original provincial court house, now a maritime museum, rose up on my right. A crowd of noisy revellers had gathered outside Harpo's nightclub and I watched them for a while. I know most of the relatively few pickpockets who are active in Victoria, and when I didn't recognize any in the crowd, I started to turn away towards the harbour. That's when I noticed something unusual—the lights were all out in Commercial Alley.

Staring into the alley's darkness, I saw a white gauze of mist suspended a few feet above the ground, and I was reminded—as happens in such moments—of my half-belief in ghosts. But after blinking my eyes several times, I decided that the apparition was real enough. It looked the way a woman's filmy nightgown might look dangling from a clothesline in a breeze. Just at that moment, Harpo's doors were flung open and the crowd began to move, and by the time I pushed my way through the revellers into Commercial Alley, the white mist had dissipated.

As I moved deeper into the alley, a flock of night birds passed overhead—their beating wings made me look up. I smelled a whiff of smoke and had the strong feeling that I was not alone, that someone or something was watching me. Turning around, I saw Harvey Cheeke standing in a deep recess, half indistinguishable in the shadows. I asked him if he'd seen anything.

"Bastards," he muttered throatily. "Those little bastards are always bugging me."

Harvey was drunk. I phoned for a paddy wagon, put one of Harvey's arms across my shoulder and dragged him onto Yates Street so that I could have a good look at him under the street lamps. He was thinner than ever, his face was pale and drawn and his bleary eyes gaped from a head nodding under the weight of too much cheap wine. And he was bleeding from a head wound.

I asked him what had happened.

"The little bastards hit me with a brick, tried to steal my poke."

CHAPTER ELEVEN

It was time to bury the remains of the young boy who had drifted onto the Warrior's beach. The requisite longhouse ceremony, orchestrated by Chief Alphonse and Old Mary Cooke, had been eagerly anticipated, but problems of protocol had delayed it. The remains had washed up in an old coffin painted with faded Coast Salish heraldic crests, but according to tradition every human interment requires a new coffin. Artie Cramp had been given the job, and now the new one, with its bentwood corners and completely waterproof, was ready.

The undertakers were experienced elders who had prepared themselves by ritual sea bathing to cleanse their bodies of human odours offensive to a corpse's soul. The bathing place, the formal procedure and the phase of the moon when these rites had been performed were closely guarded secrets, but once protected by these rites, the undertakers then ritually washed the fragile bones and took them to the longhouse. Certain bones—including the skull—were painted with red oil paint made in the traditional manner out of natural iron oxide mixed with chewed salmon eggs and spit, and it was applied with sea-lion bristles lashed to a stick. Afterwards, the skeleton was placed in its new coffin on a platform facing east and left on public view with the lid off.

That Saturday the Warrior longhouse pulsated with life and

colour. Standing together behind the coffin, three impressive men arrayed in chiefs' garments passed an argillite talking stick back and forth between them. One of them was Chief Alphonse, wearing a silk top hat and a red Hudson's Bay blanket studded with pearl buttons. The second chief was a Haida, and he was wearing an ermine-tail robe and a rope necklace dangling with bone and ivory charms, gambling sticks and head scratchers. The third was a Tsimshian clan chief wearing a black business suit and a carved and painted flying dogfish hat.

Dozens of Coast Salish dancers wearing white, green, red, and black dance aprons or blanket-robes spun and whirled around two open fires. The spectators, many of whom were wrapped in blankets appliquéd with family escutcheons, squatted on the earthen floor around the fires or watched from bleachers.

In ordinary funeral ceremonies, the relatives of the deceased have rights of precedence and show up as the first official mourners, wailing and scratching their faces. Children are generally held back. Afterwards the friends of the deceased who care to help the bereaved relatives with funeral expenses lay blankets or other expensive offerings on the coffin. Some of their friends then announce that their offerings are gifts, for which nothing is expected in return. On the other hand, if people bring gifts and say nothing, it signifies that their contributions are loans to be repaid at some future time when the lenders themselves might stand in need. This boy had come from the sea, however, and had no known relatives, so paid surrogates were acting as honorary mourners, and they put on a very convincing show of grief.

Chief Alphonse was finally prevailed upon to accept the argillite talking stick. Fortunately for the Warrior band's finances, that talking stick, literally priceless, had been donated by the Haida Nation. The three chiefs then launched into long dramatic speeches, punctuated by sweeping gestures, but few heard them because people continued to dance, groan, weep, engage in laughing contests or doze. During the speeches a carved wooden raven mask, six-feet long and sprinkled with chopped eagle feathers—and much too heavy to be danced by one man—was briefly paraded around.

After several hours of speechifying, even argillite talking sticks lose their splendour, and boredom began to take hold of me. After all, it was late spring, the season when Nature's beings create new life, and that, more or less, is what I would have preferred to be doing—given a clean bill of health, that is.

It was while I was watching other people sneak out of the longhouse to grab fresh air and gobble smoked salmon snacks or venison sausage that I noticed Charlotte Fox sitting in the high bleachers. She looked gorgeous in loose-fitting silk trousers and a clingy silk shirt. Beside her was a Native man about five foot ten, built like a linebacker and wearing stonewashed jeans and a red T-shirt. They made a handsome couple. Well, well, I thought.

Going outside for a breather, I stood beside a thunderbird totem for a few moments, but when a lightning bolt flashed high in the north and thunderclaps resounded from the Malahat Mountains, I moved away from the totem and began walking past the row of Warrior houses strung out in a line parallel to the beach. Suddenly I spotted something glittering on the ground. It was a large flake of mica and I picked it up. Our old people believe in Sisiutl, a monstrous, double-headed sea serpent with mica scales, and they tell us that such pieces of mica, shed when Sisiutl changes its skin, prove that he exists. The next bolt of lightning was closer, and I dropped the flake of mica and returned along the beach. If the serpent was still out there, I didn't want to incur its wrath.

When I returned to the longhouse half an hour later, two men from up Mowaht Mountain way were prancing around, beating deerskin drums and singing a mourning song nobody had heard before. I seated myself on a platform where I could easily see—and be seen by—Charlotte Fox and her companion, and I caught them staring at me once or twice.

When Chief Alphonse's speech finally ended, it was the Haida chief's turn. During his speech, somebody decided to rehearse a bumblebee dance, normally the first dance a Coast Salish child participates in during Winter Ceremonial. In this simple dance, a mother and a father bumblebee lead progressively smaller baby bees one by one onto the dance floor, where they trip around flapping chintsy plastic wings. When the children are led into a "beehive" at the back of the house, one child is found to be missing. The father bee circles the dance floor four times, making buzzing sounds as he searches for the lost child until, at the height of the father's agitation, the child is found hiding among the spectators and led home.

It was about midnight when the speeches finally ended, and with a fresh outbreak of loud mourning, the lid was screwed down on the coffin. It was then placed on a wooden litter, picked up by four dancers and borne outside. Carrying flashlights or candles, hundreds of us followed the pallbearers up a trail that ends on the rocky hilltop studded with Garry oaks where the Warrior band's cemetery is located. In daylight we would have seen salal, cascara, Oregon grape and amazing views of the Salish Sea. As it was, we had to watch our steps in the darkness. A grave had been dug near the foot of a red cedar mortuary pole, and the box was lifted off its litter and laid on the ground.

Out at sea, something flashed like lightning and came towards the cemetery in zigzags. We could still see this lightning with our eyes closed, and it was accompanied by a cold wind that whistled in the trees, making sounds like crying children. Old Mary Cooke told us we were listening to a thunderbird wind. The lightning continued while the box was lowered into the earth and covered up. When the storm abated, Old Mary was asked what Thunderbird had been telling us. She said, "It was telling us about Filligan."

Afterwards, the original box in which the bones had been found was laid out on the beach and burned. Then all those who had touched the bones went through a purification ceremony in the longhouse, after which the air inside was swept with smouldering cedar boughs to exorcise the ghosts.

CHAPTER TWELVE

On Monday the weather was hotter. I got out of bed and checked my laptop—Charlotte Fox's Lexus had spent the night on Moss Street. I cleaned myself up, shaved and put on pressed jeans, a white, open-necked shirt, a lightweight sport coat and a pair of cheap Chinese loafers that had looked good in the store but hurt my feet if I walked more than fifty yards in them. The laptop lay open on the passenger seat beside me as I drove into town. Charlotte Fox's Lexus was still parked on Moss Street when I went into Lou's for breakfast.

I was half-expecting to meet Bernie Tapp there but he—like most of Victoria's cops—was probably searching for those missing Harris Green boys. Coincidentally or perhaps not, a diddler had just been released from William Head on mandatory parole. It was front-page news and the public was howling for blood, but Lou's prescription for dealing with diddlers nearly put me off my sausage and eggs.

On the way to my office I checked the laptop again; the Lexus was now stationary on Meares Street. I was at my desk by nine and, remembering Cynthia's list of bad-date cars, ran a check and found that the licence plate on the BMW that had been parked across from Charlotte Fox's house a few nights earlier matched a number on the list. Intrigued, I drove across town and parked on

Meares Street near Charlotte's Lexus. Under the chestnut trees the sidewalks were littered with bud-casings that stuck to the soles of my Chinese shoes. The Lexus was unoccupied, and I thought it likely that Charlotte was breakfasting somewhere nearby. Two upscale restaurants were within easy walking distance along with several blue-collar cafes of the greasy spoon variety. Charlotte was in the Stick In The Mud, sitting alone at a table for four. She had the *Globe and Mail* open in front of her and was immersed in the op-ed pages when I went in. I found an empty table and positioned myself where—if she wanted to—she'd be able to see me in profile, and I could watch her slyly while pretending not to notice. By the time a waitress had taken my order for a toasted English muffin, marmalade and an Americano, Charlotte had sent several long glances in my direction.

A few tables from where I was seated, an old woman had finished her breakfast, and now she was painting her tight, wrinkled mouth with vivid red lipstick. Holding a compact mirror, perfectly oblivious to her surroundings, she sucked her lips in and out, eyed her own image from different angles and practised several unusual ways of smiling at herself.

When my Americano came, I stared directly at Charlotte Fox, who appeared to be wearing no makeup at all on her beautiful, olive-skinned face. She looked exotic, enigmatic and possibly dangerous. She was wearing a white cotton jacket, a lacy yellow shirt, loose-fitting white trousers, and two-inch heels the same colour as her shirt. I drank some coffee, wiped my lips with a table napkin and went across to her table. When she condescended to look up and we made eye contact, I gave her my winningest smile and said, "Good morning, Ms. Fox."

Slowly she put down her fork. "How did you know my name?"

"I made it my business to find out."

"As a policeman, I suppose, you have your ways and means,"

she said, her eyes cool and unwelcoming. "I'm not sure that I like the idea of being followed."

"I'm not following you," I lied. "Until a few days ago I don't ever remember seeing you. Now I seem to run across you all the time."

"That's an exaggeration, surely."

"Perhaps, but three times at least. Didn't I see you driving a silver Lexus SUV through Metchosin a few days ago?"

Instead of speaking, she picked up her knife and fork, cut a piece of bacon and put it into her very beautiful mouth. She was playing for time, but I didn't mind because I liked Charlotte's table manners and her general air of sexy self-assurance. "I do happen to own a silver Lexus SUV," she said at last, "but I haven't been out to Metchosin for ages."

"That's weird. I could have sworn . . . perhaps my mind is playing tricks on me. Come to think of it, you might be on my Wanted list. Could that be the reason I find you so intriguing?"

"Oh, you find me intriguing, too, do you? It's not just my car that interests you?"

"You'd be surprised. I'll check up on you when I get back to the office in case you're a fugitive or something."

"That's a bit worrisome," she said, her frosty manner now showing signs of a thaw. "Are you a detective?"

"I used to be but now I'm a neighbourhood cop. If you don't mind me joining you, I'll tell you all about it."

She said lazily, "Sit down if you like. I'm leaving soon, but please yourself."

I sat down facing her across the table. She folded her newspaper and dropped it into her large Hermes bag.

"Tell me," she drawled, "what percentage of the time do you wear a uniform?"

"About twenty per cent."

"You don't look like a policeman," she said thoughtfully. "Has anybody ever told you that you look more like a ruffian?"

"I have been told that and worse, but I have developed ways of compensating for cruel jibes. In my secret life, for example, I'm a debonair jewel thief."

"In your actual life, too, I shouldn't wonder. People say that all cops are crooks . . . and liars."

"Okay, Ms. Fox, I'll come clean. I do take bribes, only I don't come cheap. Give me ten dollars under the table and I'll take you to dinner at McDonald's."

When she laughed, a couple of red spots burned on her cheeks, but before she could speak, my cellphone rang. Call display showed Nice Manners' name, so I put the phone back in my pocket without answering it.

"There's no need to be excessively polite, Mr. Seaweed," Charlotte murmured. "You're on duty, I suppose, so I don't mind if you answer your phone."

"It was one of my colleagues and I know what he wants."

She raised her eyebrows.

"Two Harris Green kids have gone missing. He wants me to keep an eye open for them."

"How can you possibly know that?"

"Because a child molester has just been released from prison, and because at 8:30 this morning my boss' car was parked outside city hall."

After processing that, she said, "That day I saw you in Larry Trew's office—what were you doing?"

"Following you."

"But you were there before I was."

"I like to keep one jump ahead of people."

Her mouth twisted wryly. "So you used to be a detective, and now you are a neighbourhood cop. Why?"

"It's a long sad story."

"I don't like sad stories, especially long ones," she said, not quite as serious now as she had been. "But if it isn't too sad and telling it won't take too long, perhaps you'd like to explain what neighbourhood cops do all day."

"Mostly they just talk to people."

"Like now, for instance? You get paid for chatting up women in restaurants?"

"It's not always this much fun. A couple of days ago, for instance, I broke up a bottle party in that little park at the foot of Yates Street. Four girls had been drinking all night. They were sloshed to the gills and the oldest among them was only seventeen or so. The youngest was about fourteen. But I was glad they were only drinking plonk instead of smoking crack."

"People are always talking about crack, but I don't even know what it is."

"*Most* people don't know what it is. You make crack by mixing cocaine powder with baking powder. You boil the mixture down in water until it crystallizes into breakable chunks, then you smoke it in a pipe and for a few minutes it'll remove all your earthly cares. In Victoria the supply is up fifty per cent in the last couple of years so its price on the street has dropped accordingly. Right now, a chunk of crack the size of a breadcrumb costs five dollars. Then there's crank, which is the street name for crystal meth. Like crack cocaine, it's usually smoked in a pipe, but the trouble with crystal meth is that most of the people who experiment with it end up addicted."

Charlotte gave me a disbelieving look. "Why is that?" she asked.

"Crank affects the part of the brain that governs inhibitions," I explained. "People think, 'Oh, I'll try crank once just to see if I like it.' Funnily enough, they do like it—everybody likes it. And when that first wonderful high fades, they think, 'Well, that was nice, let's do it again.' The next thing they know they're living in an alley with dogs and cats and doing crank every hour. The houses and cars that they used to own have been sold out from underneath them. They are addicts with no money, no future, no friends and no family. They're covered with scabs and their teeth have rotted in their mouths. And all because they thought they'd like to try a little crank just once to see if they liked it."

" You don't have to shout."

"Did I raise my voice? Sorry."

"Those four girls you were telling me about, what will happen to them?"

"They're from Newfoundland, and I'm trying to persuade them to go home. They've already heard my lecture several times—the one that goes, 'If you're still on the street this time next year, you'll probably be drug addicts and prostitutes.'"

"Can't you just put them on a bus and send them back to their moms?"

"I wish. Doing anything of the sort would infringe their Charter rights. If you get right down to it, I'm really just an old-fashioned, anti-crime beat cop with special responsibilities in cases that involve Native people. Come around and see me some time. I've an office near Chinatown."

"You mean Natives like me?"

"Not unless that Hermes bag and those clothes you're wearing came from Value Village."

"I'm impressed," she said, laughing at last. "Most men don't notice such trifles." Then she added, "So you were walking your beat this morning and you just happened to run into me?"

"Yes, and I'm glad because I've been wondering about you and your husband since I spotted you together a couple of days ago in the Warrior longhouse."

She shook her head. "I'm not married. The man that you saw me with is my brother, George."

"You don't look alike."

"That's because George is a boy," she said, laughter in her eyes. "Our dad was White, a Calgary oilman. Mother was a Coast Salish from Washington State."

She fussed with her bag in preparation for leaving. To detain her I said, "That longhouse ceremony you and your brother witnessed—did somebody invite you?"

Charlotte shrugged. "Maybe somebody invited George, because he dragged me along. I wasn't keen to go at first, but now on the whole I'm glad I went. Your people worked some impressive stunts."

"Stunts?"

"That sudden wind, the zigzag lightning at the cemetery. My brother would give his eye teeth to know how you did it."

I grinned. "You think we can fake lightning and winds?"

Her eyes searched my face as she folded her newspaper and put it into her bag. "I have to be somewhere else in half an hour," she said with sudden briskness. "This has been fun but I have to go now." She stood up.

"Give me another couple of minutes. I want to ask you about Lawrence Trew and hypnotherapy."

She said hesitantly, "Is it hypnotherapy that you're interested in or Larry Trew?"

"Hypnotherapy, I guess. I've seen a couple of stage hypnotists. They put on a good show although it's hard to know where hypnotism ends and flim-flam begins."

My remark struck a nerve. Her face tightened and she leaned her long legs against the edge of the table, looking down at me. I stayed in my seat. She said, "The first time we met—in Larry's office—I was rude to you and I'm sorry. You were only doing your job, and I was wrong to speak to you the way I did. But you can be quite obnoxious."

"Obnoxious? Moi?"

"You seem to think I'm an easy mark. Someone easily taken in by hypnotherapists and smooth-talking street cops."

"If I offended you, it wasn't intentional. Maybe we'll meet again, make a new start. I'd like to see you again, really."

"For dinner, I suppose. Bannock and fried moose in your little waterfront cabin?"

"I was thinking in terms of a brew pub, maybe Spinnaker's. How about it?"

For answer, she picked up her bag, walked elegantly across to the cashier's desk and used a credit card to pay for her breakfast.

I wondered how Charlotte Fox knew that I lived in a little waterfront cabin.

CHAPTER THIRTEEN

It was a few minutes before noon when I got back to Pandora Street and started looking for Nobby Sumner, the autocrat who manages the office building. He was on the roof pulling weeds. He has tomato plants, potatoes, pumpkins, raspberries and a crabapple tree up there along with flower beds and a ten-by-ten greenhouse built of recycled windows where he grows orchids.

"Any chance of getting a cat flap installed downstairs so PC can go in and out of my office when she pleases and save me a lot of bother?"

Nobby snorted his amusement. "No chance whatsoever. I'm up to my yingyang as it is. See them flowers? Covered in mites. Besides, a heritage building like this, defacing a door would be strictly against regs."

"Nobby, this roof garden is against regs, to say nothing of that greenhouse."

"Yeah, but you're a co-conspirator," he returned. "You're one of the guys who carried buckets of manure up the stairs to get me started."

"How about if I gave you fifty dollars?"

"Oh, that's entirely different," Nobby said briskly. "Consider it done."

Money changed hands. I went downstairs.

I was talking on my desk phone to a fraud-squad sergeant as Bernie Tapp came in. PC appeared from behind a filing cabinet where she had been goofing off. With her tail upright and quivering, she walked on silent feet across the room and rubbed herself against Bernie's leg. Now Bernie was a bird man, not a cat man, and he was wearing very nice tan wool pants with a sharp crease that wouldn't look good with black cat hair on them. Besides, he'd made the mistake of trying to stroke PC once. So chewing the stem of his unlit corncob pipe, he shooed her away and sat in the visitor's chair.

I said casually, "I just ran into Charlotte Fox . . . a Native woman, one of Lawrence Trew's clients."

"And a looker, I guess."

"Yeah, she's quite a looker."

Bernie scowled. "You just happened to run into her, hey?"

"Yeah. I dropped into the Stick In The Mud for a cup of coffee, and there she was. She has a brother called George. The two of them showed up at a longhouse ceremony on Saturday on the Warrior reserve, so I'm kind of interested in them."

"Interested in them or interested in her?"

"How come you're all dressed up?" I asked, instead of answering Bernie's question. "Going somewhere special?" With his tan pants he was wearing a tan corduroy jacket, a cream shirt with a brown stripe in it and nicely polished brown brogue-cut shoes.

"I just left city hall. Superintendent Mallory and I had another meeting with the mayor. She's worried about those two little boys that have gone missing."

"Pederast panic?"

"Among other things. Now I'm heading out to Goldstream Park to meet a friend of yours."

"Who's that?"

"Somebody nice."

"Speaking of Nice, did he find anything interesting when he turned Titus Silverman's house over?"

"Nothing that added to or contradicted the information we already had."

"He didn't find any dead bodies, bloodstains, bags of coke?"

"Not even a smutty postcard."

"It would be really great to nail Titus for trafficking."

Bernie's face muscles tightened. "That won't happen. Due to an unanticipated turn of events, Titus Silverman now has immunity from prosecution."

"Don't tell me," I said, appalled, "that he's made a deal with the Crown already?"

"No, Titus hasn't copped a plea. Put your coat on. There's something in Goldstream Park you ought to look at before it starts to smell."

"Sorry, I can't."

"Baloney. A hike in the fresh air will do you good."

I looked at Bernie's freshly polished shoes and said, "We won't be roughing it, obviously."

"That's what you think," Bernie said.

"Just a minute," I said. "I need to check something first."

Bernie twiddled his thumbs while I phoned the Good Samaritan. Marnie Paul's condition was unchanged. Visitors were still being discouraged.

"You can drive," said Bernie, throwing his keys across the desk for me to catch.

His Interceptor has an automatic transmission and power steering so, unlike my MG, it's no fun to drive. But I slid behind the wheel and we headed north out of town. As Douglas Street turned into Highway 17, we were listening to the police channel and heard that a fifteen-year-old girl in a stolen minivan had just run a red light at Blanshard and Hillside and driven into the side of a fuel truck. The resulting conflagration was creating traffic gridlock. I switched the radio off when the dispatcher launched into a description of the incinerated girl's horrific injuries.

The ribbon developments flanking Victoria's highway north gradually give way to open countryside, and over to our left we could see Portage Lagoon, where someone was paddling a white kayak and a couple of fishermen were dangling lines from a rowboat. A guy in a red wetsuit was being dragged behind a ski boat in flagrant disregard of municipal bylaws.

Traffic speeded up after we passed the Helmcken Road hospital. Beyond Millstream Road the highway gradually narrows from six lanes to three, and we began the long, slow ascent into the rocky, forested mountains that run the entire length of Vancouver Island, forming its spine. Huge evergreens spread their branches to meet each other high above—they say that squirrels can travel the length and breadth of Vancouver Island without ever touching the ground.

As we approached Goldstream Park, we drove alongside the wide, shallow creek that was the site of a flash-in-the-pan gold play a hundred and fifty years ago. When the lode petered out, the region reverted to what it had been before—a wilderness refuge for bald eagles, cougars, black bears and nature lovers—instead of the usual tacky ghost town crammed with souvenir shops and cigar-store Indians. We pulled into the unpaved parking area now filled to overflowing with cars, buses, blue-and-whites, ambulances and fire trucks. I squeezed the Interceptor into the empty space beside a pumper truck.

A park ranger, standing on a wooden bridge that spanned the creek, was pointing out Mother Nature's unspoiled wonders to a group of schoolchildren and telling them that in a few months this creek would be thick with spawning salmon, along with the animals that flock there annually to feed on their decaying carcasses.

But the kids seemed more interested in the uniformed emergency personnel coming and going along the Mount Finlayson trail than in what the ranger was saying to them.

Lightning Bradley, a middle-aged constable with a bulging gut, was leaning against a tree drinking coffee from a Styrofoam cup. When Bernie and I got out of the Interceptor, Bradley heaved his empty cup into the bushes and wandered over. "Hi, guys," he said. "Manners is up there, waiting for you." Pointing across the creek, he added, "What you do is, you follow that path till you get near the top. Then you kind of follow a little path that juts off to the side . . ."

"Up your fat ass!" Bernie snarled in disbelief. "First thing you're gonna do is, you're gonna pick up that Styrofoam fucking cup and drop it in a garbage gobbler. Then you're gonna waddle your sorry ass back here and show us the way."

Bradley's averted eyes and tight mouth showed that he'd got the message.

Grinning broadly, Bernie popped the Interceptor's trunk, reached inside for his waterproof pants and hiking boots and proceeded to put them on.

The Mount Finlayson trail starts with an easy uphill hike over a wooden bridge and along a well-trodden path, but after a few hundred yards the ascent becomes steeper. My Chinese shoes were useless for climbing, and I was soon sliding on the damp leaves and slippery pine needles. Conditions worsened after Bradley, panting and purple-faced, led us off the main trail and along a pathless slope. Here canopies of dark, dank leaves created a perpetual twilight world, and we had to climb over barriers of rotted, fallen trees and blackberry tangles and grab at slippery, moss-covered branches for support. It took us 40 minutes to pull ourselves along the slope and up a cliff to reach a goat plateau. Nice Manners and Victoria's chief medical examiner Cliff Tarleton, along with a couple of bunny-suiters, were there already, gazing impassively at a lumpy blue tarpaulin the size of a bed sheet that was concealing a recently exhumed human corpse.

"Looks like somebody scraped a shallow hole with his boot, rolled the body into the hole and then covered things up with loose dirt," Manners told us. "By the time I got here, the scene-of-crime had been seriously compromised—first by scavenging animals, second by a hiker's dog and third by the hiker who found the body. Then the two park rangers who were alerted by the hiker trampled the entire scene before they called us."

Breathless from the climb, Bernie bent, hands on knees, and moved an edge of the tarpaulin aside to reveal the upper part of a mottled male corpse wearing a loose white shirt and grey jockey shorts. "Somebody's done quite a number on him," he remarked superfluously, gazing intently at the horrible thing lying at our feet. "Say, Doc, one eyeball has popped out . . ."

Dr. Tarleton, a scruffy-looking man of fifty, ambled over. "Decomposition gases can build up pressure inside the skull," he said. "They build up enough, it forces the eyes out like that."

"Yeah, I know. But this guy's head was bashed in, so how's the pressure gonna build up? Besides, why just the one eye? Generally they both pop out."

Tarleton shrugged. Bernie kept looking at him. Shaking his head, Tarleton said, "I don't know everything, Bernie. Sometimes there is no simple explanation."

Bradley, who had been leaning over the corpse for a good look, straightened up and said, "What I can't never get over is how big eyeballs is. Bigger'n a fucking golf ball."

A tiny white object protruded from the earth between the corpse's legs. I took a pencil from my pocket, poked for a few moments and uncovered a scrap of paper covered with illegible handwriting.

Bernie beckoned one of the bunny-suiters and said, "Put this in an evidence bag." Then he turned back to Tarleton. "So what *do* you think, Doc?"

"His face was beaten in," said Dr. Tarleton, stating the obvious, then he added, " . . . after death. It was flogged with a blunt object until it is, as you can see, unrecognizable. All of his fingers have been cut off, and I'd almost go so far as to say that they were cut off by a trained dissectionist."

Bernie shook his head. "They look to me like they were snipped off with sharp pincers. If the guy'd had an axe, he'd have cut the hands off instead of just the fingers. And I'd guess he'd smash the face in with the blunt side, wouldn't you?" Bernie suggested calmly.

"That's right," Nice Manners interjected. "But our killer was either in a hurry or he panicked, because he overlooked something. Have a look at this."

Bernie bent over again to look more closely at the grisly remains.

Using his fingertips, Manners rolled up the corpse's sleeve to reveal a hearts-and-flowers tattoo encircling the word "Edie."

As calm as a gallery goer admiring a painting, Bernie examined the dead man's partially exposed right arm. After several moments, he straightened up to ask, "Any idea how long he's been here, Doc?"

"Can't say offhand. Probably been dead for a week or ten days. There's no telling, of course, how long ago he was brought to this location." Then the medical examiner cleared his throat and added, "He was shot with a single bullet. It went through his left temple and came out the back of his head."

"Hm-m," Bernie said. "A week or ten days . . ."

"And Titus Silverman has been missing for a week or ten days," Manners commented.

"Yes, very good, Nice," Bernie replied genially. "Titus Silverman has been missing for a week or ten days. This could be him."

"Oh, it's him all right," Manners returned smugly. "I had a hunch about this and called Vital Statistics. Titus Silverman married Edith Dundern in 1984. The marriage ended in divorce eight years ago."

"Good work, Nice. What do you plan to do next?"

"Well, if you're done, we'll bring the rest of the squad up. Lay the whole area out in a one-metre grid and search every millimetre."

"In the old days we used to lay things out in three-foot grids and search every inch," Bernie mused.

"Things change," Nice Manners observed.

"They certainly do," Bernie said. "Old-fashioned villains took pride in their work. They dug graves at least six feet deep. They made life more difficult for coppers and for our hungry four-legged friends."

Dr. Tarleton decided to add his two bits. "Quite right," he said. "This park is probably full of old buried corpses."

"And I certainly hope they stay buried," Bernie chuckled. "Otherwise we'll be tripping all over the fuckers."

A helicopter hovered unseen above the trees. Bernie put a hand in his pocket and brought out his smelly corncob. In the silence after the chopper's pock-pock-pocking had faded away, we could hear the far-off roar of diesel trucks downshifting as they ascended the Malahat and jake-braking on their descent. Speaking to nobody in particular, Bernie said, "What's the easiest way in and out of this spot?"

Nice Manners shrugged.

Bradley said, "There's no easy way. If you head uphill, there's an old logging road that leads over to the Bear Mountain subdivisions and a golf course, but it's real rugged country. We better go down the way we came up."

"That's not what I'm getting at, Bradley. I'd like to know how this corpse got here."

"He didn't walk," Manners declared. "Somebody probably drove the dead body in along that logging road and slid it down here instead of carrying it up."

"That helps narrow things a bit," Doc Tarleton said. "The person or persons that you're looking for are rugged and sure-footed and clever enough to plan ahead and take advantage of inclined planes."

"How about a sidehill gouger?" Bernie said.

"How about sasquatches?" Doc Tarleton countered. "Apart from the mechanical advantage thing, a sasquatch would fit the bill in every respect."

After examining the evidence, I had to agree with Nice Manners' theory. Titus Silverman had been murdered and mutilated—or mutilated then murdered—after which his body had been dragged downhill from the logging road.

As Bernie, Constable Bradley and I began slipping and sliding our way back to the parking area, Bradley said, "Say, Bernie, what's a sidehill gouger?"

"A species of mountain goat," Bernie replied gravely, "that's seldom seen except in the Cariboo. The right legs of sidehill gougers are a bit longer than their left legs, so they can only go uphill counter clockwise. Most people only see their trails, which wind up and down the hillsides like corkscrews."

Bradley rose to the bait. "So how do they get downhill?"

"Young sidehill gougers roll down. They lose their balance when they get to the flat land at the top and just tumble downhill like drunken sailors. Old sidehill gougers go downhill backwards."

WE WERE ALMOST BACK to Victoria when Bernie mused, "About Lawrence Trew and his alleged bad temper . . . From the available evidence it would seem that he might have been involved in a punch-up in the kitchen of his house. The other guy might have been one of his acquaintances—a friend even. That assumption is feasible because, before you entered Trew's house and saw those bloodstains in his kitchen, his back door was unlocked and the security alarm had been deactivated, and that suggests Trew invited his assailant in."

"Well yes, his security alarm had been switched off but not necessarily by Trew," I objected. "It's activated by an ordinary four-digit keypad device. Some of his regular guests would probably know that keypad number—in fact, lots of people might know it. It's likely to be the last four numbers on his social insurance card or the year of his birth—something easy for him to remember. Then what happens is one of his former girlfriends or house guests is at the hairdresser's and the hairdresser mentions birthdays. They start talking about security and later it turns out that the hairdresser's son is a housebreaker . . ."

Bernie smiled charitably. "A likely scenario, except we're not talking about an ordinary housebreaking. That was Trew's blood on the floor. We're probably talking about a killer."

"How about this," I suggested. "Trew's at home when somebody rings his doorbell. He looks outside, sees Titus Silverman. Opens the door and lets him in. Trew loses his temper, blows are exchanged, and Titus Silverman ends up with his face beaten to a pulp and no fingers. According to Doc Tarleton, somebody who knew what he was doing removed those fingers, and Trew, as we know, was a doctor." I parked Bernie's Interceptor beside a fire hydrant across the street from my office and switched off the engine.

Bernie yawned, flexed his shoulders and stretched in his seat. "Deer hunters also know how to dismember animals, as do butchers. Cutting off a guy's fingers can't be too tricky—in spite of what Doc Tarleton says." He paused before adding, "There's been a suggestion that because Trew had an affluent lifestyle, he must have had a big income, possibly from drugs, but there's no evidence to support that, and I'm beginning to doubt it. He has a record, but he's not an ordinary criminal—he doesn't even park next to fire hydrants."

"Al Capone didn't have a criminal record either, till the FBI busted him for income-tax evasion." As I was getting out of the car, I said, "Trew might have gambling debts." And this reminded me of something else. "By the way, Bernie, what did you do with Titus Silverman's address book?"

He took it out of the glove compartment, climbed out of the passenger seat and gave it to me.

"I'll call you," I said.

"What Lightning Bradley told us earlier about there being no easy way to the top of that hill?" Bernie said as he walked around to the driver's side. "He's probably right, but how would he know? He sure as hell hasn't hiked up there."

"He wasn't always fat."

Sighing, Bernie drove off.

CHAPTER FOURTEEN

A few days later I was sitting in a booth in Mom's Cafe at the Fisherman's Marina, drinking coffee and having a side of New York fries. The jukebox was out of order, and an old-fashioned radio on a shelf behind the counter was tuned to KPLU. Somebody who sounded like B.B. King but wasn't was singing Billie Holiday's "Strange Fruit." I looked out the window. Because of the Japanese current, fog had formed along the outer coast and was now drifting inland and blanketing the Inner Harbour. Tonight, perhaps, the fog would rise above the mountains and give us more rain.

In another booth a couple of telephone repairmen and a man dressed like a stonemason were eating lunch. The only other customer was a guy wearing half-moon glasses and dressed in a Nike tracksuit with the jacket unzipped to his navel. He was sitting alone in a corner tapping a laptop's keys. Perspiration beaded his brow and ran down his cheeks.

Somebody slapped me on the shoulder and then sat on the red vinyl and silver duct-tape-upholstered seat across from me. It was that ink-stained wretch Fred Halloran, and he seemed happy to see me. Baring his gleaming white dentures and carefully enunciating every consonant, he said, "I was driving past and noticed your little coupe. Somebody has let all the air out of your tires, old chap, so I thought I'd buy your lunch and cheer you up."

"Buy your own lunch. I'm eating this one."

"No, seriously, I've been thinking of giving you a call."

"You need a favour?"

"What's the latest on those missing kids?"

I gave him a blank look.

"The ones from Harris Green," Fred persisted. "The pair of 'em vanished at the same time. A bit unusual, don't you think?"

"Not at all. Two boys or two girls will often run off together on a lark. In a way it's a good sign because it probably means that, wherever they are, they probably weren't kidnapped. Diddlers usually grab one kid at a time."

Fred leaned across the table and seemed about to unveil the secrets of the Sphinx when a waitress came out of the kitchen carrying a jug of coffee. When she saw Fred, she gave an agitated double take. She was about Fred's age—thin, grey–haired and wearing glasses with bottle lenses that magnified her dark eyes. The drab green dress she wore hung loosely from her narrow shoulders, and she looked careworn and exhausted. After a short pause, she straightened with a visible effort and came over to us, carrying a menu and a coffee pot.

"Just coffee, thanks," Fred said automatically without looking at her.

Her face slightly averted, she said in a low voice, "Hello, Frederick. Black, no sugar, right?"

Fred had been leaning across the table. His smile faded as he turned his head and recognized her. "Yeah, I still take it black," he said without inflection.

"Long time," she said, smiling for the first time. "You haven't changed much, Frederick."

"So," Fred replied warily, "how long have you been working here, Connie?"

"Couple of months," she said. "Do you live in Victoria now?"

"Lived here for years."

"I didn't know that," she said.

Fred's eyes followed her as she went around the room, filling coffee cups, then out of sight into the kitchen. For a minute he wasn't in that cafe with me anymore. He was with Connie somewhere else. At last he said, "I was kidding you earlier . . . about the flat tires, I mean. I was going to ask you about some character called Filligan . . . but I'd better leave that for now."

Before I could respond, he stood up.

"Hold it a minute," I said. "What's going on?"

"Nothing's going on. Why should there be?"

"I'm not talking about Connie."

"Forget it," Fred said angrily. "I wish to God I'd never come in here in the first place."

He went out, but I was right on his heels and caught up with him as he was getting into his car. "What's up, Fred?"

"My dubious past is catching up with me," he said, without looking at me. "I don't know why I'm explaining any of this to you, Silas. It really isn't any of your business."

"Maybe Connie isn't any of my business, but what's this about Filligan? Better tell me about it now, then I'll go away and quit bothering you."

"Sorry. I'll give you a call." And he drove away.

Victoria's Central Library is on Blanshard Street opposite the BC Courthouse. Those high-calorie fries needed burning off, so I walked there instead of driving. A reference librarian showed me how to log onto their e-resources website, and after scrolling back and forth among the news items that had appeared in the *Toronto Sun* in 1999, I zeroed in on May 15, the day after Lawrence Trew's wife plunged to her death. A short news story under Charles Fortunato's byline was accompanied by a photograph of the widower emerging from Toronto's police headquarters following his interrogation. Trew, pictured wearing dark glasses and a heavy overcoat with a turned-up collar, had refused to answer the reporters' questions, and he left the scene in a Cadillac driven by an unidentified female companion. A second Fortunato story appeared two weeks later at the conclusion of a coroner's inquiry into Mrs. Trew's untimely and suspicious death.

Lawrence Trew had testified that on the evening in question he and his wife had been barbecuing steaks on their outdoor balcony. Each had consumed two glasses of white wine. During the course of the evening, somebody knocked on the Trew's front door. When he answered, he found a neighbour who was returning a borrowed punchbowl. The neighbour was invited to come in for a drink, but declined. Trew put the punchbowl away in his kitchen and returned to the balcony to find his wife absent. He said that he assumed she was probably in the bathroom and thought nothing of it until several minutes had gone by and she still hadn't returned. That's when he searched the condo and realized something was amiss. When he finally looked down from the balcony, he saw a crowd gathered around an object lying on the concrete below. It was his wife. She had plunged to her death. Asked by the coroner to account for her apparent fall, Trew testified that his wife occasionally suffered from slight dizziness. He speculated that during such an attack she might have accidentally tumbled over the balcony railing.

Ralen Genova, MD, a general practitioner, was then called to the witness stand. He testified that Mrs. Trew had been his patient for the three years preceding her death and that she was in generally good health, except for moderate benign hypertension for which he had prescribed medication. In response to a question, he said that a small fraction of anti-hypertension drug users experience occasional mild vertigo. When asked if such an attack would cause an otherwise healthy woman to fall over a railing to her death, the doctor said that in his opinion it was possible although unlikely. However, he observed that alcohol potentiates certain medications and Mrs. Trew had consumed two glasses of wine, thereby rendering an episode of dizziness more probable.

After hearing further testimony from Detective Sergeant Gerald Hayes of the Toronto Metropolitan Police, who had attended the accident scene, and from Edwin Randall, a mechanical engineer who discussed the integrity of the balcony's railings, the coroner's jury retired to consider the evidence. Thirty minutes later they returned a verdict of accidental death. I checked the following weeks' newspapers and saw that by degrees, the stories concerning Mrs. Trew and her unfortunate death followed the usual downward direction from city desk to features desk and thence to oblivion.

I decided that I'd like to talk to Charles Fortunato one of these days.

RESTLESS, UNABLE TO CONCENTRATE, I walked back to the Fisherman's Marina, where I'd left my car, and drove across town to the Demi-Tasse on McNeill. I found an empty table on the outside patio and enjoyed a cinnamon bun and an espresso while browsing through Titus Silverman's address book. Charlotte Fox's name was in it. Her brother George's name was not. I bought another coffee to go, and took it to the Chinese cemetery at Harling Point. There wasn't a breath of wind. The sun was lost behind the low frothy fog that had obscured the sea all morning but was beginning to lift.

As is generally known, Canada's early Chinese immigrants spent their harsh and—for the most part—underpaid lives building railroads, sluicing gravel in icy northern gold creeks or working in cafés and laundries until they died. Traditionally, their corpses were buried until worms devoured their flesh, after which their bones were exhumed and cleaned by undertakers who specialized in the practice. The bones were then placed in wooden boxes and stored in the Harling Point mausoleum until they were to be shipped back to the old country. In 1933, however, the Chinese government banned the importation of human bones, so instead of spending eternity with their ancestors, Chinese-Canadian bones now spend eternity at Harling Point. But there are worse places than Harling Point.

Surrounded by grave markers, I stood looking out to sea. The snow-covered Olympics made a majestic backdrop for a pair of twitchy-nosed, grass-nibbling rabbits. A flock of pigeons flew in from Gonzales Bay and strutted around, bobbing their heads. I thought how nice it might be to sit here with somebody—somebody nice, that is—like Felicity Exeter or even Charlotte Fox—except Felicity seemed to have a private love life I knew nothing about, and Charlotte was undoubtedly very complicated and might even be a murderer. Besides, I still didn't know whether I had HIV or Hep C—or possibly both—so I resisted the temptation to call either of them.

Instead I would continue to keep track of Charlotte's Lexus. She'd stopped going to the Stick In The Mud for breakfast and had been patronizing the Ocean Pointe Hotel, but mostly she drove around within Victoria's city limits. Once she had driven out to Saanich and spent the night in a waterfront house near Brentwood Bay. Being nosy, I checked to see who owned the house. She did.

CHAPTER FIFTEEN

After the filing of numerous lawsuits and countersuits, stern *Times Colonist* editorials and intemperate city council meetings, Victoria's police chief was at last directed to eject the squatters from Beacon Hill Park. I watched as Police Superintendent Mallory, using a bullhorn, read the Riot Act to the noisy mob of campers, sympathizers, wackos, and protesters of both sexes who had congregated in the park. As soon as he finished speaking, a hundred uniformed cops in full riot gear drew up in close order and raised their Plexiglas shields. Mallory blew his whistle and the phalanx moved slowly forward, night-sticks clattering against their shields with a sound like kettledrums. The more militant among the mob began to throw things, but the rest broke ranks and scattered. In a bid to infuse some backbone into these cowards, the protesters began singing a bitter song, the words of which were unintelligible above the racket.

By the time the Taser guns were triggered, three officers had been injured badly enough to require hospital treatment. Thirty or so civilians were arrested and removed from the scene in various conditions of disrepair, but the park remained hazardous in those places where the hardcore rump continued to assert themselves. Sunlight filtering through the trees created a kaleidoscope of darkness and light filled with hurrying figures. CHEK TV and

A-Channel news were covering this well-publicized event, and the liberals who love the homeless as long as they stay downwind strutted before the cameras, deploring the criminal actions of Victoria's police.

It was in the aftermath of the melee that Hector Latour appeared—shivering, ill-nourished and filthy—when a front-end loader began to demolish the squat where he'd been hiding out. He was just escaping onto Cook Street when I grabbed him and frog-marched him to my car in handcuffs. Hector—high on west-coast bud—was inclined to be saucy as I shoved him into the MG's passenger seat. "Why are you treating me this way?" he whined.

"I'll ask the questions. First, I want a complete inventory of the items you burgled from Lawrence Trew's office."

"Who?"

"The hypnotherapist on Fort Street. You smashed his door and burgled his office."

Hector giggled.

I said, "One of the items was an engraved silver cup . . ."

"You're a goddamn . . ."

"Look, Hector, don't try my patience. I know you stole the cup. I even know where you fenced it."

"You got a nice line of BS. Gimme a sleeping pill and I'll listen to it for hours," Hector retorted. "Used to be you had to be a crook to land in jail. Now you only need to be homeless."

"Right. A homeless pimp who broke into Lawrence Trew's office. You and Marnie Paul."

"That's a load of crap. I'm no pimp an' we never broke into nobody's office."

"You're a liar."

"Maybe I'm just practising. Some day I might want to lie myself into the police force," Hector mocked, "but I never broke in nowhere. Ain't nothing you can say will make me change my tune neither."

I gave him a frosty stare. "You put the burgled items in a cardboard box, went over to Titus Silverman's pawnshop and popped them for cash."

Hector grunted.

I went on, "And we can prove that while you were engaged in burglary, Trew walked in and disturbed you. After inflicting a grievous wound to his head, you . . ."

"Yeah-yeah-yeah," Hector interrupted. "You're fishing. I ain't robbed nobody, I ain't killed nobody, and I ain't broke into nobody's office."

I thought of Marnie, lying brain-dead at the Good Samaritan, and I repeated with barely controlled fury, "You broke into Trew's office and burgled a number of items. Then you beaned him with a candlestick and fled. You and Marnie Paul. You might have got away with it except for a witness who saw you leaving the scene. It's a positive ID and you are facing the whole jolt."

"For what?"

"Manslaughter, criminal negligence leading to Marnie Paul's death plus whatever else the Crown dreams up to ensure you get a life sentence."

"Baloney," Hector said, although by this time his shoulders were beginning to sag and he looked a little anxious.

I bared my teeth. "Hector, you've never had any imagination, and that's why until now you've just been a small-time nuisance. But this time you figured that what worked for you once ought to work for you twice. So what you did was, you found out where Trew lived and then you burgled his home, too."

"More baloney," Hector said in a voice now reedy and fearful. "I don't even know where the guy lives!"

"You know all right. He lived on Terrace Lane. You probably got his address from the phone book. So how did you get over there? Steal a car and drive, or catch the number two bus?"

His face now waxen, Hector worked his jaws from side to side.

"You and Trew had another mix-up in Trew's kitchen. How do I know that? I've seen the bloodstains," I said, lying wildly but perhaps persuasively. "You assaulted and robbed Trew not once but twice. And you killed him. Then you administered a lethal cocktail of drugs to Marnie Paul, and she's dying, too. And when she dies, you will be going down for two slices of Murder One."

"You bastards are stitching me up!" Hector said, his voice wobbling on the edge of hysteria. "I want a lawyer right now!"

"You shut the fuck up and listen," I said. "You are going to spend every minute of the rest of your life in the house of locks. Every minute. We've got you nailed. You have a criminal record stretching back over fifteen years . . ."

"Shit, man, honest to God, I never been near that guy's house! I don't even know where the fuck Terrace Lane is," Hector wailed. "It was this way—Marnie and me was strung out, see? We didn't even have a dry place to crash except for a fucking dumpster, for Chrissake. So we was on Fort Street and it was late at night, cold and raining, and we stopped in this doorway. We figured our luck was changing because the door wasn't locked, and we went inside and spent the night flaked in the corridor. Next morning we wake up and see this office door is open. We're not looking for no trouble. We just need a fix and someplace to stay warm. I never killed the guy. I never laid hands on nobody, never. I'm a thief and a fuck-up but a strong-arm guy? That's not my style and you know it!"

That was true—strong-arming men wasn't Hector's style. He preyed upon helpless women instead, in fact, had served two separate jolts for assaults against street women. I snarled, "It's pathetic how life's treated you, Hector, when all you've ever wanted to be is an honest upright pimp and thief. Well, you don't have to worry because you're never going to touch another woman's leg. It's payback time."

"I'm no killer and I'm no pimp neither. I love Marnie. Everything's gone to hell. Shit, I never had a decent break in my life."

I'd scared Hector enough by this time so it was time, for Mr. Nice Guy. I showed him my teeth again and said slowly, "You know, Hector, maybe if I put my mind to it, I could give you a break. The question is—what will you do for me?"

Hector didn't hesitate for a moment. "I'll level with you. Marnie and me robbed that office, but it's not the way you think. We didn't do no break-in. The door wasn't locked. And I don't know nothing about no murders." In his agitation, his right knee was flexing and his foot was tapping the floor like a trip-hammer. He tried to say something more, but his mouth had gone dry. My threat to ship him down the river had really frightened him. Finally he added, "We grabbed a couple of candlesticks and a silver cup and some other stuff . . ."

"You were seen leaving the building carrying a cardboard box. I want you to imagine yourself picking things up, dropping them into that box."

He shook his head. "There was some pens . . . Hell, I don't remember . . ."

I reverted to bad-cop mode. "Fix your memory or take the high jump," I said nastily. "Your choice."

He licked his lips. "Listen, I'm an asshole all right, but for Chrissake, you know I never murdered nobody. I never carried a weapon in my life. Sure, me and Marnie took a few shortcuts, but murder? No way, man."

"Candlesticks, a silver cup, pens. What else?"

Another groan escaped Hector's lips. He made a useless gesture. "I can't remember. It's like I said already—I was strung out."

"You couldn't have been too high when you unloaded the stuff at Titus Silverman's hockshop. How much did he give you?"

"Not enough, the cheap bastard. I was making a deal with

Frankie when Tight-ass comes into the shop. She's talking fifty, sixty bucks, but Tight-ass wouldn't give us no money. Paid us in drugs," Hector said defeatedly. "That silver cup alone was worth hundreds, and the tape recorder was worth plenty, too."

"What tape recorder?"

"Oh, yeah, it's coming back. There was this tape recorder on the guy's desk. A Sony no bigger'n a pack of cigarettes."

"A tape recorder, a handful of ballpoint pens, the silver cup, candlesticks. That's it?"

"That's it. I don't remember nothing else." In response to the skepticism on my face, he added, "I'm giving you the straight goods."

"Okay, Hector, I want you to cast your mind back to going into Lawrence Trew's house on Terrace Lane."

Looking like a playground kid whose ball had just been stolen, he said, "I been levelling with you, and this is the way I get treated. I don't know nothing about no house on Terrace Lane. For all I know the guy lives in a fucking cave."

"You don't seriously expect me to believe that you don't know anything more."

The colour had drained from Hector's face. He shook his head.

I said, "So this is what we've got so far. You steal Trew's gear and take it to Titus Silverman's hockshop, where you negotiate with Titus Silverman personally."

Hector nodded. "Yeah. I'm talking to Frankie, then Tight-ass comes in and I end up making a deal with him personally. He won't give us any money. Instead he gives us some heroin and cocaine."

"Crack cocaine?"

"Yeah, heroin and a few small rocks. Tight-ass could see me and Marnie was strung, so he knew he could stiff us."

I went over the same ground again, after which Hector—who realized he had already said too much for his own good—clammed up. I adopted a friendlier tone. "One more thing, Hector—why did you and Marnie go over to Donnelly's Marsh?"

He seemed puzzled that I would ask such a dumb question. "To hide our sad asses from guys like you."

"Right, I've got that. But why Donnelly's? The place is haunted."

Hector shivered and the red-streaked whites of his eyes showed.

"Our people never spend time on the marsh after dark," I was saying when he put his hands over his ears to block my words and shook his head like a man demented.

"Shut up, shut up, for Chrissake! Don't say no more," Hector begged. "I don't even want to think about that place."

"You don't want to think about it because that's where you left Marnie Paul to die. You ran away and left her to die alone in the dark."

"Marnie was already dead, man! She overdosed. She stopped breathing. I did what I could, man. I'd have stayed with her except she was gone, and I was scared out of my gourd."

"You mean I scared you by trying to get into the house through the front window . . ."

"No, man! It was that Jesus great big grizzly! You don't have to tell me that marsh is haunted, man, because I seen that great big ghost of a bear with my own eyes. Head like a goddam balloon . . ." And Hector burst into tears.

I drove him to police headquarters, down the tunnel ramp into the underground parking lot and into an empty stall. I switched off the engine, and we sat there for a minute listening to the cars coming in and out of the tunnel making sounds like a winter's gale. Hector's high had faded and he sat beside me as quiet as a statue.

I said, "Anything more to add before I turn you over?"

He didn't respond.

I said, "There's a war going on out there because drugs have changed everything. There's so much crime on the streets now the police can't really handle it all . . ."

"Yeah-yeah-yeah, it's pathetic," Hector retorted with a burst of his former spirit.

"Just listen," I said very softly, "and don't interrupt me again."

"I'm kidding," he said, sounding as if he meant it and staring up at the MG's headliner instead of at me.

"Titus Silverman is dead," I told him. "He was murdered. If Marnie dies, I personally guarantee that you will go away for a very long time. And even if she lives, you won't have another chance to pimp young girls because I will fit you up. I will fit you up for killing Titus Silverman and, if necessary, for killing Lawrence Trew. The mayor will give me a great big fucking medal for it. I'll be a hero for a day. And don't think I can't do it, because there are a lot of people on the street who owe me favours. I will teach them how to give convincing evidence against you in court. They'll say whatever I ask them to say."

Hector had closed his eyes and he was shaking his head slowly from side to side.

"I am going to make you a proposition," I said. "Are you listening to me?"

I took it that the strangled sound that emerged from his throat meant yes.

"Good," I said. "Pretty soon you might be getting a message from me. If I do call, I'll be suggesting you either go into retirement or, failing that, move the fuck out of this province and never come back. Are you straight on what I'm telling you?"

Hector's head moved up and down.

"You'll move the fuck out of my sight forever?"

"The first chance I get I'll be long gone."

"Bright boy," I said.

I took him upstairs in the elevator and reported to the duty sergeant. After some paperwork, Hector was locked in one of the second-floor interrogation rooms. Then I walked upstairs to Acting DCI Bernie Tapp's office and gave him a rundown.

Bernie stared at me aghast. "Why, in God's name, did you accuse Hector of killing Trew? We don't even know that Trew's dead!"

"It was just an impulse, an idea that came out of the blue. It scared the hell out of him."

"It scares the hell out of me, too," Bernie said, staring at me as if I were deranged.

I waited in Bernie's office while he and Nice Manners gave Hector another grilling. Bernie's office overlooks the Memorial Arena, and I watched the people lined up outside the box office to buy tickets to the next ice hockey game. Over an hour passed before Bernie returned and sat behind his desk, staring at me without expression. I had the feeling he was a little annoyed with me. We drank several cups of coffee together and chatted about Hector for a while. About the only thing we could agree on was that Hector was a devious rat.

Bernie took a can of birdseed from a filing cabinet and opened a window. After rattling the can, he spread seeds along the window-sill. A couple of hungry pigeons flapped in immediately. When he put the coffee can away, he said, "For a guy who's screwed up royally several times, Lawrence Trew seems to have done very nicely for himself. He has a million-dollar house in Rockland. He drives a Carrera. And his only tangible income comes from hypnotherapy."

"Sounds like a nice racket."

"Maybe too nice. Nice Manners is still convinced that some of Trew's money came from drugs."

I raised my eyebrows questioningly.

"Maybe Hector and Marnie visited his office and filled prescriptions more than once."

I shook my head.

"Narcotics tell me there's been no diminution in the illicit drug trade since Titus Silverman bit the dust," Bernie continued thoughtfully. "Maybe he and Trew butted heads and Titus lost."

"So you think Trew's hiding?"

"Maybe. And maybe he's dead."

"That's a lot of maybes."

"And lots of unknowns. For example, I need to know who owns that Donnelly's Marsh house where this whole thing started."

"It's on rez land. It belongs to the Coast Salish Nation."

"Since when?"

"Since forever. The Coast Salish stopped occupying it in the mid-1800s, and some time after that it was leased to the Donnelly family, Irish farmers who ran sheep on it for the next eighty years or so. They left sometime in the 1970s, and since then it's been more or less abandoned."

"Why? It's a lovely piece of property, right there on the water."

"It's lovely in summertime and there's good clamming along the beach, but people don't like going there because it has ghosts."

"So how come Hector and Marnie hid out there?" Bernie asked, and then before I could answer, he asked, "These ghosts—are they Donnelly ghosts or Coast Salish ghosts?"

"They were there long before the Donnellys took possession."

Bernie scratched his nose. "Why did the Donnellys move off?"

I shook my head.

CHAPTER SIXTEEN

The case was going nowhere. The man—or woman—who had killed Titus Silverman might have killed Lawrence Trew as well, and my mood was gloomy because murder, like every other form of extreme behaviour, is addictive. That killer had to be caught and quickly, so I went back to first principles and made a list of all the dubious characters in the case. That list included the late Titus Silverman, the elusive Lawrence Trew, Charlotte and George Fox, Tubby Gonzales, Hector and Marnie, and Joe McNaught. Harvey Cheeke's name was down there, too. Over the course of the next few days, I tracked down and questioned the friends, enemies and associates of all the people on my list. My questions all tended in one direction—what threads, if any, connected these mismatched characters?

Days passed fruitlessly. I gathered little information and discovered no promising leads. In the meantime, I was still keeping tabs on Charlotte Fox. Her activities followed a familiar pattern. She seldom ate at home and spent a lot of time and money in Victoria's high-end rag shops, beauty salons and day spas. She attended a couple of gallery openings, several cocktail parties and a concert by the Victoria Symphony Orchestra.

Then suddenly after a couple of weeks of this, the pattern changed. One afternoon Charlotte abruptly left town. After driving her Lexus through Goldstream Park and up Highway 17 into the Malahats, she hightailed it non-stop past Mill Bay and Arbutus Ridge, her average speed about 100 kilometres an hour. She took a five-minute pit stop at the McDonald's Restaurant in Duncan, after which she continued north for another ten minutes before leaving the coast and heading west into the Beaufort mountains. At that point I came out of my office onto Pandora Street on the run, fired up the MG and, with the laptop open on the passenger seat, went after her.

Victoria was very hot and muggy that day. If you're used to a cool wet climate, as we are around here, every hot day seems the worst in history. But this one really was, because rainfall and temperature records were falling all over BC. As I ascended into the mountains, it became a bit cooler, but vehicles with raised hoods and steaming radiators jammed the viewpoint parking area at the top of the Malahat. While they waited for engines to cool, the sweating tourists aimed their cameras and VCRs at Brentwood Bay and Saltspring Island and off to the east, where North Saanich's farmlands and vineyards were dehydrating beneath layers of mist. As I roared past, I could see out in the middle of Saanich Inlet that somebody was building a house on an acre of tree-covered rock. Beyond the summit, the road descended into the heat again. Scorched air, rising above the blacktop, made the horizon shimmer.

At Duncan my MG's gas gauge was showing half a tank. According to my laptop, the Lexus was stationary a few miles short of Songwet, an out-of-the-way Native village at the head of one of Vancouver Island's deep coastal inlets. I gassed up at the Shell station, checked my tires, water and oil, and stopped at McDonald's long enough to grab a coffee. Ten miles past the Cowichan Lake turnoff, I headed west along unpaved logging roads towards the Beaufort Range. Small tree-girt lakes and mountain peaks dominated the scenery. A mile short of Songwet, I came to a fork in the road. A rough wooden sign pointing down the left fork said: PRIVATE LOGGING ROAD. DANGER. NO PUBLIC ACCESS. I ignored the sign. Five hundred yards later, a locked gate and an unmanned sentry hut brought me to a stop. My laptop told me that the Lexus was somewhere beyond that gate. I backed up to a sideroad and parked.

High clouds roiled with red and yellow fire, lit by a sun that was now invisible below the western horizon. I walked back to the sentry hut, climbed the gate, and looked around. Down to my left, half-visible through forest, a saltwater inlet rippled. Loons and cormorants floated silently, and immense trees leaned over the water, lending an air of mystery to the silent landscape. I began following the road down toward the water.

It was nearly dark when I came out into a clearing dotted with Oregon grape and blackberry thickets. In the middle of it was a rustic cottage lit by kerosene lamps. Music and smoke spilled out of the open windows and doors. A half-dozen revellers had gathered on the shore. All the laughter, canned music and rowdy voices drowned out the approach of a woman who came up from behind, threw her arms around me and told me how much she'd always wanted to be an Indian. She had black and red markings daubed on her face and was wearing a red and black cape hung with ermine tails and bear claws, but she wasn't a Native. She was White and middle-aged. Standing close in her embrace, I smelled the breathy funk of dope.

"Are you one of the dancers?" she asked breathlessly.

I said that I was, escaped her clutches, and stepped back into the trees. From this vantage point I could see that Charlotte Fox's Lexus was parked in a grassy area near what seemed to be a traditional Coast Salish longhouse. Nearby were a twenty-passenger school bus and a war-surplus ambulance. On the adjacent level

ground a wood fire glowed within a shallow pit that was about
fifteen feet long and four feet wide. It had obviously been burning
for many hours so that now it was largely reduced to hot ash and
small embers.

But as I drew closer, I realized that things were not as they
seemed. The longhouse was a Quonset hut with a false, lime-
washed housefront crudely decorated with paintings of thunder-
birds, whales and otters. The front door of the longhouse was so
low that, when I pushed it open, I found it necessary to stoop
before I could look into a gloomy room lit by a small fire burning on the ground inside a circle of stones. A wooden screen at
the back of the house was partially draped with black curtains.
Instead of entering, I went around to the rear of the building
where I found a door that opened on the narrow area that lay
behind the screen. In a traditional Native longhouse this back
part of the house behind the screen is where shamans and sor-
cerers store the equipment used to create magical effects, because
tricks and wild dances—many of which simulate murder, canni-
balism, and other bloody dramas—are an essential part of West
Coast Native initiation rites and ceremonies. But here I could see,
after my eyes adjusted to the darkness, that the area was filled
with theatrical props of various kinds, including long dark curtains, painted canvas flats and black boxes large enough to accommodate human-sized objects. Robes, blankets and papier-mâché
animal masks dangled from hooks.

When I heard the longhouse's front door open, I put an eye
to a peephole in the screen and watched a man enter with an arm-
load of wood with which he built up the fire and then went out
again. Moments later several more men wearing long robes and
carrying masks entered the longhouse and stood around the fire,
talking in low voices. I grabbed a wolf mask and a robe, put them
on, went out the back door and made my way in the dark back

into the trees bordering the parking lot. The clouds above were now black smudges in a starlit sky.

Then gradually I became aware of an eerie, smoky-yellow light. Several feet long and suspended above the ground, a river of flame was travelling past my hiding place, headed towards the inlet. The effect was unnerving until I realized its cause—half-screened by the underbrush, a long line of masked, dark-robed individuals carrying flaming wax torches were walking in single file towards the inlet, where a crowd waited. After the procession passed, I joined the back of the line. Nobody paid any attention to me. I wondered which mask hid Charlotte Fox's pretty face.

A large dugout canoe had been drawn up on the shore, and as our procession snaked past the cottage, a dozen "Native" handlers, all of them disguised as crazy men, grizzly bears, wolves or cannibals, dragged a struggling shaman out of the cottage and threw him into the canoe, where he lay as if poleaxed. The people watching along the shore began to shout and clap.

The shaman's hair dangled in loose, matted strands to his shoulders. He was naked except for a leather breechcloth and knee-high leggings hung with small bells and deer-hoof rattles. Carved bone charms dangled from a ring around his neck, but the rest of his bare body and his face were black with filth. Cedar-bark bracelets entwined with bones, sticks and feathers encircled his wrists.

The handlers wrapped a heavy chain around the shaman's neck, pushed the canoe into the inlet, leapt aboard and paddled out into deep water. Then, as we all watched, the shaman was thrown overboard. He didn't protest and he sank from sight instantly. The handlers paddled back to shore and beached the canoe. By this time the crowd had grown silent, and after waiting eight or ten minutes to see if the shaman would resurface, the procession reformed and straggled back up to the longhouse to mourn the shaman's death.

Once inside the longhouse, people set their torches upright

in stands positioned around the room on the earthen floor. It was evident that this ritual was a new experience for some of them, as they had to be shown what the stands were for and how to set their torches in them. There was a certain amount of confusion before things were sorted out. A few of the older people then sat on three-legged stools while the rest of us crouched in a half-circle on the bare ground, facing the fire and the screen and encircled by the torches. The smell of burning wax was strong.

After a woman placed a rack hung with bear claws, teeth, rattles and carved wooden headgear in front of the fire, a dancer carrying a paddle and a miniature canoe suddenly appeared through an opening in the screen. He pretended to paddle the canoe down a raging river, mimed getting washed overboard, and then did a series of sleight-of-hand tricks with things that he drew out of the canoe. As a finale, he pulled a raven mask out of the canoe and put it on his head. To our astonishment, another mask jumped out of the box, apparently of its own accord and it, too, landed on his head. Then another mask jumped out, and another. As a magic act, it impressed the hell out of me.

Authentic West Coast Native musical effects are produced by whistles, drums, rattles and human voices, but it was electronic harps and keyboards that produced the faint melodic sounds we next heard as three dancers emerged from behind the screen. Beating drums and wearing animal headpieces, their bodies draped in blankets decorated with traditional crests, the barefoot, singing, swaying dancers circled the spectators and the fire, its glow picking up the rainbow colours of their abalone-shell necklaces and bracelets.

Then still singing, the dancers passed through the screen and returned with a boy about ten years old. They seated him on a mat in front of the fire. In the silence that followed we could hear him weeping. An owl called, and the drummers commenced a frenzied beating. At that moment the shaman, still wet from his recent immersion in the sea, emerged from a hole in the dirt floor. Wild-eyed and shaking a carved beaver rattle, he jumped and spun in circles as violent contortions shook his whole being. When he squatted beside the weeping boy, the shaman shook his wet head with enough violence to fling water on the terrified child's face. Then, using a pair of wooden tongs, the shaman grasped the boy's head and, calling out the name of various animals and spirits, dragged the boy around the fire, first in one direction, then the opposite one, before pushing him roughly onto the mat again.

While this was going on, a large black wooden box had appeared in the smoke hole and descended to the ground. Shaking and singing, the shaman's gyrations took him behind the black box so that the lower half of his body vanished. The drumming intensified whenever the shaman raised his arms to shake his fists at the sky.

Then a woman appeared carrying a carved wooden whale about four feet long, which she set upon the black box before departing. Arms still raised, the shaman faced the whale. His body trembled as the whale slowly rose into the air, the shaman apparently defying gravity by the power of his will. The whale levitated until it was four feet above the ground, then the shaman grabbed it and began to sing. The whale seemed to be very heavy as its weight slowly bent the shaman double until his face was half-concealed by his long hair, and he moved crabwise around the fire, seeking something and shaking with rage because he couldn't find it. The drums resumed their beat, quietly at first, and every once in a while the shaman's song would be interrupted by strangled wails from behind the screen. Gradually one of the phrases he sang came to predominate. I could make no sense of it until the shaman and the whale suddenly vanished behind the black box, whereupon someone shouted the word, "Filligan!"

Two female assistants dragged the boy to his feet. The drums, rattles and whistles were making a tremendous racket when a ghostly shape materialized from the frightened boy's mouth. This ghost was floating away when the shaman reappeared, captured it inside a bag and disappeared again into the earth.

That seemed to be the end of the show. Everybody trooped outside, and one of the masked dancers directed us to line up alongside the firepit. Then, with a sudden theatrical howl, the shaman emerged from the longhouse with the boy, who was barefoot, and began forcing him to walk along the firepit.

There is nothing remotely West Coast Native about firewalking, so it seemed like a good time to leave. But walking towards the parking lot, the hairs on the back of my neck started prickling, and I looked back over my shoulder. Two of the masked cannibal dancers were right behind me.

"What the fuck are you doing here?" one of them asked.

I didn't hear the third man come up behind me, and the blow he struck on the back of my neck numbed me to my toes. As I fell to the ground, they put the boots to me. It was three against one, and I didn't stand a chance.

I WOKE LYING FACE down on a wet beach, pulses hammering deep inside my head. My clothing was soaked and my hands were freezing. I tried to move and couldn't. But gradually I became aware that the tide was coming in, and when ripples of salt water began creeping slowly along my arms, I drew my elbows up and rocked myself until I was kneeling. The camp had apparently been abandoned, and I had the night to myself. I started crawling. After a while my body warmed and my brain started to work.

I smashed the window in the cottage door, slipped the latch and went inside. I fumbled around in the darkness till I found a bed, took my wet clothes off and crawled naked beneath the covers.

CHAPTER SEVENTEEN

It was one of those quiet, clear, Sunday afternoons. Rooks cawed up in the trees, squirrels feasted on acorns cached since last fall. Kids were building sandcastles on the beach. Joe Paul was using a double-bitted axe to chop driftwood and pile it into a wheelbarrow. Everyone was enjoying life except me. My head ached, I had a bruise on my stomach that looked like a gaudy example of modern art, and every time I moved, my bones ached. I washed two aspirins down with two ounces of Scotch and went out.

A friendly Airedale, curled up in long grass beside the pathway, woke up and trailed at my heels as I took an evening hobble. To my surprise, clerks were busy in the Warrior band's office, and looking through a window, I saw Maureen working at a computer. The dog flinched when I stooped to pat its head. "There's a good boy," I said. It stayed on the doorstep as I went inside the office.

"I'm glad you came in, Silas," Maureen said, looking up from her computer. "I've been wanting to talk to you about something."

"Sure, go ahead."

"Need coffee?"

"No thanks," I said, sitting across from her desk.

"I've just had an email from Provincial," she said. "There's a fraudster targeting bored New Agers with trust funds—retired stockbrokers, property developers, dot.com millionaires, rich people generally that are sick of travel and shopping. What they want now is personal transformation and inner growth, and they think it'll be groovy to find their inner Indian. You know, commune with nature in the deep woods. Co-exist with noble savages. Enjoy shaman sweats in a nicely scented sauna. Run around waving mass-produced sacred objects. Smoke peace pipes stuffed with sacred marijuana, get a little buzz on, enjoy some sacred sex."

"Yeah," I said, "you've got it down pat."

"I went on the Internet, boned up."

"Native American spirituality workshops started popping up in California thirty years ago," I told her. "It was just a matter of time before they reached us."

"These workshops don't come cheap," Maureen said. "The going rate for a weekend introductory course on core shaman-ism is between $250 and $1,000, and that doesn't include travel and accommodation. These guys don't even advertise. They have a core group of devoted followers that vet potential recruits. Newcomers are sworn to secrecy and made to feel special, part of the chosen few."

It was getting on towards sunset when we finished talking. I was leaving when Maureen stopped me by saying, "What's the matter, Silas? You don't seem your normal self."

"Let me ask you something … do you ever get up in the morn-ing, look around, and say to yourself … "

Maureen interrupted with, "You need a holiday."

I went outside. I was looking around for the Airedale when I saw a boat round the breakwater and head in toward the jetty. The setting sun was shining directly into my eyes, so I didn't rec-ognize the boat until it was two hundred yards offshore. It was the *Ednorina*, Johnny Mack's 36-foot troller. Screeching gulls were flapping around it, hoping there'd be offal to fight over. I went down to the jetty in time to catch Johnny's heaving line, and as we tied the boat up, the seagulls tried to settle on railings and pilings. The Airedale chased up and down, apparently unaware that an Airedale has never in the entire history of dogdom outwitted a gull.

The *Ednorina* had five thousand dollars worth of spring salmon, cod and halibut in its hold, and Johnny brought a couple of fifteen-pound springs ashore and gave one to me. I hooked three fingers into its gills, took it home, scrubbed its silvery scales off with a wire brush, filleted, cleaned and decapitated it and cut off its tail, then threw what I wouldn't eat onto the beach. Seagulls had borne every scrap aloft within seconds.

Feeling a bit livelier, I called Bernie Tapp. He arrived promptly with a case of Labatts. He popped a couple of caps and we drank while I scrubbed new potatoes, put them on to cook, washed broccoli, sprinkled ground pepper onto four salmon steaks and fried them in butter till the flesh was slightly brown.

Dinner went down well. Bernie cleaned his plate, congratulated the chef, slackened his belt and offered me another beer. I hesitated.

Bernie said, "What the hell, Silas. You've probably got AIDS as well as clap by now. Yellow jaundice and death may be just around the corner. Do you think another beer's going to make things any worse?"

He was right.

Bernie interrupted my reverie. "Now tell me what's happening."

"Yesterday I followed Charlotte Fox out to Songwet."

"Where's that?"

"In the back of beyond, way west of Duncan."

"No, you didn't."

I gave him a dubious look.

"Charlotte Fox wasn't in the bush west of Duncan yesterday.

She was in town," Bernie declared flatly. "My wife has been bugging me to take her to see *The Illusionist*. It was on at the Cinecenta. I've been busy lately and kept putting it off, but we finally went to see it last night. And Charlotte Fox was in the audience. She was sitting three rows in front of me, her and another woman. I had them both in sight the whole time. Not only that, but their car was parked near mine."

"It sure as hell wasn't Charlotte's Lexus."

"I never said it was a Lexus. It was a Mercedes 280. Belonged to Charlotte's friend, I suppose."

"Then what? Where did they go?"

"I don't know where they went. They drove out of the parking lot before I did. In any case, I have no interest in Charlotte Fox." Grinning, Bernie went on, "She's dragging you around by your dick, pal. You're a dopey sod sometimes, especially where women are concerned, but I'll say this for you—you've got one very endearing quality, which is why, I guess, a lot of women go for your particular line."

"Which of my many endearing qualities is that?"

"Your charming capacity for making an ass of yourself."

I shook my head. "Yesterday I trailed Charlotte's Lexus—without actually having it in sight—to a fake longhouse west of Duncan. That Lexus was definitely there."

"How do you know it was her Lexus?"

"I checked with Motor Vehicles. It's registered to her. While I was at it, I checked to see if there were any liens against it. There aren't. She owns that Lexus free and clear."

"In that case, Charlotte either lent the Lexus to somebody else or it was stolen."

"It wasn't stolen. The last time I checked my GPS gizmo—which is about two hours ago—that Lexus was parked outside her house on Moss Street."

"I thought I warned you about that! You know damned well that bugging peoples' cars is a big no-no!"

"I must have forgotten. It's a good thing I did, though, because I found out something interesting. There's this cult thing happening out Songwet way, and last night they staged a hokey healing ceremony. The audience was White and probably thought they were watching something genuine. They weren't. But everybody was wearing Indian masks so I borrowed one and watched the show."

"Where are we going with this?" Bernie inquired cynically. "If a bunch of consenting adults want to dress up in weird clothes and have fun out in the bush, so what? Paintball warriors do queer things out there every weekend. And what the bears and rabbits do in the bush is also nobody's business."

"It may not be your business, Bernie, but I've made it mine."

"Don't tell me you take this shaman crap seriously?"

"Coast Salish shamans believe that sickness is caused by magic and soul loss." I grinned. "This may come as a surprise to you, Bernie, but people have two souls. One's in your head, the other is in your heart. When you're asleep, these souls can be frightened away from your body by ghosts or stolen by people who want to harm you. Shamans find missing souls and bring them back to the sufferer."

"Where do missing souls go?"

"Mostly to the Unknown World."

"Sounds like a long way off, so I guess a good popular shaman can build up frequent flyer points pretty fast," Bernie said, popping another can. "This Unknown World can't be much joy, though. So maybe shamans use their points on fun trips, take their wives to Acapulco or Fiji, right?"

"In fact, a shaman's wife can build up her own frequent flyer points."

"In *fact?*"

"At a healing a shaman often sings along with his wife, and they sometimes use a wooden bowl full of water to reflect the universe."

"That's it? No drums, none of those goofy, feather dream catcher gizmos?"

"Sometimes, if a patient has a suppurating wound, say, the shaman uses a hollow bone and sucks the pus out. But you don't see much pus-sucking these days."

"That's the truest thing you've said today," Bernie murmured, taking a long swig of his beer.

CHAPTER EIGHTEEN

About a week after my Songwet experience the sun came out in Victoria again. Extravagantly brief miniskirts blossomed like summer flowers all over town. Ice cream shops along Government Street ran out of stock. Old folks hugged the shade. And for no discernible reason the inside of my office began to smell like wet paint. I wanted to tackle Charlotte Fox, but wasn't quite sure how to handle the matter. I decided that grasping the nettle might work. When I phoned, she answered immediately. I said, "It's Tuscan night at the Med Grill tomorrow. Four courses, only $16.95 plus taxes. How about it?"

"Does that include wine?"

"No, but Med Grill wine isn't all expensive, and you don't have to buy any if you don't want to. What I do is buy a bottle of Italian red at the liquor store, hide it in an inside pocket and have a little rubber tube running up the sleeve of my jacket so I can siphon a drink when the server isn't looking."

"When you invited me to dinner, I was imagining the Empress, maybe even the Latch."

"Sorry, you must think I'm Warren Buffett. This is Silas Seaweed."

"Is it? Good lord, let me check my calendar." There was a pause. "Heavens! I'm booked till Christmas! Sorry, bye."

I shrugged. It was time to deal with ordinary reality. Headquarters had updated my missing-kid list, and I noted that the two Harris Green boys were still missing. The mother of one was a high-class call girl, and her son had been more or less fending for himself. It had been days before she even noticed his absence.

I began an aimless drift around the streets and ended up outside Capital Iron. Folks were clustered around a hot-dog stand, where a girl with a yellow ferret draped across her shoulders like a scarf was feeding it bits of pink meat. When they'd finished eating, she crunched the hot-dog wrapper into a ball and heaved it into the gutter. The ferret leapt to the sidewalk, pounced upon the wrapper and tried to carry it away, until it was hauled up short by the string tied to the girl's belt.

The Good Samaritan Mission was only two blocks from there, and I knew I ought to go over there and get the results of my blood tests, but something was hauling me up short, too. Instead, I walked over to Moran's Gymnasium, a single, long, narrow room situated on the upper floor of a red brick, two-storey building so decrepit that the next time Victoria has an earthquake, Moran's gym will probably be reduced to rubble. I climbed the outside staircase and opened the door at the top. Going into Moran's is like stepping into a time warp—nothing ever changes. The place has been short of a good mopping since 1980. It lacks proper ventilation and always smells of embrocation, sweaty feet and dust. Fortunately, after a while nasal paralysis sets in and you don't notice.

Young hopefuls who might otherwise have been robbing banks or riding unmufflered motorcycles were exchanging blows in a boxing ring. Retired scrappers were reading newspapers and arguing about the Mariners' latest disaster. Moran himself, chewing an unlit cigar and wearing a shiny blue suit, yellow shirt, red tie and brown fedora, was wandering among the punching bags and weight-training machines and occasionally stepping into the ring to explain a point of basic ringmanship. The rest of the time he lurked behind his lunch counter, hoping somebody would be dumb enough to buy one of his month-old wieners or a cup of yesterday's coffee. As usual, the octagonal poker table was littered with newspapers and outdated copies of *Ring* magazine.

Tony, the masseur, wearing a white T-shirt, white pants and white tennis shoes, was sitting on his massage table chewing a plastic swizzle stick. He was swarthy, heavily muscled and almost as tall as Danny DeVito. He looked at me with sad brown eyes.

"I need a rubdown, Tony."

"You need more than that," he said in a voice like Tony Soprano's.

I took my clothes off in the shower room, hung them in my personal locker and went back to Tony in my jockey shorts. He placed a fresh towel over his massage table. I stretched out on it face down and said, "Treat me gently. My head aches and my bones are fragile."

"It's not only your bones. Face it, Champ, you've gone to pieces. You are a mere shadow of your former self," Tony said, pouring oil onto my back. "I guess AIDS kicks the stuffing out of a guy."

"I don't have AIDS."

"That's not what I heard."

"I'm being tested for HIV. It's not the same thing."

"That's like the girl three months late saying she's only a little bit pregnant. And what happened to your head?"

"I slipped on a banana peel. By the way, what are people saying about Titus Silverman?"

"They're saying the nasty prick got what was coming to him," Tony said, gently kneading the loose skin at the base of my neck with his strong, smooth hands. "They're saying it was a mob hit."

"Mob hit? Give your head a shake, Tony. I come in here for

a massage and some polite conversation. All I get is Hollywood Noir and hackneyed expressions."

"What do you expect with a thirty-buck massage, David Letterman?"

"I could go a bit higher if you've got something hot."

"Okay, try Crazy Legs. She's fifteen to one in the two-thirty at Saanich."

"The last time you gave me a horse, she came in last."

"Certainly she did, but that tip didn't cost you anything. You want solid information, you've got to pay for it."

Moran came over and stood watching us. He was holding his head to one side and seemed to be listening to something—voices inaudible to the rest of us, maybe, or tinnitus from sixty years of timekeepers' bells. He jiggled his cigar from the middle of his mouth to side and said, "There's a poker game here Friday night. Are you guys in?"

"Sure, I'll be here."

"Me too," Tony said.

Moran went away then came straight back. "By the way," he said to me, "Joe McNaught dropped by earlier. He said to say there's a message for you at the clinic." He ambled off to sit behind his lunch counter.

Tony was working on my pectorals. "Forget Crazy Legs," I told him. "Tell me who croaked Titus Silverman."

"I ain't heard nothing," Tony said, "but my nephew might know. He's in William Head."

"Doing what?"

"Eight years. When I visit him on the weekend, I'll whisper between the bars. Maybe he'll know something."

I had a shower, ate lunch at Lou's Cafe and meandered in a daze to the Good Samaritan Mission, wondering about the news awaiting me there. Joe McNaught was absent, and nobody knew where he was, so I stopped by the clinic and asked about my blood tests. The results had come in, but Dr. Auckland had pinned a note to my file stating that he wished to break the news to me personally. I fretted in the clinic's waiting room for several minutes before my name was announced and I was ushered into Dr. Auckland's office. He was sitting behind his desk, writing in a folder. "Hi, Silas, take a pew," he said jovially, but he kept on writing and didn't look at me properly. There's an old saw that when juries arrive at a guilty verdict they avoid looking at defendants, so I expected the worst. Finally he closed the folder, leaned back in his chair and gave it to me straight. The news was still sinking in when he came around the desk, tapped my head lightly with a forefinger and said, "Does that hurt?"

"Only when I laugh."

"That's the spirit," he said, his voice faintly satirical. "Come with me."

THEY HAD TAKEN MARNIE out of the emergency ward and she was now in a regular hospital bed in an ordinary private room. It was dark in there, apart from a small bedside lamp with a 15-watt bulb that illuminated the top of her head and threw the rest of her into shadow. Joe McNaught was on his knees at the foot of the bed, snivelling like an infant, his hands clasped in mute supplication to whatever Christian saint he was addressing. When he heard Dr. Auckland and me come in, he rose to his feet and said with a catch in his voice, "It's God's will, Silas. It's the will of God." And he staggered out like a stricken elephant.

Marnie had lost quite a lot of weight in the weeks that had passed since I'd found her unconscious at Donnelly's Marsh, and she'd been skinny even then. Drained away by her battle against death, her face was gaunt—loose skin laid upon unfleshed bones. The blankets had been turned down to her chest, and both of her cold, skinny, tattooed arms were uncovered. Her heart-lung machine had been switched off, and IV fluids no longer dripped into her blue-veined arms. Her eyes were closed and she looked asleep.

I kissed her pallid cheek and sat down beside her.

Smiling remotely, Dr. Auckland left the room.

I took Marnie's left hand and gently squeezed her fingers. They were cold and unresponsive, although at my touch her eyes seemed to flicker behind lids as fragile as butterfly wings. I got up from the chair, went around the bed, tucked her exposed right arm beneath the covers, went back to the chair, sat down again and held her left hand as before. Gradually her fingers got a bit warmer, and mine got colder, but it was very quiet and peaceful sitting there. I was thinking about my blood tests and about Marnie and about how peculiar life is sometimes and I dozed off—or maybe I went into a meditative state for a while—and when I checked my wristwatch again it was ten minutes past four. I knew I'd entered Marnie's room at two o'clock.

Her eyes were wide open and she was looking at me. She said quietly, "I've been sleeping and dreaming. Sometimes I don't know what's real and what isn't. Like that time out on Donnelly's Marsh when you came into that kitchen and started kissing me. Do you remember that, Silas?"

"I remember something like that."

"You looked the way you always look, Silas, but I was in this kind of dream and you acted different to the way you usually do. It felt real, but I knew it was a dream because I could fly. Besides, you never kissed me like that before. It was pretty sexy, you know."

Oh dear, I thought. "Was it?"

"Yeah, because you're a sexy guy, Silas. I was lying on the floor, you were kneeling down, kissing me, and then I sort of floated up to the ceiling and I could look down and see us. I've always had dreams about flying, ever since I was little. Then these ambulance guys came in and you stopped kissing me and I lost track . . ."

"They've been pumping you full of chemicals for weeks, Marnie. It's bound to affect your mind."

"Yeah? I guess that's explains it. I've been wondering what's been happening to me. I've been singing a spirit song that I haven't heard since I was a little girl, and I haven't even seen the inside of a dance house for years. Yet there I was in my dreams singing my spirit song inside a dance house."

"Was anybody in the dance house with you?"

"Not at first. It was a big dark place, and the only light was a tiny fire ringed with fir-bark. After a while I saw Old Mary Cooke sitting about six feet from the fire, spinning an ivory bobbin." Marnie smiled up at me. "Life's a mystery, innit?" And she went on talking about Old Mary Cooke and ivory bobbins until her voice faded, her eyes closed and she fell silent.

I walked along to McNaught's office, tapped on the door and went in. He was sitting behind his desk, leaning back with his eyes closed. When he heard my footsteps, he opened his eyes and said, "I left a message with Moran. Did you get it?"

"I did. I tried to reach you but sometimes you're hard to find."

"Harvey Cheeke is missing and I'm a little worried about him. Did you know he had tuberculosis?"

I nodded.

"He really ought to be in a TB hospital." McNaught tipped his chair up and rested his arms on his desk. "This is Harvey's second home—he eats here at least five times a week. Sometimes he checks in, stays a couple of days. In the meantime his condition keeps getting worse."

"Spreading germs?"

"Shit, no. We know how to deal with people like Harvey. He's not the only chest case out there. Anyway, bottom line, Silas, is do what you can to find him."

I went back to my office and put Harvey's name on the wire.

CHAPTER NINETEEN

Charlotte Fox didn't want to see me, but I wanted to see her, wanted to find out how a Calgary oil baron's privileged half-Native daughter lives. That evening I drove over to Moss Street and parked, admiring the dusky blue fall of the Sooke Hills into the purple sea. It was a pleasantly cool twilight, and a fugitive breeze brushed my cheek. I was wearing a khaki safari jacket, a white knit shirt with thin brown stripes, pressed jeans, and profligate Mephisto loafers to replace the Chinese shoes I'd had to junk. No socks, good fake Rolex. My head had stopped aching, and I had a bottle of wine in a paper bag. I walked up to Charlotte's front door with a pleasant sense of anticipation that lasted until George Fox answered my ring. He was wearing a white dinner jacket, pleated shirt, black bow tie, black trousers with satin stripes down the legs, and black lace-up patent leather shoes. His lips were stretched in a grin as if my arrival amused him in some obscure way.

"Long way from the reserve, aren't you, bud?" he said, his grin widening as he looked me up and down. "Sure you're not lost?"

"Maybe I am," I replied politely. "I thought this was a private house, but maybe it's a restaurant. Are you the maitre 'd?"

He was still deciding how to respond to that when I told him I had a delivery for Miss Fox.

"I'll take it," he growled, holding his hand out for it.

"No, you won't. My instructions are to deliver it into Ms. Fox's hands."

"She's busy," he said brusquely, "and I doubt if she'll see you."

He stepped back, but if he had expected me to wait on the steps, I disappointed him by following him inside the large entrance hall. It was well-appointed and attractive—although for me at that moment its principal attraction was George Fox himself. I'd seen him at a distance at the bones ceremony in the Warrior longhouse, but this was the first time I'd seen him up close.

Soft piano music played somewhere deep inside the house, but what caught my attention was the sound of footsteps on the wooden floors above. Suddenly Charlotte Fox appeared on the landing at the top of the stairs that led up from the hall. She paused dramatically and perhaps deliberately in front of a stained glass window, its ambient light behind her, before coming down, her left hand trailing along the banister. She wore a beige silk jacket with matching silk trousers that were loose around her ankles and tight around her thighs. When she got closer, I noticed a blue-diamond seahorse gambolling across the aubergine shirt that draped the impressive waves of her upper body. The alligator-skin handbag clutched beneath her arm had evidently been crafted by the same genius responsible for her pointy-toed shoes. It was an impressive entrance—straight out of *Vanity Fair* or Hollywood, Charlotte being the star attraction, George the obnoxious prig, and I presumably the kid from the pizza shop.

George said, "Some Native guy with something for you, Charlie."

I handed her the paper bag. She took it, realized what it contained and, without looking to see what kind of bottle I'd brought, murmured dryly, "A jug instead of flowers. How original. It's lovely to see you, Mr. Seaweed. Sorry our meeting will have to be brief because I'm tied up this evening."

"That's too bad. But if you have a minute, there's something I'd like to ask you."

She inclined her head slightly. "Let's go into the lounge." And she led the way through an open doorway into a lounge no larger than a church hall with a twelve-foot ceiling, hardwood floor, a lot of Asian rugs and a half-dozen ornate lamps set upon antique cabinets and tables. A youthful Charlotte looked out of one of the frames hanging from a picture rail. George tagged along behind us. She set the bag I'd brought down on a miniature table and sat in a big chair on one side of the unlit fire. I took the chair on the other side, all the while trying to think of a diplomatic way of telling George to get lost. Charlotte may have been thinking the same thing because, her eyes gleaming with mischief, she said, "I think drinks would be nice, so Georgie will do the honours. I'll have my usual. What's yours, Mr. Seaweed?"

"Rum and coke, please. No ice."

She repeated, "A rum and coke for Mr. Seaweed, Georgie. No ice."

Brother George froze for a second before he ambled to a cabinet, opened it, and standing with his back to us, brought out various bottles and glasses. With much unnecessary clatter he made three drinks, put them on a silver tray and carried it over to his sister. She took a glass of red wine. Then, instead of offering the tray to me, he set it on a low mahogany table, helped himself to a glass of red wine and went to stand with his back against a bookcase. My rum and coke had three chunks of ice in it, and the mahogany table lay beyond easy reach.

I leaned back in my chair, smiled, crossed my legs and stayed put.

His eyes upon me, George looked like a man deep in amusement.

Charlotte gave me a chance to pick up the glass myself. When

I didn't, she rose from her chair and said coldly, "That'll be all, Georgie. We won't be needing you anymore. So why don't you just toddle off and play somewhere else?"

Instead of moving, George maintained his faintly scornful look and tasted his drink. Charlotte's attempt to dominate her brother had failed dismally. Flushing, she dumped my drink into the fireplace and carried the empty glass to the cabinet. At that moment the doorbell rang, and George casually detached himself from the bookcase and went to answer the door. We heard his footsteps crossing the hall, followed by voices. Two or more visitors—elderly females to judge by their tone—had arrived.

"Some of George's clients," Charlotte explained as she made me a fresh drink. When she brought it to me, her hand briefly touched mine—she was shivering with suppressed rage.

I was enjoying myself, had already decided that coming here tonight was a very good idea, and I raised my glass to Charlotte and grinned as I tasted the rum and coke.

"Don't mind Georgie, it's nothing personal. It's just that he's very protective of me, and sometimes he forgets his manners," Charlotte advised, adding pointedly, "Maybe the fact that you're a Native has something to do with his attitude."

Stifling the obvious rejoinder, I said, "Fine. It's clear that he plays second fiddle, that his opinions don't carry much influence with you."

"You're seeing us at our worst," she countered. "It's not always cat and dog with us. And in case you're wondering, George is only staying here temporarily. Generally he has his own place, but he's going through a bad patch right now."

"You mean he's out of money and out of a job?"

"Well, he's never really had a proper job," Charlotte said, and then added defensively, "Father had high expectations for his only son, expectations that nobody could possibly have lived up to.

From the time he was little, George was pushed to succeed, to be somebody big like his dad. So of course he has an inferiority complex."

"Does George know this, or is that your take on things?"

"What do you mean?"

"George might have disappointed his father, many of us do, but he has responsibilities to himself and he's screwed up there a few times as well."

Her eyes hot with sudden anger, she said, "Why do you think he called you a Native just now? It was so ridiculous that you ought to feel sorry for him instead of being angry."

Obviously I'd pushed that line far enough. I said with a grin, "This is a beautiful house. When you were coming downstairs just now, with your brother in his monkey suit dancing attendance, I was thinking that it was like a scene from a movie."

"What—*Andy Hardy Meets Nancy Drew?*"

"No. *Sunset Boulevard*, except you're too young to play Gloria Swanson, and George has too much hair to play Erich von Stroheim."

"But you see yourself as William Holden, I suppose, observing everything with sad cynical eyes and making judgments."

"Nope. I see myself as Adventurous Boy Detective, fighting hopeless, valiant battles against the forces of evil. As for making judgments about people—if we didn't make judgments, life would become rather complicated."

She raised her eyebrows.

I went on, "For example, the way you look—with those beautiful, expensive clothes and that diamond seahorse pinned to your shirt—tells me several things about you. It's why I'm here, after all, instead of eating hot dogs with somebody who keeps ferrets."

"You said you had something to ask me. But now you say you came because you like the way I look."

"Sure, and I'm crazy about the way you live, too, and I love this house. I like the way George's highly polished shoes reflect the deep hues of polished oak and coloured glass."

"Do you have a question for me or not?"

"A question sends a message, doesn't it?" I said, finishing my drink. "My question is what's stopping us from getting out of here and going for a drive? Find some place nice and have supper."

"Oh dear, you are persistent. Well, to be frank, I've already eaten," she said, smiling. "However, we still have a couple of minutes before I have to kick you out, so there's time for another drink. What kind of plonk did you bring me?"

I collected the bottle from the table, held it with the proper reverence and let her read the label.

Charlotte's eyes narrowed, the tip of her tongue appeared and brushed her upper lip. "You're full of surprises. NK'Mip Qwam Qwmt Pinot Noir," she said, pronouncing the words correctly. "And here I've been thinking of you as a lowly wage slave."

"I know somebody who owns a large chunk of the Okanagan. He sends me a case of this stuff occasionally."

I opened the bottle, let Charlotte sniff the cork, poured a thimbleful into her wineglass and watched her eyes glaze over when she sipped it. Instead of telling me what she thought it tasted like, she sighed. I filled her glass and one for myself, looked deeply into her eyes and said, "Cheers."

"Mmmm," she said, holding my gaze for a long moment before concentrating on the nectar in her hands. A minute passed in a reverential silence during which we could hear George and his guests talking and laughing together in a distant room.

Charlotte's leather bag lay at her feet. She tucked it beneath her arm, stood up and said, "Will you excuse me for a moment? I'll be right back."

I stood politely and watched her trip off in her high heels.

From her footsteps and her partially audible voice, I knew that she was speaking to somebody on the hall phone. When she came back, I was stretched out in my chair, admiring the moulded plaster cherubs flying across the room's ceiling.

"You don't need to stand up every time I move," she said, as I struggled to get to my feet. "I prefer things less formal."

I laughed outright. "Informal, Ms. Fox, in this lovely old house?"

"Call me Charlotte," she said, sitting down. "And this lovely old house, as you call it, was an empty lot when I bought it five years ago." Her voice and manner were as changeable as the wind. Now she went on cautiously, "I hope you'll forgive me for being a bit standoffish, but I've heard certain things about you. Your visit here tonight, for example—it's been interesting and occasionally amusing, but I can't forget that you're a cop."

"Even cops have social lives."

"They have professional lives, too, as well as secret lives, and not-so-secret sexual lives."

"You *have* been busy."

"That's not very reassuring."

"It wasn't meant to be. Everything I've said tonight goes. I'm here because I've been thinking about you in a certain connection. I didn't want more days to drift by without talking to you again."

"In case you're wondering, I'm not just playing hard to get. I actually do have another appointment for this evening, which I've just tried to cancel. Unfortunately, it can't be done. I'm sorry." She paused and then said, "So if that's all you came to ask me . . ."

"No, it isn't. Lawrence Trew has been missing for several weeks now, and I think you might know why."

"Whatever put that idea into your head?"

I waited.

"I don't know where Dr. Trew is. I wish I did. I am worried about him, but not for the reasons you might think." Choosing her words with care, she went on, "I know somebody who is being blackmailed—one of my women friends—and I'm not sure how to advise her. I'm not sure it's safe to confide in you, though I suppose you could tell me things that might help her to deal with the problem. At the same time, I've been hearing things about you."

"If you've heard I have AIDS, forget it. I don't."

She smiled.

I said, "This friend of yours—what's she been doing that she shouldn't have been doing?"

She was silent for a moment and then abruptly stood up. "Forget it. I'm sorry I said anything."

The glass in her hand was empty, and so was mine—we'd wasted a whole bottle of very good wine. Instead of savouring it slowly, we'd been swigging. "Take it easy," I said. "I won't put you through an inquisition. Anything you can tell us that will help nail a blackmailer, we'll treat confidentially. If your answers don't help us, fine, that'll be the end of it."

She put her glass on the table. "No, I won't say any more. And I really must ask you to leave now."

I didn't argue.

Going through the hall, I saw George Fox in a room opening off the lounge. He was with three well-dressed matrons of the furs-and-pearls set, and they all seemed to be enjoying themselves. I realized instantly that I'd seen one of the matrons before, but I was outside the house before I placed her. The last time I'd seen her, her face had been daubed with red and black paint.

AFTER LEAVING CHARLOTTE'S house, I went over to the Parrot Lounge, a rooftop restaurant about a half-mile from my office. But instead of enjoying the billion-dollar view, I turned my back on it and sat at the bar. The bartender came over promptly. Her name is Gloria. She's about thirty, a buxom-phase Renee Zellwegger, and that night she was wearing a white Foster's T-shirt that fitted her like shrink wrap and a pair of jeans with a high waist as tight as a corset. A while back, about three years before I met Felicity Exeter, Gloria had played a big role in a recurring dream that also involved a five-barred gate, a sewing machine and a bowling alley. The dream never made sense, but one night I got drunk and confided in her. She gave me her take on it, we had a good laugh and have been pals ever since. Now I ordered a Bacardi and coke, no ice.

I finished the first drink, decided to have another and signalled Gloria again.

"Your money's no good here," she deadpanned, looking me straight in the eye.

"You're buying?" I asked.

"Not me. You've got another friend," she said, pointing.

I turned on my barstool and saw a woman sitting alone at a table. She was examining me the way some people examine pictures in a museum. Though they've seen reproductions of the same pictures many times, the originals are sometimes quite different and sometimes vaguely disappoint. I had the feeling I disappointed this lady.

I gazed at her for quite a while, remembering what I'd been missing. Felicity Exeter's long hair was like polished bronze with yellow-blonde tints. The face beneath it was heart-shaped, the nose straight and patrician, the mouth wide and soft, and she had the imperious air that rich girls acquire after years of civilized mollycoddling. She was wearing a short, shiny, green silk dress almost the colour of her eyes, a pearl necklace and three very good diamond rings. Underneath all that, she looked troubled.

"Attaboy, Silas," Gloria said. "Go get her."

I carried my drink over to Felicity's table and sat down beside her. Close up, her green eyes were colder and darker than I remembered.

"It's been a long time," she said. "I'm glad you came in here tonight because you never call me any more. Sometimes I have trouble remembering exactly what you look like."

"I don't have that particular problem. Maybe it's because I think about you all the time."

"Really," she said.

Her cellphone rang and we both stared into space. At the fourth ring, the caller gave up.

Felicity relaxed, and a glimmer of warmth appeared in her eyes.

YAWNING, FELICITY EXETER flung the bedclothes aside, stretched out one long shapely leg and looked at her bare foot. Still yawning, she wiggled her toes, got out of my bed, and walked naked across the cabin to where her clothes and mine lay jumbled together on the floor where we'd dropped them the night before. Some women dislike being seen naked, but Felicity doesn't mind in the least, so I hoisted myself higher on the pillows and watched her dress.

"My goodness," she said calmly, looking at the tiny watch adorning her wrist. "It's nearly seven o'clock."

"Stay and I'll make breakfast," I said. "Or we could go to John's Place."

"No, thank you," she said sweetly, zippering and buttoning her lovely body out of my sight. "I'm a farm girl, remember? You're not the only goat in my life."

"Goat! Is that fair?"

"Perhaps not, darling, but lying in bed with you before you've brushed your teeth, you do sometimes remind me of a fluffy little black kid with morning breath."

"I hate these goodbyes," I said.

"You hate hellos, too," she said, coming over and planting a sisterly kiss on my brow. "But you know what you can do about that, don't you?"

"Do I?"

"Of course you do, darling," she said, opening the cabin door. She stood for a moment in the doorway. Gazing back at me fondly she said, "Somebody told me you'd been ignoring me because you had AIDS."

"Somebody told me you'd been ignoring me because you'd met somebody else."

She blew me a kiss and went out. A minute later I heard her Land Rover start up.

CHAPTER TWENTY

Several days passed before I spoke to Old Mary Cooke about her latest trip to the Unknown World. For some reason that she hadn't explained, she had moved off the Warrior Reserve and was living in a wickiup on a beach lying below a cliff of lichen-mottled rock. It looked like a bonfire ready for burning. Her sons had built it for her out of driftwood, but they hadn't sawed the wood up, just used it any length as it came from the sea, though it was mostly straight, longish tree trunks rubbed smooth by rocks and tides. The roof was draped with tarpaulins and had a stove-pipe sticking out of it. They'd made the door from derelict planks. The fence around Old Mary's small parcel of land matched the rest of the place.

I rattled the gate, which was padlocked—who knows why?—and after a while she came and let me in. She was wearing a long black skirt, a thick woollen Cowichan sweater and a knitted toque.

"I brought you a smoked salmon," I said, handing her that propitiatory object.

"Thank you, Silas," the old woman said, laying the salmon down on the piece of salvaged plywood she had obviously been using as a cutting board. The wickiup was dark inside, but in the light of the fire I could see a jumble of upright logs in the centre of the room that provided a small private sleeping space. Beside the fire were two ancient sofa chairs upholstered in blue tapestry that had gone green and furry in places. The old woman sat on one of the chairs. I was wearing a pair of $80 black trousers, but after some hesitation I sat on the other chair.

Strings of onions hung from the roof along with miscellaneous cooking utensils, lengths of rope, and a collection of fishing floats. There was a strong pervading smell of iodine and smoke. What looked suspiciously like a dead dog lay against a box of kindling.

"That's a bad wind," she said. Then, sitting upright with her head cocked as if listening to something I couldn't hear, she filled a short stubby pipe with dry leaves taken from a tin box and lit them with a sliver of wood from the fire. The tiny flame illuminated her wrinkled brown face before it flickered out and left us in semi-darkness again. "I knew Hector Latour's grand-dad," she said at last, inhaling with evident satisfaction, although to my mind the burning leaves stank like old gym socks and must have tasted worse.

"He was a log salvager, lived up Stewart Island way. They nicknamed him Seal Whiskers because he was so prickly. He was a gambler. Instead of congratulating winners and taking his losses with a smile, Seal Whiskers called the people who beat him trick-sters, and he didn't always pay what he owed. Seal Whiskers was married, but he took up with his neighbour's underage daugh-ter. He did not love that girl. He did it to spite that girl's father. Somebody killed Seal Whiskers after he'd been gambling one night. Few people came to his funeral."

The strong smell of woodsmoke mingling with the smoke from the old woman's reeking pipe was making my eyes water, and I closed them for a minute. She was still talking about Seal Whiskers when I went into a doze. I didn't fall asleep entirely but when I opened my eyes, she was going on about log-salvage swindlers—how thieves in speedboats steal up to floating log rafts at night, cut the corner chains with oxyacetylene outfits and help themselves to thousands of dollars worth of prime BC timber. But somehow Old Mary's voice had gained strength, and in the slow swirling smoke of her fire, I could see that her hair now appeared sleek and black. She'd stopped being a fat, grey-haired old woman and had become an upright, shapely, barefoot young woman dressed in what might have been deerskins.

I told myself that it was eyestrain, a trick of the light, and closed my eyes again. A minute later I heard the wickiup's door open then close. I got up and went outside. Beyond the beach the ocean had a purple sheen. Old Mary had walked across a shelf of rock and was following a footpath into the trees. I followed. An hour later I'd gumshoed her as far as the Johnson Street bridge, but since it's very dark along there, I was sure she didn't know she was being followed. That illusion lasted until we reached Fisgard Street and a diesel pickup went by, laying an exhaust smokescreen. By the time the smoke cleared, Old Mary had given me the slip, and the woman I was now following was a bimbo, thin as a whippet, wearing high heels and a power suit. I lost sight of her as she strode past the Good Samaritan Mission, its grey concrete exterior as featureless and harsh as a prison wall. I went on, still hoping to catch up with Old Mary, but a half-hour later I knew I'd lost her. I circled back to the Mission and went inside, wondering if Joe McNaught might be in his office. He was. Seated behind his monster desk, he was eating a steak sandwich.

He said, "Find Harvey Cheeke yet?"

"Not yet. There's a Canada-wide on him."

"In that case, what do you want?" he asked ungraciously.

"Five minutes ago I could have given you an answer, now I'm not sure," I said, and told him about my walk. "It crossed my mind she might be coming here."

"I hope she's not the old woman who was here a half-hour back. She created a riot in Marnie Paul's ward and upset the medical staff."

"Doing what?"

"Smoking, doing incantations. She was wearing some sort of necklace." He paused. "Some of the staff found it rather . . . unsettling to look at."

"Why?"

"I didn't ask. Things like that are highly subjective. It's like being afraid of spiders or heights." McNaught bit into his steak sandwich. Speaking with his mouth full, he said, "Want me to phone a taxi for you?"

"Not right now. I'll phone the station later and see if there's a patrol car to drive me home."

"If the general public knew how you cops operate, there'd be trouble."

"No, there wouldn't. The general public already knows that cops and preachers are all the same—idle, grasping bastards. Tell me about this necklace."

He put down his sandwich long enough to make a circle with his pudgy hands. "It had these flat disks on it about the size and shape of a CD," he said and picked up his sandwich again.

I realized McNaught was describing one of Old Mary Cooke's ivory bobbins. They have two holes in the middle with a piece of string looped through them. She grasps each end of the loop and swings the bobbin with a rotary motion to get it spinning and then, by alternately loosening and tightening the string, she can make the bobbin rotate back and forth.

"It made a whistling sound," McNaught said, his mouth full again.

CHAPTER TWENTY-ONE

I'd been patrolling the Old Town's streets for two hours, and it was cold—by local standards, that is. On Vancouver Island's southernmost tip, even in May, sudden gales howling in off the Salish Sea can lower the temperature by several degrees in an hour. If it is wet as well as cold and you don't know how to stay dry, hypothermia can kill you in a hurry. I was wearing a quilted jacket, boots and waterproof pants and still had to step lively to keep warm.

I was looking for Harvey Cheeke, but around midnight I found a girl prostrate in a doorway. I knew her well by sight, although I didn't know her name. She'd been panhandling on Fort Street, and the last time I saw her she'd been singeing the hairs off her skinny white arms with a cigarette lighter. Now her eyes were closed, but she wasn't asleep. She was dead. I phoned for an ambulance. Tony Roos was driving the one that showed up. Victoria's homeless shelters had been full all week, Tony said, although he figured she could have squeezed herself into the Good Samaritan if she'd wanted to. But maybe she hadn't wanted to.

Apart from an occasional passing car, Government Street was deserted after the ambulance departed. I turned down towards the Inner Harbour and Bastion Square just as it began to rain. A hundred and fifty years ago—before sections of the Inner

Harbour were filled in—the spars of sailing vessels had jutted above waterfront warehouses now buried beneath fifty feet of rubble. The remains of an old sea wall, a hundred yards from the nearest water, can still be seen down here if you know where to look for it.

I switched on my flashlight and followed its yellow beam into Commercial Alley. The cold night wind sighed and sobbed in the dark corners. Rats sniffing around on the cobblestones fled at my approach. Rain dripped and gutters overflowed. My cellphone rang, and I sheltered beneath an awning for a minute while I answered. It was Moran, reminding me about a poker game. I put the phone away and switched my flashlight on again. Last time I'd been down this way there'd been a dumpster parked beside the awning, and the pavement was still dryish where it had stood. Now I noticed faint traces of black soot surrounding a circular iron manhole cover in the middle of the dry area.

My heart began to pound. I remembered something Harvey had said.

I punched in 911 and then hauled the manhole cover aside. The air that rose up was foul. Iron rungs stretched ten feet down to a tunnel. With the flashlight in my mouth, I stopped breathing, put my foot on the top rung and started down. I stayed below ground long enough for a quick look along a brick-lined tunnel about seven feet high and six feet wide that stretched into unrelieved blackness in both directions. Above my head, no sounds were audible.

When I climbed back up, I was gasping for clean air. Emergency sirens wailed towards me along Yates and Wharf streets. The first vehicle to arrive was a shiny red pickup driven by a fire captain who explained that the tunnel had originally connected the Driard Hotel to a laundry. But he wanted to do things by the book— install air blowers and ventilate the tunnel thoroughly before letting anyone go down. We were arguing the point when Bernie Tapp showed up. I told Bernie what I had in mind and why. The fire captain was overruled and Bernie and I put on breathing apparatus and went down the manhole.

We shone our flashlights across brick walls and an arched ceiling. As the floor was pierced here and there by drainage holes, the tunnel was perfectly dry but it was icy cold. We turned left, walked fifty strides or less and came up against a brick wall. The mortar protruding from the joints told us that it had been bricked up from the opposite side. We retraced our steps and then continued for another fifty paces or so beyond the manhole to reach a second bricked-in dead end. But there was a vaulted recess, ten feet deep, jutting off to one side. And this was where Harvey Cheeke had found himself a sanctuary. He was dead, laid out neatly in his sleeping bag. What appeared at first glance to be a pile of jumbled clothing nearby proved to be the boys missing from Harris Green. They were huddled together beside the remains of a fire they had lit to keep themselves warm. They had been dead for weeks.

"It's COLDER DOWN THAT tunnel than it is on the street," Bernie said. Daylight was creeping over the city as we sat in his office. "Doc Tarleton reckons the boys died of hypothermia," he continued. "Harvey Cheeke was luckier. He died of natural causes."

"If death by tuberculosis is natural these days," I said sourly.

Bernie didn't take it personally. He filled his pipe and leaned back in his chair. With the pipe clenched between his teeth, he reached into his pocket for a match before remembering that his office was a smoke-free zone. He put the pipe back in his pocket, clasped his hands together and twiddled his thumbs. He was waiting for me to say something.

"I can understand it in a way," I said slowly. "Some people are born tramps. They hate walls, rules, bosses. Most of them hate cops. Like a lot of other people I know, Harvey would rather sleep in a doorway than check into a shelter or a hospital."

"Yeah, well. He went his own way to the last, but what good did it do him? They say he was talented. With a bit more common sense, he could have had his own studio."

"True. Anyway, I ought to have twigged that he was living in a tunnel. He told me he just had to pull the lid down on his squat. Then I remembered he'd complained that some kids had hit him with a brick and tried to steal his poke. I guess when they didn't get it, they followed him . . ."

"Probably spied him going down that manhole," Bernie said. "It must have seemed like fun, going down there."

"Then what happened, somebody decided to fix a roof along Commercial Alley. The roofing gang parked their dumpster on top of the manhole, trapping Harvey and the boys."

Bernie shook his head sadly. "Two kids trapped inside a tunnel with a dying man. It must have been a fucking nightmare." He stopped twiddling his thumbs, got up, went across to a filing cabinet and brought out a can of birdseed. Two pigeons patiently waiting on Bernie's windowsill had puffed up their feathers to stay warm.

I said, "Harvey had a portfolio—dozens of drawings and paintings. The kids burned 'em to keep warm."

"Pity," Bernie said.

CHAPTER TWENTY-TWO

I walked through Chinatown to my office, went inside and closed the door. PC entered through the cat flap almost immediately afterwards and sat there on her haunches, eying me with her head tilted. When I opened the window blinds, sunlight put a silvery gloss on her smooth black fur. I parked my backside in the roller behind my desk and said, "Hi, Pussycat."

She jumped onto my blotter, assumed a Sphinx-like pose and began to purr. I was seriously thinking of stroking her when a woman called to complain that amorous raccoons had learned how to take her garbage can lid off and were trysting by night amidst her trash.

"There's no law against it," I said.

My caller was responding intemperately when Charlotte Fox came in. "Love makes the world go round," I told my caller and put the phone down. PC had jumped off the desk and hidden behind a filing cabinet.

Charlotte wore a green blazer over a white top and her smooth, shapely legs went from sight beneath a white skirt that ended four inches above her knees. Her green sandals had two-inch heels. She seemed preoccupied and, instead of saying hello, she stood near the window with her head turned away, gazing out at the bricks-and-mortar brigade across the street.

"Is that what you really think?" she said without looking at me. "That love makes the world go round?"

"Come to think of it, I guess love makes the world go *smoothly*," I countered. "It's sex that makes the world go round."

"What about money?"

"Money helps, sure. But people survived for thousands of years before money was invented. A few probably still manage quite nicely in economies where money isn't important."

"Name one."

"Igloo City?"

She shook her head and ran her fingers through her hair. Emotion wrinkled her smooth brow. She began to talk about how nice it would be if we had dinner together after all—somewhere quiet where we could have a cozy tête-à-tête—but I was very hard to read, so she didn't understand where I was coming from half the time, and besides, she was alone in the world without a single real friend as most of the people she knew were shallow and facile. Her voice was breathy as if she'd been running, and instead of looking at me directly, she remained half-facing the window. However, I was close enough to see a little pulse beating in her throat.

I said, "Forgery's not a crime, Ms. Fox, unless you try to pass it off as the real thing."

She turned to look at me, frowning. "Once again I haven't the least idea what you're getting at."

I shook my head. "Your talents are really wasted. You should be on the stage. The Belfry Theatre is doing Shakespeare again this year. I think you should audition for Macbeth's wife."

Her eyes widened. "You are a bastard."

"And you're a liar."

Her cheeks went as red as if I'd just slapped her. At last she said, "Perhaps I deserved that. I haven't been completely honest. I told you that I had a friend who was being blackmailed . . ."

"Uh-huh. I remember. I just didn't put any stock in it."

"Well, it's not a friend, it's a bit closer to home. I'm the person being blackmailed. He phoned me again this morning and I'm frightened."

"Surprise, surprise," I said sarcastically.

"I have to trust you because I have little choice, Silas. But if you pass on what I tell you to anyone higher up, I'll deny everything."

"I suppose that could work, since you're not under oath."

The planes of her pretty face tightened. She was holding herself together, but the effort was costing her plenty.

"So you're being blackmailed. Why?"

"I can't tell you that."

"Have you paid anything yet?"

"Once. I made one payment," she replied. "Shortly afterwards I received another demand."

"How much?"

She hesitated. "Ten thousand."

"That's a lot of money. But blackmail is like cancer—a tragedy for its victims. However, nowadays most cancers are treatable if caught early enough. Victoria's police department deals with blackmail cases regularly. Even so, we know that many more cases go unreported because people know that if they report it, the first thing police will ask is why they're being blackmailed."

"I did something wrong, something I deeply regret."

"Confession is good for the soul."

"The hell it is," she said bitterly. "It was talking too freely that landed me in this mess."

"Whatever you say to me, Charlotte, I will be discreet, but if I do get involved, there's no way of knowing what I'll stir up. When you put ferrets down holes, it isn't just nice furry rabbits that pop up."

She turned back to the window. "Perhaps coming here was a bad idea. Maybe I should hire a private detective."

"Things probably won't improve if you do, and maybe they'll even get worse."

She said after a long pause, "I'm being blackmailed by a man I was seeing."

"Seeing as in 'dating'?"

"Yes," she said, coming over to the desk at last and sitting across from me. "It wasn't serious. It didn't go anywhere. But I told him something I now regret. A secret."

"Have you confided in anyone else?"

"Certainly not."

I didn't say anything because I was trying to interpret Charlotte Fox's body language. She'd stopped looking me in the eye and she was smoothing her hair with a fluttery hand. She continued evasively, "Who was it that said that nobody can look back on their lives without self-contempt?"

"Dr. Phil?" I said mockingly.

"Maybe I'm misquoting. Anyway, this thing, this secret, is something I'd rather you didn't know either. The details, I mean."

"In other words, you trusted a casual boyfriend but you don't trust me?"

She had been looking into space. Now she raised her eyebrows and stared at me. Her eyes were cold and dark. "Don't make it so difficult. I want you to think well of me. Is that so terrible?"

"Charlotte, here beginneth the first lesson: blackmailers are heartless. They are pathologically greedy, uncaring, vicious and unprincipled by definition. Do you think the man blackmailing you is somehow different?"

"If he is who I think he is, I know he doesn't fit the ordinary profile."

"Have it your own way then," I snorted. "He's a nice guy . . .

as blackmailers go. Only, greed brings out the worst in people, Charlotte, even blackmailers. Face it. This affair will get even nastier unless this guy is stamped on."

"Can I rely on your discretion?"

"Up to a point, but I'm sworn to uphold the law, and I have to assume that somebody's putting the bite on you because you've done something dishonest, probably criminal and actionable."

She managed to smile, but it was quite an effort. I let her think for a minute before I said, "Are we talking about Lawrence Trew?"

She didn't answer.

I continued, "Because if we are, he's already the subject of a police inquiry. Officially we've listed him as missing, but he might be dead."

She shook her head. "Oh no. Larry's very much alive."

I sat upright. "You've seen him?"

"No. I've just heard from him."

"You're accusing Lawrence Trew of blackmail?"

She turned pale and pressed her hands together between her knees. Eventually she nodded.

"Ms. Fox, you've been lying to me since the minute we met," I snarled. " I don't know what game you're playing or why, but if you really do have a serious problem, give it to me straight, because all I've had from you so far are half-truths and evasions."

Her shoulders slumped as misery overwhelmed her. She burst into sobs. Little drops of moisture appeared in her nostrils, tears washed mascara down her cheeks and she made little racking noises deep in her throat.

I took a couple of Tim Hortons coffee mugs from the bottom drawer, splashed two fingers of my cheap Scotch into each and shoved one to her across the desk. "Here," I said harshly. "Drink this."

"God, what a fool I've been," she exploded, her wet eyes glittering with abrupt hatred. "I'm worse off now than I was before."

"You and me both," I snapped as she stood up and rushed out of the office.

I drank my Scotch, licked my lips in satisfaction, poured her drink back into the bottle, took both mugs out to the lavatory, rinsed them under the tap and dried them on the roller towel. When I got back to the office, Charlotte Fox had returned and was once again seated in the visitor's chair. She'd done nothing to repair her makeup and was dabbing her eyes with a cambric handkerchief edged with fancy lace. I put the mugs back in a drawer and sat down. As I watched her, I was thinking that, like most of us, Charlotte had two identities—the one she showed to the world and the one she kept hidden. I figured she had shown Lawrence Trew the one that was concealed from the rest of us.

She said, "Do you have to be such a bastard?"

Scowling, I slid deeper in my chair, clasped my hands together and gazed at her over my crossed fingers.

"A little while ago, Larry Trew asked me to lend him ten thousand dollars," she said in a sudden rush of words. "I'm reasonably well off and ten thousand isn't much, I suppose, in the grand scheme. I asked him why he needed it. He told me that he'd lost money in a hedge-fund meltdown. That was probably a fib, but instead of turning him down flat, I said I'd think about it. I'd been seeing him once a week for ages, and I knew he had plenty of clients and he charged hundreds of dollars an hour. So the question was—why did he need to borrow money? I decided against helping him. Besides, I'd reached a point where I no longer benefited from our sessions. His asking for money precipitated my decision to wind things up, so I cancelled my upcoming appointments, mailed him five hundred dollars in lieu, thanked him for his services and wished him well."

"Did he send you a receipt?"

"No," Charlotte said, adding, "A few days later I received his first blackmail demand. A letter."

"He signed it?"

"God, no. Larry isn't that stupid."

"Then how can you be certain that Trew sent the letter?"

"I've already told you that I'd confided in him. I told him something I've never told anyone else."

"Are you certain of that?"

"Absolutely."

"This blackmail letter. Was it delivered by regular mail?"

"Yes," she said.

Turning away and addressing the wall instead of me, she said. "Stupidly, I burned the letter."

I said, "You claim that Dr. Trew asked you to lend him ten thousand dollars. On the face of it, it's an odd request from a man who drives a Porsche and owns a million-dollar house."

She laughed bitterly. "Larry only lives like a millionaire. I found out his house is leased, and I'll bet that Porsche is leased, too. Still, I was incredibly shocked when his letter arrived. I didn't do anything about it for a couple of days, just kept reading it over and over again. Eventually I calmed down, burned the letter and did nothing. A week later I got a phone call."

"You recognized his voice?"

"No, it was muffled but I know it was him."

"Tell me exactly what happened next."

"He gave me a week to come up with the money or he would expose me. He told me to get used banknotes, put them into a large envelope and take it to Beacon Hill Park. There was a map showing the exact spot I was to go to. It's in an open area about ten feet from a park bench and a garbage can. He told me to sit on the bench and wait for my cellphone to ring. He said he'd be watching me and that if he saw anybody in the neighbourhood who looked like a policeman, I'd be sorry."

"You followed his instructions?"

"Exactly. I was sitting on the bench, holding the envelope with the money in it, when the call came. He told me to drop the envelope in the garbage can and leave the park immediately. I did exactly as he said, and more fool me because a couple of days later I received another letter saying the next installment was due."

"It came by regular mail again?"

"Yes."

"Did you keep that one?" When she nodded yes, I said, "Let me see it."

"It's at home, locked away," she said lamely.

That was an obvious lie, but I let it go. "How much have you paid him in total?"

"I only paid him once. That ten thousand in the garbage can. I guess it would have been better if I'd given him the money straight off when he asked for a loan. I might have saved myself a lot of heartache."

I brooded for a minute before saying, "You and your brother are Coast Salish . . ."

"Half," she said, interrupting me. "Our mother was Coast Salish from Washington State. Dad was a White man from Calgary."

"I know. But what I don't know is what brought you to Victoria, and why I didn't know of your existence until recently."

"There's no reason why you should know about me. I'm not ashamed of my Native blood, but I'm not interested in living on a reserve or involving myself in Native affairs. Neither was Mother. She got off the reserve when she was barely sixteen. When she and Dad met, she was a legal secretary and hadn't set foot on a reserve in ten or twelve years."

"Where did you go to school?"

"Calgary, mostly. After high school, I went to California and got a degree from UC Berkeley."

"What in?"

"Art history."

"Tell me exactly when and under what circumstances you first encountered Dr. Trew."

"I met Larry about two years ago. It was a bad time in my life. Father had just died. I've had mild insomnia most of my adult life, and a doctor had prescribed sleeping pills and I was becoming dependent. I was drugging myself to sleep at night and feeling half-bagged all day. A friend recommended Larry Trew."

"Why did you give him that ten thousand bucks?"

"Because I'd rather give it to him than spend years in a jail," she retorted angrily.

"Years?"

Instead of answering, she shrugged.

I said, "What were your first impressions of Larry Trew?"

"I guess I'm a poor judge of human nature, because I liked him right off the bat. Not everyone is a good subject for hypnosis, but it appears that I am. He weaned me off sleeping pills after a few sessions, and I started having good natural sleeps for the first time in ages. He really is a terrific therapist. He was always so kind, so considerate. That's why I was terribly shocked and hurt when this blackmail started."

"Did you even wonder why he was practising hypnotherapy instead of conventional medicine? He's an MD, after all."

"Yes, I did wonder about that at first, but he told me he'd suffered from asthma his whole life until an acupuncturist cured him. After that his approach became holistic. He was open to traditional Chinese medicine, hypnotism, whatever. He'd even experimented with orgone-box therapy. As for him being an MD, so what?

He was principally a counsellor. Psychiatrists have MDs, and what do they do except counsel people?"

Suddenly a jackhammer started up across the street, and neither of us said anything, waiting for it to cease. When silence came, I said, "You told me that you burned Trew's first letter. Why don't you want me to see the second one?"

"I didn't say that I didn't want you . . ."

"I know. You told me the second letter is locked away at home. That's a lie, isn't it?"

Her chin quivered. She opened her bag, removed a business-sized envelope and slowly shoved it across the desk towards me.

The envelope was stamped and addressed. It had been delivered by regular mail to Charlotte Fox's Moss Street house. The enclosed letter, written in large childish block lettering, was undated. I read it out loud:

YOUV BEEN A GOOD GIRL SO FAR GET ANOTHER TEN THOUSAND DOLARS REDDY FOR ME INSIDE OF TWO WEEKS YOUL BE HEERING WHAT TO DO WITH THE MONEY BY FONE NO TRICKS

I put the letter down on the desk. After rereading it, I flattened the envelope—which had become slightly creased—by running my hand lightly across it once or twice. "Sent by some half-smart guy pretending to be completely ignorant," I said, "but you'll notice that where accuracy is required—I'm speaking about the ten thousand—he can spell properly. What's really tragic is that you burned the first letter."

"Why tragic?"

"There's no telling what a police graphologist might have gleaned from it."

"But the first letter was written on a typewriter."

I'd been slumping in my chair. I sat upright and said urgently, "This might be very important so please try to remember. Did that letter have the same kind of spelling mistakes and syntax? Did it lack capital letters and punctuation—periods, commas, exclamation marks?"

"Well, yes. There were no capital letters, and there were stupid spelling mistakes. And no punctuation."

"Do you know anybody who uses a manual typewriter?"

"No, I can't think of anyone."

I tried to remember where I had seen one lately. And suddenly it came to me—the Underwood in Titus Silverman's office.

"Banks flag large cash withdrawals nowadays," I mused aloud. "Raising ten thousand in cash without setting off alarms must have been quite a challenge."

She didn't say anything. The phone rang and we both looked at it. After the fifth ring, the caller hung up.

Charlotte relaxed a little. She said, "I thought you liked me."

"I used to."

"What changed?"

"You did."

"And now you think you've got me hooked, you're playing hard to get," she said, only half-joking. She stood up, opened her mouth to say something more, and then her glance fell on the blackmail letter lying on my desk. She snatched it up, waved it in my face and said excitedly, "I've just remembered something! That first letter, the one I burned . . ."

"The one you *said* you burned."

"No, I really did burn it. But listen . . . when I got that first letter, I took it into my office at home and I just got madder and madder. I remember figuring I had to get rid of it before it drove me nuts, and I threw it into the fireplace," she said, her face alive with eagerness. "But the envelope that it came in, I'd dropped it into the wastebasket when I came into the room. It's probably still there!"

"Right," I said cynically. "It's still there unless the cleaning lady emptied your wastebasket last week, in which case it's gone to the recycling depot."

I leaned back in my chair and put my hands behind my head. Charlotte came around the desk, cradled my face in her hands, and she was just going to kiss me when somebody gave a low whistle. Bernie Tapp had just come in. Charlotte fled.

CHAPTER TWENTY-THREE

"Sorry," Bernie said. "I saw a woman's handsome backside and I just naturally assumed it belonged to Felicity Exeter."

"I ought to hate you," I told him. "That was a beautiful, unscripted moment."

"Unscripted? If you ask me, in another minute you would have been undressed. And you'd have whistled too, buddy, if you'd seen what I saw. She had nothing on underneath that little white skirt and all I could think of was . . ."

Bernie was driving, and we were heading north along Douglas Street in his car. An hour earlier we had visited Charlotte Fox at her residence and confiscated the contents of her office wastebasket. Against all my expectations, the discarded white envelope that we were interested in was lying crumpled at the bottom of it. It was an ordinary four-inch by nine-and-a-half-inch envelope, and I for one was very relieved to see it, because I'd been ready to tag Charlotte as a total liar. Typewritten and addressed to Charlotte Fox at her Moss Street house, it had been mailed and postmarked in Victoria. The second blackmail letter and both of the blackmailer's posted envelopes were now in the police lab. But photocopies of the second letter and of both envelopes were also in Bernie's briefcase.

Pulling up outside Titus Silverman's hockshop, Bernie said,

"Charlotte Fox is playing games with us. None of her testimony is reliable."

"What can we do about it?"

"For starters, tap her phones and put her house under surveillance."

"Surveillance? Sure, she's playing games, but you think it's worth allocating those kinds of resources?"

Bernie muttered something I didn't catch.

"By the way," I said, "where's Inspector Manners?"

"Putting fires out. There was a gaybashing outside the Prism when it closed last night. And another derelict died in an alley."

"A natural death?"

"Foul play not suspected."

Bernie tucked his briefcase under his arm, and we went inside the pawnshop. Frankie Nichols was behind the counter haggling over a pile of CDs with a gaunt young guy wearing a padded jacket and greasy jeans. His face was the colour and texture of a squeezed-out orange, and his eyeballs seemed coated with Vaseline. Everything about him said "junkie." He was one of the end losers in a gravy train that had steamed into Victoria all the way from the golden triangle.

"About time you assholes came back here," Frankie said tersely. "I hope you're returning that property you stole from Titus' office."

"Take it easy, Frankie," Bernie said sternly. "We'll talk when you're done with your customer."

The young guy turned at the sound of Bernie's voice. He gave him a brief glance before his attention slid to me. His gummy eyes were now black between narrowed lids.

I said, "Hello, Johnson. How you been?"

He shrugged and turned his head away.

Frankie slid the CDs across the counter and into a plastic bag just out of Johnson's reach and in exchange gave him a pathetically small bundle of cash. He scooped the money into his pockets and slouched outside.

Frankie leaned back, folded her arms and said tonelessly, "My life will become a helluva lot simpler if you're returning Titus' address book."

Bernie and I assumed expressions of wounded innocence.

"That book is valuable," Frankie said with a rising inflection, "and Tubby Gonzales is blaming me for being dumb enough to let cops inside Titus' office in the first place."

"You can stop worrying about Tubby Gonzales," Bernie said. "As soon as we get done with you, I'll go right on over there and straighten him out."

"Like hell you will! The last thing I want is cops stirring things up between me and Tubby," Frankie snapped. "Things are bad enough. If you haven't got the book, just clear off! The air in here's beginning to stink."

That's when Bernie showed Frankie our search warrant. Without even glancing at it, she reached for an old-fashioned wall-mounted telephone and made a call. When her party answered, she said, "Tell Tubby the pigs are rooting around in here again." After a listening pause, she went on angrily, "Yeah, didn't I just tell you? They're here right now. If Tubby don't like it, he can come over and handle things personally. I don't give a rat's . . . " After another short pause, she yelled, "You fucking deal with it then because I'm outta here."

Frankie slammed the phone down on its base, locked her cash drawer, put its key behind a mantel clock on a shelf behind her, reached inside a closet, grabbed a shoulder bag and headed out through the back door of the premises.

"Wait a minute!" Bernie said, grasping her arm as she strode angrily past.

"Get your hands off me, you bastard, or I'll scream the house down!"

Bernie let go.

"Last man out, bolt the doors," Frankie yelled. "Anybody wants to know, I'm at the welfare office."

"Wait a minute," Bernie said again, but it was too late. Frankie had gone.

We swung around behind the counter and went into Titus Silverman's office. The door was open, and the place was filthier than ever. It didn't need a vacuum cleaner. It needed a ten-horsepower leaf blower. The dust covering the leather recliner suggested that it hadn't been reclined in recently, the room's four-bulb pedestal lamp still lacked a shade, and the shag carpeting was perhaps a shade greyer where people had walked in and out, perhaps to borrow one of Titus' paperbacks. The Underwood manual typewriter that we were interested in, however, wasn't there anymore.

Bernie sat behind Titus's desk, took a pair of latex gloves from his briefcase and, after some rummaging, removed a half-dozen business-sized envelopes from a drawer. He was stowing the envelopes into his briefcase when his cellphone rang.

"Fuck Alexander Graham Bell and all his tribe," Bernie muttered.

While he talked on the phone, I went outside and stood on the street with my back to the hockshop door, absorbing the area's olfactory barrage of burning garbage and hot exhaust pipes. A couple of sparrows were shopping for groceries in the gutters of a house across the street, and a blue Mustang convertible with a jacked-up rear-end went north doing 90.

I thought about Bernie Tapp's recent interrogation of Charlotte Fox. He'd been pretty rough with her, even tougher than I had been, but Charlotte wouldn't tell him why she was being blackmailed. Just then Frankie Nichols emerged from the back of a nearby vacant lot astride a man's bicycle. She gave me a wave as she rode by. She was wearing a skirt, and I tried not to look at her underwear as I said without raising my voice, "Hey, Frankie. What happened to Titus' typewriter?"

Frankie kept going for about half a block, did a U-turn and pedalled back.

"Maybe I was a bit hasty, pulling the pin like that," she said, stopping the bike and standing with her legs immodestly straddling the crossbar. "Whaddaya think, Silas?"

"You know the system, Frankie. Better file today, because you won't get welfare for over a month."

"I know, it's a bastard. The thing is, I live from paycheque to paycheque."

"Go back to the pawnshop and force 'em to fire you. That way you'll get EI benefits instead of nothing."

She pushed off again. "Oh, I nearly forgot," she shouted over her shoulder. "That typewriter's over at the depot. Tubby uses it now."

Frankie disappeared from sight around the corner.

Bernie Tapp came out of the hockshop, and I told him what Frankie had said about the typewriter. He reached into his briefcase, extracted the photocopy of Charlotte's first blackmail envelope and gave it to me.

He said, "Something just came up. Wait here until Nice Manners drives over and picks you up. Then I want the two of you to go over to the recycling depot and find that Underwood typewriter. If its typeface matches the lettering on this envelope, seize it. And don't give Manners any shit."

"He won't like working with me."

"You guys should try to get along. In case you've forgotten, Nice is a good cop," Bernie said before climbing aboard his Interceptor and driving away.

Half an hour passed before Nice showed up in a blue-and-white. Mendelssohn's second violin concerto was tumbling out of his speakers when I got into the passenger seat.

He glowered at me and said, "You're supposed to be a neighbourhood cop. So tell me—why do I have to put up with you?"

"You don't. It's all about choices. For instance, if I were driving this heap, we'd be listening to Gatemouth Brown's guitar instead of Itzhak Perlman's fiddle."

He grunted, put the car in drive and headed into the traffic. He said, "Okay, Seaweed, gimme an update."

"It's a blackmail case . . ."

"For Chrissake, I know that already," Manners interjected.

I went on as if I hadn't heard him. "So far, the blackmailer has sent his victim two letters. The first one arrived in a typewritten envelope. The second envelope was addressed by hand."

"Cut to the chase. I haven't got all day!"

"This case started when I found Marnie Paul and Hector Latour hiding out at Donnelly's Marsh. Previous to that, Hector and Marnie had burgled a doctor's office . . ."

"Trew's not a doctor! He's a fucking hypnotist."

I thought pleasant thoughts and said calmly, "After burgling Dr. Trew's office, Hector and Marnie took their loot to Titus Silverman and hocked it for drugs. When Bernie and I investigated, we noticed a manual typewriter in Titus Silverman's office."

"This is all crap. Titus Silverman is dead and the second blackmail note was posted after he died. As for Lawrence Trew . . ." Nice, continuing sarcastically, turned to face me.

"Keep your eyes on the bloody fucking road," I snarled.

His face turned pink. He drove on in careful silence till we reached Titus Silverman's recycling depot. Instead of getting out of the car, he said petulantly, "You're supposed to have AIDS. How come I'm always getting stuck with you?"

I got out of the car, went through the doorway marked TRASPASSARS KILLED, said hello to the poker players— who didn't even look up from their game—and went into Tubby Gonzales' office. Nice Manners trailed at my heels.

Gonzales was snoring in a chair behind his French provincial dressing-table-cum-desk. His circa 1954 Austin hubcap was full of cigarette butts as usual, but the aroma of freshly smoked BC Bud alleviated the grimy room's usual stink. The typewriter we were interested in sat on the floor in one corner. Gonzales was still in dreamland when I went down on my knees, threaded a sheet of paper into the typewriter and typed "the quick brown fox jumped over the lazy dog." When we compared typefaces, it was obvious—the first letter mailed to Charlotte Fox had been typed on this Underwood.

Nice Manners stared at Gonzales. "Think he's drunk?"

"What's wrong with your nose? The fucker's stoned out of his gourd."

Manners put a hand on Gonzales' shoulder and shook him violently.

Waking up, Gonzales flopped backwards until his chair was balanced on two legs and he began to windmill with both arms. Just before he crashed to the floor, one of his flailing fists struck Manners' face, giving him a nosebleed. Manners, enraged at his nice white shirtfront being covered in blood, knelt heavily on Gonzales' chest and put him in handcuffs. It took both of us to drag him out of his office. The poker players, intent on their game, paid no attention because there was a massive pot on the table. Gonzales' arrest was nothing to them.

Interrogated at police headquarters, Gonzales denied everything. He didn't even know who Charlotte Fox was, he said, and it was outrageous to suggest that he'd stoop to blackmail. The kilogram of BC Bud found in his office must have been planted, he insisted, because he didn't smoke dope and he didn't associate with lowlife pot smokers. Unfortunately for Gonzales, Bernie Tapp had an ace in the hole, namely that Gonzales was an illegal alien. But Gonzales stuck to his story even after we threatened to send him back to Mexico. We couldn't budge him.

CHAPTER TWENTY-FOUR

The city works department van that the Victoria Police Department was using for surveillance purposes was parked on the street across from Charlotte Fox's house, its audio equipment and a video camera surreptitiously recording everything happening both inside and outside the house. As a result, the detectives inside the van noted the delivery of the morning paper, watched Charlotte step out onto the porch to pick it up and saw George Fox leave the house for his regular morning jog at 6:55. But they hit the jackpot at 7:15 when they intercepted the black-mailer's next call. The phone message—made from a public box by a male caller using an artificially muffled voice—was short and direct. Charlotte was told to put ten thousand dollars into an envelope, take it by car to the Ada Beaven rose garden at nine that same evening and await further instructions.

I sat in my office waiting for Charlotte to report the black-mailer's call. Two hours later I was still waiting. Feeling vaguely let down, I popped next door to Lou's, got a coffee to go and ordered breakfast sent over. My desk phone was ringing when I returned to the office, but it was Mumbai trying to interest me in a once-in-a-lifetime opportunity. Eleven o'clock came and went. Noon dragged by. Bernie came in to see me at one o'clock. Charlotte finally showed up at two when, as it happened, Bernie had popped into Lou's for a cup of coffee. Although subdued and lacking her usual confident manner, Charlotte looked as lovely as ever in a summery print dress cinched at the waist with a silver belt. Her hair was a bit shorter than a few days earlier and seemed to have more blondish streaks.

"You look nice," I said, smiling. "Been to the hairdresser?"

"Yes, I have actually," she said in a neutral voice. She sat in the visitor's chair with her knees together and her silver handbag on her lap. "I had an appointment with Henri at ten. That took an hour and a half. Afterwards I had lunch at Ottavio's. I thought of inviting you to join me because there's something I wanted to tell you . . . but obviously I didn't."

"Too bad. I was free for lunch today. I would have enjoyed it."

"Would you?" she said absently, cocking her head slightly. "The reason I didn't call, I suppose, is because the last time we met, you and that detective inspector were quite negative towards me and what I really need right now is moral support."

"Having a haircut and lunching alone brought you down?"

"I was down to begin with," she said, opening her handbag, looking inside, and then closing it again. She went on, "You think I'm a complete fraud, don't you?"

"Not completely. You lie to me sometimes, although you don't do it very professionally."

"So if I were to tell you that Trew called me this morning, you wouldn't believe me?" she said, looking me straight in the eye.

"I might. What did he say?"

Charlotte's pink tongue slid along her painted lips. "He told me to take ten thousand dollars to the Ada Beaven rose garden at nine o'clock tonight."

I waited a moment before saying, "Are you going to do it?"

"No. I've come to my senses at last. To hell with him."

"Is that wise? Trew will undoubtedly follow through on his threat to expose you. Your secret, whatever it is, will become common knowledge if you don't play ball."

"It doesn't matter," she responded, giving way to bitterness. "He's not getting any more money from me. I remember what you said about George—that people have responsibilities to themselves. I've taken those words to heart. I want to be free of the bastard whatever the cost to my reputation."

"Very courageous, but there's a downside. If you don't show up with the money tonight, we may never know the blackmailer's real identity. Your secret will be out and he won't be penalized."

"I *know* who he is. He's Larry Trew. I've already told you so."

"Right, but we've no concrete way of proving that. It'll be your word against Trew's, and we don't even know where he is. When we do find him and try to haul him in front of a judge, his lawyers will be all over us. Things will become very messy, Charlotte, unless we catch him red-handed."

"What do you mean?"

"We can nail him when you drop the money off and he tries to pick it up."

"No! I can't! You're asking me to do the impossible. Don't you understand? I'm really scared, Silas," she said. "I can't carry on with this."

"You made the first payment safely," I said, coming around the desk and reaching for her hand. "He won't hurt you physically— it's your money he's interested in."

"Things are different now," she said in a manner I found unconvincing. "Did you know he killed his wife?"

"Who told you that?"

"Nobody," she said, pulling her hand out of mine. "I googled him, something I should have done a long time ago. The whole story about how he killed is wife was all over the Toronto newspapers. And he didn't decide to stop practising medicine—he lost his licence!"

"He was never charged with murder ..."

"But everybody knows he did it!"

Footsteps sounded outside and Bernie came in, glanced at Charlotte, then closed the door behind himself and leaned against it with his arms crossed.

"Ms. Fox has received another blackmail demand," I said to preserve the fiction that we were ignorant of her private phone conversations. "The blackmailer's told her to take ten thousand dollars to the Ada Beaven rose garden at nine o'clock tonight. She's worried, naturally, although I explained that this plays into our hands because it gives us a chance to catch him."

"I'm more than worried," Charlotte said. "I'm frightened. Silas wants me to act as a decoy, presumably while police lurk among the rose bushes, but I can't face it."

"There's little or no danger to you," Bernie said. "We've a certain amount of experience in such matters. What usually happens is that the victim is sent to an intermediate place—in this case the Ada Beaven rose garden—from which he or she is directed to a new location. The blackmailer, of course, is already there, waiting and watching. At the merest suspicion of a double-cross, the blackmailer vanishes."

"If that's the case, you won't catch him," Charlotte responded.

"Maybe I'm repeating myself, but that's not the way things usually work. If the victim cooperates, we generally get our man. You *do* want him caught?"

"I guess so."

"You guess so?"

"I want him caught, obviously ..."

"Well, I'm glad to hear that because the relationship between blackmailer and victim is often quite complex," Bernie said. "But now, Ms. Fox, I have to ask you some personal questions . . ."

"That's another of your standard lines, I suppose," Charlotte interjected. "Silas said the same thing to me in almost identical words."

Bernie grinned. "When we interview people, we do tend to fall into certain habits of speech. But I can assure you that if what you tell us doesn't help us get our man, we will, as far as possible, treat your replies with discretion."

"Does that include immunity from prosecution?"

"That depends," Bernie said good-naturedly. "By your own admission, that blackmailer knows something about you that you'd rather the world didn't know. We won't know how serious that something is until you tell us."

"I've been over that ground with Sergeant Seaweed. I did something rotten and wanted it off my chest, so I confided in Larry Trew. I've no intention of telling anyone else."

"Trew will sing like a bird when we catch him, Ms. Fox. You're only delaying the inevitable . . ."

"Then I won't help you catch him," Charlotte said. "There's no way I'll face him personally." And she left the office. Short of arresting her, there was no way to prevent it.

"Goddamn," Bernie said. "Now what the hell do we do?"

After a minute's thought I said, "How about getting Cynthia Leach to act as a decoy? She's tough. And she's very similar in size and shape to Charlotte."

Bernie frowned and then picked up my desk phone and punched numbers. When Cynthia Leach answered, he said, "This is Acting DCI Tapp. I'm calling to brief you on the job you've volunteered to do for us tonight . . ." While he talked to Cynthia, I set off after Charlotte. We were going to need her SUV and her cellphone if this trick was going to work.

CHAPTER TWENTY-FIVE

The Ada Beaven Memorial Rose Garden, located at the southeast corner of Windsor Park, is one of the city's most tranquil and beautiful public gardens. About the size of a double city lot, it is surrounded by tall, sculptured hedges and trellises.

Bernie Tapp had set up a command post on the top floor of the Windsor Park Pavilion from which the rose garden's high hedge was visible—just beyond a cricket pitch and a soccer field. Male and female plainclothes police officers patrolled the neighbourhood on foot and in unmarked vehicles. The evening was overcast. A cool wind blew in from the sea bringing with it an occasional light drizzle. An elderly woman had been walking in the rose garden earlier, but after she left at 8:30, there were no further visitors.

From up in the command post we saw Charlotte Fox's Lexus SUV appear on Windsor Avenue at five minutes to nine, turn right onto Newport Avenue and park across the street from a mock-Tudor apartment building. Cynthia Leach got out of the Lexus and disappeared from sight into the rose garden.

She was wearing a mike pinned to her collar and carrying a Nokia cellphone patched into Charlotte's personal phone. "I'm walking between the rose beds," she reported. "I'll sniff the roses for a minute and then sit in the arboretum."

She was seated on a park bench when at exactly nine her phone rang. But instead of Cynthia answering, it was Charlotte who took the call. Unfortunately, it was one of Charlotte's woman friends, trying to fix up a date for lunch, and Charlotte quickly got rid of her. Another several minutes passed before the phone rang again. This time it was the blackmailer.

Obviously male, but speaking in a muffled voice, he said, "Have you got the money?"

"Yes."

"Good girl, you know how to follow orders. Now I want you to drive your car to Cattle Point. You know where it is?"

"It's that marine park off Beach Drive where people launch their boats."

"Right. Go to Cattle Point now. There'll be some cars and trucks with boat trailers parked there. Park beside them and walk to the boat ramp. You'll see a white five-gallon plastic pail beside the ramp. Put the envelope into the pail, go back to your car and drive home. Understood?"

"I understand."

The line went dead.

"We've got him! The only way in or out of Cattle Point is along Beach Drive!" Bernie shouted exultantly. The two of us discussed strategy briefly before Bernie switched his radio mike on and started barking orders. He was still organizing his people when I ran to my MG.

I barrelled north along Beach Drive for half a mile, swung down a side road to Willows Beach, where I left the MG, and then sprinted up a steep, narrow pathway that I figured would bring me to Cattle Point, a rocky, heavily treed promontory bordering the sea. I don't know that neighbourhood intimately, but I judged the boat-launching site to be two or three hundred yards distant. That whole woodsy area is criss-crossed by footpaths, and

I hurried along a likely path that curved slightly away from the shore. On a clear day San Juan, Discovery and Chatham islands are all easily visible from there, but it was getting dark now and the drizzle was turning into rain so that the marine horizon was screened as if by a grey curtain. I was slowed down by Garry oaks, alders and tall bushes until I came out on a point overlooking Cadboro Bay. Forested land sloped down to long shelves of smooth glaciated rock that descended into the sea. The boat ramp was a fifty-yard strip of poured concrete flanked on its right-hand side by a steep bank that partially obstructed my view. To the left of the ramp, driftwood lay on a section of sandy beach exposed by the low tide.

From my position nose-down in a patch of brush, I saw Charlotte's Lexus arrive. Driving slowly, Cynthia parked it below me alongside a Ford Aerostar van with an attached boat trailer. I watched her get out of the Lexus. Carrying a conspicuously large envelope, she walked towards the boat ramp. From my position, I couldn't see the five-gallon pail that she was aiming for, and I lost sight of her for an instant after she went behind the bank overhanging the ramp. Moments later she reappeared without the envelope. At almost the same instant, a minor avalanche consisting of loose soil, gravel and vegetation poured down the bank and spread out on the ramp. By night, forest shadows can play strange tricks upon the nerves, especially upon nerves already stretched, and Cynthia, momentarily panicked by the avalanche, cried out.

At the same moment a green rowboat appeared from around a headland and came inshore. As quietly as I could, I moved twenty yards to my left to get an unobstructed view of the boat ramp and the blackmailer's white pail. Meanwhile, Cynthia had gone back to the Lexus, and when she drove away, the incoming rowboat and its lone occupant were still about a hundred yards out.

Staying among the trees, I was moving cautiously towards

a point directly above the boat ramp when someone wearing a black neoprene wetsuit emerged from hiding below me, snatched Cynthia's envelope from the white plastic pail, shoved it into a shoulder bag and dove with it into the sea. In seconds the swimmer had vanished from sight around the headland. Cursing, I ran from my hiding place down to the boat ramp, clambered up the adjoining bank and began running across the headland. However, at one point my feet sank to the ankles in a patch of loose muddy soil, and by the time I'd pulled myself loose and crossed through the trees to reach a lookout point, the blackmailer had gone. A small black shape that appeared momentarily between me and the lights of the houses lining Beach Drive might have been a man paddling a kayak, but it also might have been my overwrought imagination playing tricks.

We'd lost him.

IT WAS LONG AFTER midnight, and the Coast Guard and its helicopters had abandoned the search for the aquatic blackmailer. Bernie Tapp and I were sitting in his office with the Fox file—now large enough to bulge an accordion folder—lying open on his desk.

"That," Bernie said, "was a humongous fuck-up, but you've got to hand it to the guy—he is one smart individual." He began sorting through the reports that had been deposited in his in-basket while we were out chasing the blackmailer.

"The question is, what will he do now? Instead of ten grand, he's got a mitt full of scrap paper."

"He'll blow the whistle," Bernie predicted. "We came so damn close to nailing him that he won't take any more risks."

"Bernie," I scoffed, "we never came anywhere near catching him. And the kayak he used to make his getaway was probably stolen . . ."

"If that really was a kayak you saw!"

"Whatever. There are a hundred places within an hour's paddle of Cattle Point where he could go ashore unnoticed." But something else was bothering me. "You know, Bernie," I said, "from what we know of Trew, I wouldn't have expected him to be that athletic, that smart. He's as cunning as a fucking weasel."

Bernie looked up from the report he'd been scanning. "Mr. Weasel isn't as smart as he thinks he is, because now we've got DNA samples."

Astonished, I straightened in my chair. "Since when?"

"Take it easy, Silas, I haven't been holding out on you. This is the DNA lab report that just came in. Remember the letters that the blackmailers sent to Charlotte Fox?"

"Slow down, Bernie. Did you say blackmailers? You mean there's more than one?"

"That's the way it looks. Whoever they are—or were—the senders were dumb enough to lick the envelopes sent to Charlotte Fox. This report says that at least two people are involved, perhaps more. The DNA on that first envelope—the one typed on Titus Silverman's Underwood—doesn't match the DNA found on the second, hand-written envelope," Bernie said, grinning sardonically as he filled his pipe.

I didn't say anything.

"They're certain that Silverman licked the envelope containing the first blackmail demand. However, the lab won't commit to anything definite on the second envelope yet because there's a problem. The DNA on it closely matches the blood found in Lawrence Trew's kitchen, but that blood may or may not be Trew's. I told them to check it with Charlotte Fox's DNA, too."

When I got over my astonishment, I remarked lamely, "I wasn't aware that we had obtained a sample of Charlotte's DNA."

"Nice Manners took care of it. Followed her to a cafe some-where and picked up a paper napkin she'd discarded. It was his idea."

"Good thinking, but where does it get us? Are you suggesting Charlotte is blackmailing herself?"

"Stranger things have happened ... We only have her word for it that she paid out to the blackmailer the first time, and she refused to carry the money tonight ... "

I shook my head. "I'm lost. It's like being trapped in a laby-rinth. You know there must be a way out, but ... "

"All we can do now is wait till the DNA lab specialists get finished. They've promised us a definite answer within a couple of days."

I was lost in thought.

Bernie went on, "Well, what do you think, Silas?"

I shook my head.

Bernie shrugged.

"I'm tired," I said, standing up and going to the door. "Something is staring us in the face but my brain's dead, I'm going home."

Going home, going home ...

Those words kept repeating themselves in my head as I unlocked the door to my cabin and stepped in out of the rain. It was cold enough for a fire that night. I opened a fresh bottle of Scotch, poured myself a couple of ounces and stood by a window, looking out to sea and trying to unravel the puzzle.

Calmed by the rain and the absence of wind, the sea looked like hammered pewter. White foam bubbled along the shore-line. I finished my drink, rejected the idea of having another and cleaned my teeth instead. Undressing for bed, I took all the stuff from my pockets and laid it on the night table, and that's when I noticed that my cellphone had been switched off for an hour or two. I switched it on and read a couple of text messages. Fred Halloran, ace reporter, wanted me to give him a call. I glanced at my watch—it was after three. I switched the cellphone off, finished undressing, climbed into bed and spent most of time until morning examining the ceiling above my head. It stopped raining about six.

APART FROM A FEW scraps of grey cloud floating above the Sooke Hills, the day had broken crisp and clear. I was frying bacon and eggs when Fred Halloran phoned. "No comment," I said, interrupting his opening remarks.

"Yeah-yeah, I know. There's a media blackout on last night's Cattle Point debacle, but de genie's out of de bottle."

"What debacle?"

"The word on the street is that it was a drug bust went wrong."

"Sorry, Fred. It was probably one of Bernie Tapp's operations. I can't tell you anything," I said sweetly before hanging up.

The bacon was crunchy, my two eggs were slightly brown on both sides, and my whole-wheat toast was a bit overdone, which is exactly how I like it. I was just chowing down when Halloran called again. I switched the phone off, finished eating, washed the dishes and then went out to the MG and drove to work. On the construction site across the street a member of the bricks-and-mortar brigade was deepening a hole with a shovel.

An idea that had been gnawing at me for several hours grew stronger.

I phoned Bernie Tapp and said, "Anything new?"

"Nothing."

"Fred Halloran has called me a couple of times. He's asking about last night, thinks it was a drug operation."

"Yeah, that's the line we're feeding the media. Unofficially."

"Is Charlotte Fox's house still under surveillance?"

"No. I pulled the guys off because my overtime bill is through the roof." After a pause Bernie added, "You know how short-staffed we are, especially since last night."

"That's too bad, because I need a couple of good stout constables with shovels to do a little digging."

"What for?"

"Last night in all that rain there was a minor landslide at Cattle Point. A couple of yards of loose muck washed down a slope and onto the boat ramp. I didn't think anything of it. A minute or two later when I was chasing along the trail in the dark, my feet sank into a patch of loose dirt. I didn't think anything of that either. Not then."

"You've lost me," Bernie growled, "but keep talking."

"I've been wondering what sort of natural phenomenon would cause that soil to be loose in the first place."

"You think somebody's been digging."

"Yes, well, it's a bit improbable, I suppose, but . . ."

CHAPTER TWENTY-SIX

It was about four in the afternoon before I drove across town to Charlotte Fox's imposing Moss Street house. Bernie Tapp had scheduled a news conference for five, and I wanted to speak to Charlotte first.

I got out of the MG, crossed the street and knocked on her front door. As I waited, I was aware of the sun shining and the hummingbirds buzzing among the flowers. Nobody answered my knock. I followed the concrete pathway that ran between the side of the house and a tall evergreen hedge and opened onto a flagstone terrace dotted with large terracotta urns abloom with geraniums and nasturtiums. I was admiring a bronze sundial mounted on a granite plinth when I became aware of a movement off to my side. Ten yards away, Charlotte Fox was watching me from the doorway of a sunroom that jutted from the back of her house. She wore a woollen robe over yellow silk pajamas, and her hair was tousled as if she'd just crawled out of bed. I said hello. She gave me a deadpan look and, leaving the door open, disappeared into the sunroom. It was very warm in there. Bamboos, bougainvillea and hibiscus grew in profusion from more huge terracotta urns and planters. Water flowing endlessly from a naughty bronze boy's anatomically correct, uncircumcised pecker trickled into a small rectangular lily pond banked with clivia and azaleas.

Six black wicker chairs with white cushions and a circular table draped with a white linen cloth complemented the sunroom's black and white floor tiles.

"Sorry for barging in unannounced," I said. "When nobody answered my knock, I guessed you might be round the back."

She shrugged. To judge by the dark crescents beneath her big brown eyes, she hadn't slept well either.

"I'm sorry about last night," I said, sitting across the table from her. "You handled your end well and we let you down."

"It's what I expected," she said ungraciously. "Do you have any news, or is this a social visit?"

"Just checking in. There's nothing new to report," I lied. "The blackmailer's still out there. I'm not entirely happy to find you here alone, however."

"Why?"

"A quasi-paternal instinct."

"My father would be a hard act for you to follow."

"All the same, I think you need to be kept company, at least for a day or two until we catch him."

"That's hardly reassuring. You were supposed to catch him last night."

"We slipped up. He outsmarted us."

"Well, if you police can't look after me, I'll have to count on George, I suppose."

"Does he know what happened yesterday?"

"Yes and no," she replied, her voice turning to bitterness. "He probably realized I'd had a bad night."

"You didn't explain what had happened?"

"Of course I didn't!" she snapped impatiently.

"Why 'of course'? You've decided not to pay any more black-mail, so George is bound to find out what's going on soon."

Her eyes registered scorn.

It was no time for argument. I stood up and said, "Okay, I'm butting in. You don't want any more of me so I'll clear off. Only it's as I said—I don't think you should be left alone. Can you call someone, a friend perhaps, to keep you company?"

"No, don't go," she said apologetically, her changes of mood as unpredictable as the weather. "I'm being thoughtless, blaming you for something that's my own fault."

"But you're right—we screwed up."

She stood up and gently stroked my arm. "I'll call someone to come and stay with me later. Would you care for some coffee?"

"Sure."

"I'll make a pot. Just give me a few minutes."

She went out of the sunroom. I heard her moving about in the nearby kitchen before she went upstairs. Looking around from my comfortable chair, I saw an elaborate, multi-storeyed, wooden birdcage dangling amid the conservatory's lush tropical greenery. Instead of live birds, it contained coloured glass Christmas tree ornaments. The slightly funereal odour of lilies, fat tropical plants and moist bedding soil was beginning to get mildly oppressive, when suddenly there was a loud, metallic click as the room's arrangement of thermostatically controlled fans switched off automatically. As soon as they stopped, I overheard faint distant voices. As I went from the sunroom into the house, the voices grew louder, and I found that they came from a portable radio playing in the lounge. It was tuned to the police channel.

I returned to the sunroom. Charlotte Fox rejoined me soon afterwards carrying cups, saucers, cream, sugar and a carafe of coffee on a tray that she placed on the table. She'd brushed her hair, but was still wearing her robe and pajamas. Before sitting down, she adjusted the sunroom's thermostat. The fans clicked on and the air became breathable again.

"Did you find it all right?" she asked.

I raised my eyebrows.

"The bathroom. When I looked in here just now, you were somewhere else."

"I wasn't looking for a bathroom. I was being nosy, just poking around your handsome house."

"That ought to make me nervous, I suppose," she said, pouring coffee. "Cream and sugar?"

"Black for me."

"Find anything interesting?"

"Mildly. That radio in your lounge is tuned to the police channel. Not what I'd call easy listening."

"That's George. He's an insomniac. Instead of taking a pill, he comes downstairs and either watches TV or listens to the radio. I guess he finds the police band more interesting than the chat shows you get on the radio after midnight."

"Slightly off the topic—but George doesn't like me very much, does he?"

She looked startled. "Is there any reason why he should?"

I shrugged. I decided that I didn't want to get into after all.

Then, out of the blue, she glared at me and said, "My dad used to hunt game. When I was a kid, our deep-freeze was always full of venison and moose meat. Then he gave it up. He told me that when the season opened, there were some places with fifty hunters for every deer. He said there were too many hunters crashing around in the woods. But Dad didn't give up hunting because it had become dangerous. He gave it up because he got sick of it." She stopped talking but she didn't stop glaring. I was wondering where she was going with all this when she continued maliciously, "Cops are hunters, and George has always been a target for them. I'm sure you know all about George's checkered career, but there was a time in his life when George needed a break. He didn't get it. The cops had him in their sights. Now why don't you get the hell out of here and leave us both alone for a while?"

I wagged my head. "Whoa, Charlotte. I'm on your side, remember?"

Hands trembling, she refilled her coffee cup, spilling a little into her saucer. I reached for a paper napkin, folded it into a square and placed it under her cup.

"Thanks," she said without looking at me. "Do you think I'm a coward?"

"No. I find you mysterious, but that's a very attractive quality. Besides, if you're anything like me, you're a mystery to yourself. I look back at my own actions sometimes and think, what in God's name made me do that?"

"Right. But you'd probably feel better about me if I'd been the one in Ada Beaven's rose garden last night instead of letting that policewoman take the risk."

"You did it the first time, remember?"

Her eyes widened.

I said, "When the blackmailer contacted you the first time, you made the drop all by yourself. That took courage. Especially when you were sitting on that park bench, waiting for his phone call, and that dog came over and snapped at your ankles."

"Oh sure, the dog," she said lamely. "To be honest, I don't remember much about it. It's all a blur now. I was scared senseless actually."

She was sitting tense and upright.

I watched a black and purple butterfly—one of a pair that had been flapping about the sunroom—land on a cactus as green and spiky as a hedgehog.

Abruptly Charlotte said, "I'm sorry, I've a busy day ahead. I really must ask you to leave here now."

I said goodbye. I might have appeared sad going out of

Charlotte Fox's sunroom, but I wasn't as sad as I looked. One thing was certain—conversations with her were often frustrating, but seldom unrewarding. In fact, I was beginning to see a tiny candle flickering dimly at the end of a very long tunnel.

I drove to the foot of Moss Street and turned right along the waterfront. I was trying to work something out, but it was a beautiful day and there were many distractions. Even apart from glorious mountain and ocean vistas, there were windsurfers, kite flyers and bikini-clad sunbathers lying on the beaches. Three paragliders hovered in the thermals above the Dallas Road cliffs. One had had risen about 300 feet, and were it not for the day's obscuring heat haze, I figured he'd have been able to see as far east as Mount Baker, as far west as the Pacific Ocean. A stilt walker came by juggling three orange balls, and for just a moment he obscured my vision of a war canoe coming around Ogden Point. Paddled by a dozen of my Native brethren, it was on course for the Olympic Peninsula, twenty miles across the Salish Sea.

CHAPTER TWENTY-SEVEN

It must have been seven o'clock that evening before I finally returned to my office, and it took me a couple of hours to dispose of the routine paperwork that had accumulated. Then I switched the lights off and was all set to pull the blinds and go home when PC—who, when she's not prowling Chinatown's back alleys for mice, does the same thing in this old building— came in through the cat flap that Nobby Sumner had installed at such great expense. She complained noisily until I opened a can of anchovies and dumped the contents into her personalized stainless steel bowl. PC likes anchovies, but instead of eating, she sat on her haunches, eyeing me mysteriously.

"You're a funny one," I said. "What's going on inside that head of yours?"

She was busy scratching her neck with a hind leg when footsteps sounded in the hall outside, and she vanished into the shadows behind my filing cabinets as my door opened and Fred Halloran came in. He was wearing a brown fedora and a brown raincoat with bulging pockets. I switched the lights on again.

"Silas," he said, his dentures gleaming like alabaster tombstones at high noon, "you're a hard fellow to nail down."

"You're the Word Man, Fred, not me, but is that a tautology or a non sequitur? We spent an hour together not so long ago."

"Hardly a tautology. If you ask me, it's a sophism, an example of what—before women invaded newsrooms and a lovey-dovey courteousness became the norm—we used to call feminine logic," Fred replied with uncharacteristic savagery. "Are you planning to pour me a drink voluntarily or do I have to come right out and beg?"

I reached for the office bottle. It was half full. I splashed some into my Tim Hortons mugs and shoved one across the desk.

"That was quite a performance Bernie Tapp put on for the TV cameras," Fred remarked insincerely. "It was all over the news."

"I didn't see the news."

"It'll be repeated later. Bernie gave you a very flattering mention, said you were involved in the Cattle Point stakeout last night and in this morning's follow-up," Fred said, draining his glass and pushing it forward for a refill.

"Did Bernie say what we found?"

"Sure. What you found and who. Bernie thinks you're a hell of a guy."

"And so I am," I answered modestly, refilling our mugs and thereby emptying the bottle.

"Feel like telling me the whole story in your own words?"

Suspicious by nature, I picked up the phone, dialled headquarters and asked for Acting DCI Tapp. When Bernie answered I said, "I'm with Fred Halloran. He tells me that you told the world all about Cattle Point this morning. Is that correct?"

"Sort of, we're still playing it close to the chest in that we haven't mentioned the blackmail angle. But we've come clean about who we found buried."

"Thanks. I'll see you later," I said, hanging up.

I leaned back in my chair and sipped a little whisky. "As you probably know, you need a machete to get through some of the vines and blackberries in the brush around Cattle Point, but last night somebody—blundering around in the dark—noticed a patch of loose earth out there. It was dark at the time and we were busy with other stuff. But this morning when we went over there with shovels, we saw that the patch was about six feet long and three feet wide, roughly rectangular. We started digging. It was a shallow grave, and it contained a male corpse."

Fred Halloran eyed my bottle. It was empty. He reached into his capacious pockets, produced a mickey of Chivas Regal and refilled our cups. "Right," he said then, reading from his notebook, he went on, "The body was identified as that of Lawrence Trew, a doctor. He lives on Terrace Lane and practices hypnotherapy on Fort Street. He'd been missing for a while." Halloran looked up from his notes. "I never knew the gentleman. What was he like?"

"I can't answer that because I never met him personally. It's probably fair to say that during his lifetime Lawrence Trew was sometimes improperly and unfairly maligned."

"A chap who shoved his wife off a balcony?" Fred made a sour face. "Well, maybe you're right, Silas. But you can't say the same for Titus Silverman or Tubby Gonzales."

"What's Tubby Gonzales got to do with this?"

"Nothing," Fred said, laughing self-consciously. "His name just popped into my head, I don't know why. Thirst must be making me light-headed," he said, reaching for the mickey.

CHAPTER TWENTY-EIGHT

The mickey had been drained, and Fred Halloran had departed. I sat in the dark for a while thinking before I switched the lights on once again and phoned Chief Alphonse. As usual these days, he wasn't home. I opened my computer. Charlotte Fox's Lexus was stationary somewhere inside Donnelly's Marsh.

I phoned her home number. Nobody answered, not even the voice mail. Instead of leaving a message, I said goodnight to PC, locked up and went outside. Pandora and Government streets were choked with late-evening traffic. Pedestrians jammed the sidewalks and parked cars lined the curbs. A parking ticket was tucked under the MG's wiper blade. I resisted a boozy temptation to tear it asunder and stowed it instead in my glove compartment, where it joined a dozen of its neglected cousins.

I drove down Highway 1 again to the View Royal turnoff, past the north end of Esquimalt Harbour, past the Great Canadian Casino and the used-car lots. When the Donnelly house loomed up ahead, I stopped the car. The night was warm and full of stars, and a sliver of moon had risen above the trees, but as soon as I turned the MG's headlights off, the house became just a black rectangle in the darkness. I reached underneath the driver's seat and carefully detached my Glock from its magnetic clip. The gun felt heavy and awkward when I slid it into my shoulder holster, but its presence was comforting.

I had locked up and was just putting the keys in my pocket when a familiar voice said, "We finally figured out how you did it." Charlotte Fox was sitting on the porch in one of the old Cape Cod chairs. "Now come on up here and have a drink," she said, "and tell me *why* you did it."

"What are you doing here?"

"I should be asking you that question."

"Ladies first," I said.

"If I told you I was waiting for you, Silas, would that make you happy?"

"I'm always happy when I'm near you, Charlotte. But how did you get here?"

"I drove, of course. The Lexus is behind the house. Come on up and have a drink."

I went up the steps. She held a glass of wine, while a bottle of wine and two empty glasses were beside her on the porch railing. "It's a Pinot Noir. Help yourself," she said, her voice strangely amused. "Sorry there's no rum and coke."

I poured myself a drink and sat on the chair next to hers. In the moonlight I could see she was wearing a shimmery copper tube top, a short, light-coloured skirt and low-heeled shoes. "Skoal," I said. "It's a nice evening and you look lovely, Charlotte. May I call you Charlie?"

"Of course. Would you like to kiss me?"

"Yes, I would, Charlie," I said, the lie coming easily to my lips, "in a minute, but I see you have a third glass here. Are you expecting more company?"

"Who knows?" she said, laughing lightly. "But listen to this—I'm sure you'll find it interesting—Georgie took my Lexus to the dealership for its fifty-K checkup . . . and guess what the mechanic found?"

"Mud?" I suggested. "A busted shock absorber from driving around back-country roads?"

"Oh, the mechanic didn't mention shock absorbers. What he found was a cellphone duct-taped under the dashboard." Charlotte's voice still carried the same highly amused tones. "The phone had a GPS chip, so it must have been put there by someone wanting to keep tabs on me. A lovestruck swain, perhaps. What do you think, Silas? Should I be flattered?"

"Evidently I have a rival for your affections."

"What on earth do you mean, Silas?" she asked, cocking her head to one side as she smiled at me. "What rival?"

"I don't know, my dear. Whoever he is, thank goodness he's not here now."

"But he is here, Silas," she said, laughing. "You're the one who put the phone there, aren't you?"

"Well, no," I lied, "but let's pretend that I did do such a crazy thing. That wouldn't explain how you and I both came to be here tonight."

"Oh, but it does, Silas. Instead of smashing the cellphone, we took it to an electronics shop. It's your cellphone, and it's on the seat of the Lexus right now. So you're here now for just one reason."

"And what reason is that?"

Playfully she said, "The same reason that prompted you to 'accidentally' run into me at the Stick In The Mud. You're here because you're still following me. Now will you kiss me?"

I placed my glass on the porch railing, stood up and was moving towards her when I saw her eyes widen and one of her hands fly to her mouth. She screamed.

I turned. Lumbering towards the house was a bear—massive, immense, silent—and it was walking upright on two legs. Unlike my first encounter with this bear, my mouth didn't go dry. I didn't feel

my heart bouncing against my ribs. But Charlotte was still scream-
ing in fright and the bear was almost upon us. After an instant of
inertia, I dragged my Glock from its holster. Before I could aim and
shoot, Charlotte leapt from her chair. Scampering towards the door
to the house, she jolted my arm and my shot went wide. The gun
clattered to the floor and slid off the porch. The bear was now only
ten feet from the steps, and I raced into the house and slammed
the door in its face. Somewhere in the dark interior behind me, I
could hear Charlotte moaning, and I felt my way along the hallway
until I found the kitchen door. When I opened it, she was dimly
silhouetted against windows. "It's me," I was saying as she slid to the
floor in a dead faint. Her head cracked against the floor with a hor-
rifyingly loud thud. I took my jacket off, put it beneath her head as
a pillow and straightened her out on the floor.

Beads of sweat trickling down my face, I went back along the
hallway to a room at the front of the house and looked out into
the moonlit night. There was no sign of the bear. Nothing moved
out there except a slight breeze swirling in the grass. I returned
to the hallway and slowly opened the front door. My Glock was
out there and I needed it. I was standing on the porch, trying to
decide where the gun would have landed, when feet scraped on
the decking behind me, and a powerful arm came around my neck
and jerked me backwards. As I tried to turn and grapple with my
assailant, I caught a glimpse of a face, but it was no more than a
white blur in the darkness.

"You had plenty of warnings but you never listened," he said.

The blow to the back of my head buckled my knees. Then,
with his arm still around my neck, he delivered a second blow. I
don't remember hitting the deck.

I CAME BACK TO life slowly and unwillingly. Bathed in sweat, I was
lying in the dark on a dirt floor with my wrists lashed together.

My ankles were tied. When I moved my head and tried to sit up, galaxies of white stars appeared. Groaning, I waited until the stars faded. On my third attempt I managed to sit upright and began working on the ropes that bound my hands and feet, trying to loosen them.

The surrounding darkness was not quite absolute—faint slivers of vertical light showed here and there. After a while I heard a vehicle approaching, its engine labouring when the driver floored the accelerator in low gear, and as it came closer the vertical slivers of light grew brighter in the glare of its headlights. When the vehicle's engine was cut, its lights went out, but by then I knew where I was—inside the longhouse on Donnelly's Marsh. Another ten or fifteen minutes passed in silence before a man came in through the longhouse's frog-door. He was carrying a flashlight, and he focused its beam on me. "So you're still alive?"

I knew the voice. It was George Fox. I said nothing.

"Enjoy it while it lasts," he said and walked toward the back of the longhouse. I heard him moving about for a while before he re-emerged from the darkness, stuck a dozen long wax candles in a circle on the floor and lit them. His back to the frog-door, he switched off his flashlight and sat cross-legged inside the circle of lights. I could see that he had got himself up in a cedar cape and a conical cedar hat, but what really caught my attention was the gun he held in his hands. It was my Glock.

"You've tied my wrists too tight, George," I said. "I've lost all feeling in my hands. How about loosening them up for me?"

He laughed. "No chance, Seaweed. You're a cunning fucker . . . That GPS cellphone stunt was very clever."

"Not as clever as the tricks you've been pulling, George." When he didn't answer, I said, "So what are you up to here, Georgie? What's this all about?"

"This place is sacred to me," he announced in a strange high voice, "because it's where I opened myself up to the Great Spirit. I denied myself everything, gave myself up to fasting and prayers and songs . . . and I was led here and felt the Creator's presence . . ."

"Oh come off it, Georgie! We've known all about your fake-Indian con game for weeks now so . . ."

"I'm not a fake Indian!" he snarled. "I'm real!"

"No, Georgie, you're only a half-Indian pretending to be a reincarnated witch. And that witch you're pretending to be— that Filligan character—he got whacked in the end, you know," I taunted him.

"I've learned from his mistakes."

"Yeah, you pick on rich old ladies instead of other men's wives. But let's face it, that hokey longhouse up by Duncan had its limitations. You needed something better. Something more genuine and closer to town. And that's where this place came in for you, didn't it? And it would have been perfect if you could have made it work." George's teeth shone in the candlelight as he smiled. "Go on."

"But I came looking for Marnie Paul and I ran into Hector Latour as he went hightailing it out of here. You'd been using your bear trick to frighten people like him and Marnie off the property. For you this land isn't sacred, Georgie, so stop trying to kid me. Everything you've done has been for money. Everything."

"But I scared the shit out of you, Seaweed!" he said. "You went running for your life!" And he laughed.

I said, "I'll level with you, Georgie. That bear act of yours did scare me . . . until I did a bit of investigating."

George couldn't seem to stop laughing now. "You were scared shitless!" he chortled. "Scared shitless!"

At that moment the candles flickered as the door behind him opened briefly and closed again, as somebody came inside and moved silently to a place across the longhouse from me. George didn't seem to notice.

"So, Georgie," I said suddenly, "what did you do with the ten thousand dollars your sister gave you to pay off the blackmailer?"

George Fox's smug grin vanished. In my best storytelling voice I began, "Hector Latour and Marnie Paul took the stuff they stole from Lawrence Trew's office to Titus Silverman's pawnshop and exchanged 'em for drugs. Among those items was a Sony tape recorder and some tapes, because Lawrence Trew taped his hypnotherapy sessions, and during one of his sessions with your sister, she confessed to a crime, a very serious crime. Unfortunately for Charlotte, when Silverman, presumably out of idle curiosity, played the tapes, he came across her confession, and he decided to squeeze her. When Charlotte ignored his blackmail letter, he phoned her. She told me that after she got his phone call, she got ten thousand dollars together, put it in an envelope, and took it—as per instructions—to Beacon Hill Park and dropped it into a garbage can." I looked George in the eye and said, "How am I doing so far, Georgie?"

He shrugged and looked away.

"But your sister lied to me. She never went to the park. How do I know this? Well, first, you see, Charlotte gave me two different accounts of how that initial money transfer took place. Second, she was too afraid to help us with the second money drop. She said she couldn't bring herself to go to an isolated place at night where there was a possibility she'd meet her persecutor face to face. So I knew she had never made the first drop either."

The candle flames surrounding George flickered briefly again as the door behind him opened and closed again. Another person had entered the longhouse, but this one remained near the door.

I said, "I suspected from the beginning that she'd used an intermediary to do the job, but I didn't figure out that it was you until a day or two ago. You went to Beacon Hill Park as directed, but instead of handing Charlotte's money over to Titus

SEAWEED ON THE ROCKS   215

Silverman, you killed him and took his body to Goldstream Park and buried it. But before you killed Silverman, you tortured him until he told you exactly how Charlotte had laid herself open to blackmail. Then you killed Lawrence Trew as well. We found a sample of the killer's blood in Trew's kitchen, sent it for DNA testing and got a very peculiar reading—that sample closely matched Charlotte's DNA."

Nearly a minute passed before George spoke. He said, "I didn't bury his body right away. I was going to frighten Charlotte with it . . ."

"Why, for God's sake?"

"Why not?" he demanded, and then, without waiting for my answer, he sneered, "You don't know the real Charlotte, because you're infatuated with her like all the others. Charlotte is a ruthless, controlling bitch." His voice had become unnaturally high and strained again.

I said, "But why kill Lawrence Trew? Killing Silverman makes sense in a way, but you had nothing against Trew. Why kill him?"

"To divert attention from myself, of course."

It was a crazy answer. I said, "Do you expect to go free, George?"

"I've never been free," George Fox said bitterly. "I've had to climb over walls all my life." Then suddenly he laughed. "It's funny, Seaweed. I've been waiting for you to ask me how Charlotte laid herself open to blackmail. Don't you care?"

I shook my head. But George went on, "Charlotte's a murderer, Seaweed. She killed my father. She overdosed him on sleeping pills, ground them into a powder and mixed it into his glass of scotch. When he still wouldn't die, she held a pillow over his face." He paused, apparently reliving the scene, then said, "He never left me a cent. He always said that Charlotte was going to get it all, and she did. He wanted me to beg for it but I wouldn't."

Suddenly George got to his feet. Still standing in his circle of candles, he waved the gun at me. "But I'm on a roll now! I've got suckers lined up in droves. I'll bring them here, do a little magic, show 'em a few tricks . . ."

"It won't work, Georgie."

"I'll make it work. Some of your people came out here a while back for a look around. I dressed myself up in deerskins, hung a few plastic skulls around my waist, scared 'em shitless. They won't come back in a hurry."

"Face it, Georgie, the game's up."

"There you go again, pissing me off." And he raised the gun, giving it the two-fisted grip you see on *Crime Scene Miami*—the one where the gunman stands with one foot ahead of the other, scowling fiercely.

But the shot that rang out didn't come from the Glock. It came from a rifle. When Chief Alphonse stepped from the shadows after pulling its trigger, George was writhing on the ground, his right elbow shattered where the bullet had gone through it.

Chief Alphonse pointed his rifle at George's head. "Think I should kill him now, Silas, or do we let him bleed to death?"

I didn't answer.

Chief Alphonse picked up one of George's candles and held it high so that we could see Charlotte Fox sitting with her back to the longhouse wall. She'd heard everything her brother had said.

After the chief cut me loose, I led Charlotte outside. My cellphone, the one with the embedded GPS chip, was lying on the driver's seat of the Lexus. Charlotte sobbed softly as I used it to call headquarters.

CHAPTER TWENTY-NINE

The view of Victoria by night from the eighteenth-floor Parrot House is certainly worth seeing, and a few nights later Felicity and I and three waiters had the view all to ourselves.

I said, "Some of our old people think that because stars survey the whole world, they can empower their protégés to discover things. Things like lost vitality, for instance."

"What do you mean, protégés?"

Instead of answering directly, I said, "About eighty years ago, when she was a young girl, one of our people went to Harling Point and built herself a wickiup on the rocks below the Chinese cemetery. One evening as she lay in the wickiup, something that made a noise like a mallard crashed inside and fell onto her bed. The girl killed it with a stick. But when she reached to throw the mallard outside the wickiup, the mallard turned itself into a two-headed snake, which bit the girl and wrapped itself around her body until morning. Later her people came and found her paralyzed and they took her home. They gathered medicines in the forest and collected the bark of a certain tree that they charred in a fire. A shaman smeared the girl's face with this charred bark, and she recovered from her paralysis. Afterwards she was able to cure others with the same illness. She was the snake's protégé."

"Very interesting." Felicity spooned some crème brûlée into her lovely mouth, and then added, "But I never know whether you're pulling my leg."

I leaned back in my chair and grinned at her.

She put her spoon down. "Why don't you tell me about George Fox."

"The whole thing was very cleverly done," I said. "It started when George Fox came down to the Warrior Reserve very early one morning when it was blowing a gale and put a dugout canoe into the sea. The canoe contained a coffin. He then spread a rumour that there was man out in the bay, paddling a dugout canoe. The sea was wild, full of driftwood. Because people expected to see a paddler and were actually looking for a paddler, a paddler is what they saw."

"Even though there was no paddler?"

I nodded. "It was an exercise in mass hysteria. So when the canoe drifted ashore with a porpoise and a young boy's coffin inside it, the Filligan myth was reborn."

"Was it always just a myth, or is there a grain of truth in it somewhere?"

"Some of us bought into the Filligan myth, but Chief Alphonse never did. He spent hours in ritual, trying to figure things out. Eventually he got to the truth."

"Where did George Fox find that young boy's skeleton?"

"We don't know yet. George won't tell us. He might have disinterred it from a graveyard—maybe a Coast Salish graveyard. Let's hope so, because a Coast Salish graveyard is where his bones are resting now."

"But what about that bear you saw and that shaman disappearing and reappearing?" Felicity asked. "That wasn't a case of mass hysteria."

"It took me a while to figure that one out," I said. "It wasn't until I saw a stilt walker in the park doing juggling tricks that it hit me. Dressed up in a bear costume, a man on stilts that make him twelve feet tall is pretty impressive. And dressed in a different sort of costume and on black stilts, a person can even appear to hover above the ground, disembodied. In the dark, that is. That kind of stunt couldn't work in daylight."

We were both silent as we looked out over the city. Then I said, "Nearly all of the people involved in this case were liars. Charlotte Fox especially, although initially I found her lies convincing, because she mixed in enough truth to make her stories plausible."

"Did she really murder her father?" Felicity asked.

"He was dying of cancer and in constant pain, and he asked George to put him out of his misery. George hated his father and refused. He wanted to see him suffer as long as possible. The old man then appealed to Charlotte, and she gave him an overdose. When he didn't die right away, she used a pillow to smother him. It was a mercy killing, but technically she's a murderer."

"Patricide."

"Correct. If she were to be charged for it and found guilty, she'd get life."

"Will she be charged?"

Instead of answering, I said, "When the deed began to weigh heavily on her conscience and she couldn't sleep or eat, she ended up with Lawrence Trew. At some point she told Trew what she'd done. Her confession was a terrific cathartic release, and after months of sleeplessness and angst she could finally relax. Her peace of mind crumbled again after Trew asked her to lend him ten thousand dollars. She figured it was thinly veiled blackmail. But that's when things started to get screwy. See, shortly afterwards, Hector and Marnie burgled Trew's office—just a random, opportunistic break-in by a couple of addicts—but among the things they stole was the cassette tape of Charlotte's hypno-therapy sessions.

"Titus Silverman listened to Trew's tapes and decided to put the bite on her. Charlotte assumed Trew was the blackmailer. She was frightened, but she tried to ignore it. Then Silverman, disguising his voice, phoned and told her to hop to it. At this point Charlotte, frightened out of her wits, asked her brother to help. She gave him the money, he took it to Beacon Hill Park, confronted Silverman, killed him and took over the blackmail scheme himself."

Felicity, shaking her head in disbelief, said, "But why on earth did George Fox kill Lawrence Trew?"

"To destroy every connection between his sister and the blackmailer."

"What about this Hector character and what's her name, Marnie?"

"Hector Latour and Marnie Paul? Hector cleared off and we've lost track of him. As for Marnie, Joe McNaught pulled some strings and got her into a private rehab clinic over in Vancouver." I gazed at the empty glass in my hand, thinking about the little girl that I used to drive to ballet classes.

Felicity filled my glass, then reached across the table and held my hand. "But there's a lot more to this, isn't there? About Donnelly's Marsh, I mean."

"Oh yes, there's more," I said. "I'll tell you all about it very soon. Right now, I have other plans for you."

Instead of drinking the wine, I stood and helped Felicity to her feet. We left the restaurant and went out into the night.

Catch Silas Seaweed in his next adventure in
SEAWEED IN THE SOUP

SEAWEED IN THE SOUP EXCERPT

Victoria was hot like Tucson is hot. I brought the office bottle out and had a stiff one. Last week, CFAX's weatherman told us that our present climate is the way it was in northern California 50 years ago. I'm beginning to believe it. Farmers are ploughing up potato fields, planting vines and calling themselves vintners. People grow peaches in their backyards instead of apples. I had another drink, put the bottle away and went out. I was sweating by the time I'd walked the few blocks to View Street. The sun blazed above the rooftops, wisps of steam rose from manhole covers. Half a dozen Harleys were parked outside Pinky's, a hole in the wall bar. A red neon motorcycle being driven by a green neon pig rotated up on the flat roof. Inside, Pinky's has low ceilings, bad-smelling air and is furnished with the kind of seedy mismatched oddments that marginal restaurateurs pick up at fire sales. Bearded men with tattooed arms were drinking beer at tables set around a small dance floor. Rock music poured out of giant speakers. Female patrons were dressed in clothing suitable for hanging about on street corners after dark.

Fred Halloran—a reporter who covered the crime beat for a local rag—sagged against the bar. Thin and elderly, with a gloomy expression, large horn-rimmed glasses and ill-fitting dentures, Fred wore a brown fedora and a scruffy beige raincoat that had been out of fashion since the Beatles left Liverpool. I sat on a barstool and said hello.

"Jeez, this weather," Fred replied.

Pinky's Irish beer slinger, a tall beer-barrelled mutt named Doyle, was behind the bar picking his teeth with a plastic cocktail fork. Doyle wore a Foster's apron, a starched white collarless shirt with the sleeves rolled up, and black pants supported by green suspenders.

"Glory be to God, it's the filth, so it is," said Doyle. "And here a fellow was telling me only half an hour ago that you'd been swept to your death down a drain, so he did."

"And the best of Hibernian luck to you too, Doyle. I'll have a cheeseburger and fries, a bottle of Foster's, and give that ink-stained wretch over there whatever he's drinking."

"Bless your tiny heart, Silas. A double Scotch will set me up nicely, so it will," Fred Halloran responded in a fair imitation of Doyle's rough Belfast patter.

Doyle shouted "Cheese and fries!" through a hatch behind the bar, poured the drinks, set my Fosters in front of me and slid the Scotch along to Fred. Doyle then leaned against the bar's back counter and resumed work on his upper molars.

Fred stopped ogling a long-legged woman across the room, clinked his glass against mine and said, "Here's looking up your old address."

"I seem to recall that you covered the crime beat in Vancouver before you moved to Victoria."

"I was with the *Vancouver Province* in the sixties. Those were investigative journalism's glory days," Fred said wistfully. "Jack Webster and Jack Wasserman were writing back then. Ben Metcalfe and Doug Collins were doing great columns as well. They're all gone now."

A mirror behind the bar gave me a good view of the whole

room. I watched a swarthy Hispanic man come in from the street with a young blonde. She had freckles across the bridge of her nose, but she was thin and twitchy, and the lids covering her blue eyes were at half-mast. I didn't recognize her but he was Tubby Gonzales. Gonzales, according to the drug squad, was buying a single kilo of cocaine a month from Vancouver, cutting it to make three, selling it down the line to his sidemen, and pocketing twenty thousand dollars every month—close to half a million dollars a year. Gonzales glanced casually around the room, but his eyes swept past me without recognition. It was probably just as well. I saw him escort the woman out of sight behind a screen at the back of the room.

Doyle edged closer. He removed the cocktail fork from his mouth, eyed it speculatively, and said, "Unless my eyes deceive, that was Tubby G. There'll be a hot time in the old town tonight, begorrah."

I was already sick of Doyle. An empty table had come up beside the dance floor. I picked up my drink and said, "Okay Fred. Let's you and me sit over there."

We crossed the room together and sat down. The bikers who had used the table ahead of us had left empty glasses and crumpled Dorito packages in their wake. Eunice Murnau cleared up and wiped the table with a damp cloth.

Eunice is my age, about 40. A good-looking waitress, she was wearing a Che Guevara T-shirt that she must have purchased in a weak moment. She'd either switched to wearing elastic-waisted jeans or was losing weight. The skin raccooning one of her eyes showed purple beneath its makeup. I asked Eunice to bring us another round.

After Eunice went away, I said, "I expect you still know your way around Vancouver, Fred. You'd know all about the Big Circle Gang, I suppose."

Fred had been slumped in his chair. He straightened up and returned my gaze warily. "I know a little. Why do you ask?"

"Casual interest," I said—sharing info with newspapermen and begging them to keep secrets is like trying to herd cats. I was careful not to mention Raymond Cho's name.

"A few years back I did some investigative journalism on gang activity for the *Province*, which the wire services also picked up," Fred said, awakening fascination showing on his face. "After my stories went to press I received threatening phone calls. Such calls are part of the territory; reporters get used to such things. Still, those particular calls made me nervous, I'm glad to be in Victoria now, instead of Vancouver. To be honest, just *talking* about those crazy bastards makes me nervous. What do you want to know, exactly?"

"What can you tell me about the Big Circle Gang?"

Fred looked at me directly, his horn-rimmed glasses accentuating his narrow face. "Are you involved with the Raymond Cho murder?"

I raised my shoulders and said, "I'm just a neighbourhood cop."

"A neighbourhood cop till you bailed from the VPD's crime squad. You never got around to telling me why?"

I humped my shoulders.

"You and Bernie Tapp are as thick as thieves, so you must have locked horns with somebody else," Fred went on.

"I'm enjoying what I do now, working with street people and setting my own agenda."

Fred sipped a little whisky and said, "Big Circle Boys, or Dai Huen Jai, are brutes first and last. It's not strictly accurate to call them a gang. The Big Circle Boys are a loose network of interlinked cells usually consisting of ten members or less. The head of the organization—if there is in fact a head—is rumoured to live in

Hong Kong. The Big Circle Boys originated on the Chinese main-land. They first showed up in Vancouver in the 1980s, although it was several years before they made a blip on police radar. The Boys arrived in Canada via Hong Kong, travelling on false docu-ments. Raymond Cho may have been a Big Circle boss. Now that he's dead we may never never know for sure."

Fred stopped talking when Eunice brought our drinks, along with my burger and fries.

"What *are* these things?" I asked, pointing at the interlocked strawlike objects covering my plate.

Eunice smiled. "They're waffle fries. What do they look like?"

"They look like deep-fried hairpieces," I said. "I hope the chef didn't fry 'em in Brylcreem instead of cooking oil."

Eunice sauntered away.

I said, "Okay, Fred. You talked about a leader who may or may not exist. But the Big Circle Boys didn't arise out of thin air."

"No, the Big Circle Boys arose out of China's Red Guards—a paramilitary arm of the Cultural Revolution who murdered intel-lectuals and the upper classes during Mao Tse Tung's era. The very mention of their name used to put the fear of God into people. After Mao died, the Chinese People's Liberation Army stamped the Red Guards out. Viciously. Many Red Guards were killed by firing squads, some were tortured, then buried alive. The rest were locked up in prison camps outside Canton City. On local maps, the prison camps were shown inside a big circle—hence the name. A few prisoners managed to escape. Some escapees ended up in Hong Kong. Afterwards a few came to Canada, posing as refu-gees. They are all very hard men."

I tasted my cheeseburger. After two bites, I pushed the plate away.

Fred has a strong stomach. He popped one of the waffle fries into his mouth, washed it down with Scotch, and said,

"My research suggested that back then—I'm speaking of ten years ago—there were no more than fifty Big Circle Boys in Vancouver. I doubt if there are many more than that number even today."

"How do you know? You said earlier that each cell consists of ten members or less."

"That's right, I stand by it. However many there happen to be, the Big Circle Boys are alive and well and operating in Vancouver. They're into every kind of mischief. Drug trafficking—primarily heroin brought in from the golden triangle. Lately I hear the Big Circle Boys have branched out into cocaine and BC weed. Prostitution, gambling, massage parlours. Loansharking. Extortion. Human smuggling. Vancouver is a big city, there's plenty of muck to wallow in."

He sipped a little more Scotch. After a pause he said, "All due respect, Silas, but if you're getting any information from the Mounties, I'd advise you to take anything they tell you with a dose of salt. Their take on Asian gangs isn't reliable."

"Why?"

"Several reasons, by and large it has to do with language. Most cops are Canadian-born high-school graduates. Their first and usually only language is English or French. Many big-time Canadian gangsters were born overseas; they conduct business in Mandarin or Vietnamese or Russian," he said. "What do you think happens to English-speaking cops when they try to infiltrate Urdu-speaking gangs?"

"I think they end up with their feet in buckets of concrete."

"Or worse. The RCMP is recruiting foreign-language speakers, but for the most part they still rely on paid informers. What they are getting for their money is sometimes worse than useless. It's fiction."

Fred finished his drink and licked his lips. I offered him a refill. To my surprise, he declined. We shook hands, he went out.

An alley cat slunk into view from behind a screen at the back of the room. Her name, she once told me, is Candace. If she weighed ten pounds instead of a hundred, I'd put a rhinestone collar around her slender white neck and keep her in my office as company for my cat.

After scanning the room, Candace made a beeline to my table. Her face had coarsened slightly since I first knew her, but Candace still had very good bones. She was wearing a cocktail dress with a low-cut top, and six-inch stilettos. Putting both hands on my table and leaning towards me, smiling as if she meant it, Candace gave me a chance to admire her new implants before saying huskily, "Remember what I told you the last time I saw you in here?"

"No, but I remember what I *thought*. I thought that you were bad news, but that you have a beautiful ass and nice legs and that your figure is lovely. In fact, it's lovelier than ever. When you pull your shoulders back like that, your nipples point straight up."

"What I *said*, Copper, was there was a time when they didn't let Siwashes inside places like this."

"They've amended the Indian Act since then. Besides, I'm not a Siwash, I'm Coast Salish. Would you like a drink?"

"A drink will do for a start, but what I really want is to get laid. It'll set you back two hundred. Cash or VISA. Special deal, because I like you."

"You've got VISA now?"

"Certainly. In my business you've got to keep up to date. My ass isn't the only thing that moves with the times.

I didn't want to know what had been in the mouthful of cheeseburger I'd just eaten, but whatever it was, it had taken my appetite away. I raised a hand for Eunice.

"I can hardly wait," Candace said. "Let's go over to my place and get it on."

When Eunice arrived, I gave her a twenty and said, "I'm leaving now. Candace can have whatever she wants, as long as it comes out of a government-approved bottle. I'll settle with Doyle the next time I come in."

Candace was disappointed when I left. I was too, in a way.

I went outside, walked half a block, and stood outside Peacock Billiards for a minute.

Looking north along Douglas Street, I pondered my next move. The sky was clear. The city was warm, noisy, bright. Victoria is a port city. The downtown sidewalks were a blur of colour because a French aircraft carrier had just dropped its anchor in Royal Roads. Matelots on shore leave and local girls with sun-bleached hair were strolling back and forth arm-in-arm—flirting and enjoying themselves. Skateboard kids were doing toreador acts between moving cars and taxis. Street buskers and jugglers and ice-cream sellers were all cashing in.

I strolled north. The town-hall clock told me that it was eight p.m. In six or seven hours Victoria's nightclubs and bars would be closing. That's when the masculine propensity for birdbrained aggression reaches its peak. The streets would get a little rowdier. Fights that began over perceived dirty looks would turn nasty. Pissed-off drunks would end up with slashed faces or punctured livers. Bicycle cops, ambulances, and France's shore patrol would arrive. One or two losers were liable to wind up on marble slabs, or start the new day in front of a judge.

My MG coupe was still parked where I'd left it on Johnson Street. I got in, cranked it up, and listened to its four-cylinder engine purr for a while. Instead of driving straight home, I detoured through Chinatown, looking at its garish coloured lights, flashy chop-suey cafes, and the gaudy imported wares displayed in its shop windows, but I was wondering what secrets lay hidden behind its red-painted doors and silk window curtains.

ABOUT THE AUTHOR

STANLEY EVANS' previous novels are *Outlaw Gold, Snow-Coming Moon* and the first three books in the Silas Seaweed series: *Seaweed on the Street, Seaweed on Ice* and *Seaweed under Water*. Stanley and his family live in Victoria, BC.

ISBN: 978-1-894898-34-8   ISBN: 978-1-894898-51-5   ISBN: 978-1-894898-57-7

"Makes great use of the West Coast aboriginal mythology and religion."
—*The Globe and Mail*

"The writing is wonderful native story telling. Characters are richly drawn . . . I enjoyed this so much that I'm looking for the others in the series."
—*Hamilton Spectator*